The Days of Elijah

Book Four:
The Seventh Vial

Mark Goodwin

Technical information in the book is included to convey realism. The author shall not have liability or responsibility to any person or entity with respect to any loss or damage caused, or allegedly caused, directly or indirectly by the information contained in this book.

All of the characters, places, and incidents are products of the author's imagination or are used fictitiously. Any resemblance to actual people, places, or events is entirely coincidental.

ISBN: 1973997584
ISBN-13: 978-1973997580

DEDICATION

And there came unto me one of the seven angels which had the seven vials full of the seven last plagues, and talked with me, saying, Come hither, I will shew thee the bride, the Lamb's wife.

Revelation 21:9

To the faithful, the true followers of Messiah who have purposed to keep themselves separate from the wicked Babylonian system which has permeated our culture, our news and information channels, our education system, our music and entertainment, and even our apostate churches. This book is dedicated to the true Church of God—the pure, beautiful, holy, loyal, and wise Bride of Christ.

ACKNOWLEDGMENTS

Special thanks to my beautiful wife and faithful companion. Thank you for your love, encouragement, and support.

I would like to thank my Editor in Chief Catherine Goodwin, as well as the rest of my fantastic editing team, Ken Elswick, Jeff Markland, Frank Shackleford, Kris Van Wagenen, Sherrill Hesler, Paul Davison, and Claudine Allison.

CHAPTER 1

And he spake to them a parable; Behold the fig tree, and all the trees; When they now shoot forth, ye see and know of your own selves that summer is now nigh at hand. So likewise ye, when ye see these things come to pass, know ye that the kingdom of God is nigh at hand.

Luke 21: 29-31

Thursday afternoon, Everett Carroll kissed his wife on the head and gave her a big hug.

"What time do you think you'll be home?" Courtney asked.

He sighed as if he were already exhausted from the task which had yet to begin. "Late, I'm sure.

You know how the members of the Knesset are. I've never seen people who like to argue and deliberate as much as them. They're like addicts to controversy."

She looked at her husband with compassionate eyes. "When we came to Batumi three years ago, the two rabbis of the Chief Rabbinate Council were going to run everything like a theocracy. Why did they bring back the Knesset?"

"I guess Rabbi Weismann and Rabbi Herzog got tired of having only each other to bicker with. The Knesset offers them a pool of twelve additional opponents. It's like oratory chess to them, and no one seems to enjoy it more than the two rabbis."

She walked him to the door of their simple cottage nestled along the river in the Lesser Caucasus Mountains. "I know the incessant squabbling won't make your job any easier tonight, but at least you had the good sense not to throw your hat in the ring to be in the Knesset."

"They'd have never elected a gentile."

"I'll have to disagree. It seemed like everyone in the valley was begging me to get you to reconsider after you said you weren't running."

"You never told me that." He turned as he walked toward the door.

Courtney smiled like the cat who ate the canary. "I wanted you all to myself. I wasn't about to twist your arm to run for office."

He pressed his lips together with a faint grin. "Still, it would have been nice to know."

Ali called out from across the road as he walked down the stairs of his cottage. "Everett, Courtney, how are you?"

Courtney stepped out onto the small porch and waved to Ali. "We're great. And you?"

"Wonderful, thank you very much. It is such pleasant weather we are having."

Courtney chuckled as Ali sprinted toward their home. "Early August in the Goshen Valley is pretty nice. Temperatures in the mid-seventies aren't going to help your case."

Ali looked at Everett when he arrived. "Yes, but the members of the Knesset are very wise. I am sure they will make the right decision."

Everett's mouth twisted. "After hours of quarreling, speculation, and contemplation, I agree; they'll eventually do the right thing."

Tobias came out the same door Ali had exited moments earlier. "You guys ready to go?"

"Depends on how flexible you are with your definition of *ready*." Everett gave Courtney one last kiss and descended the stairs of his porch to join Tobias.

Tobias waved to Courtney. "Gideon and Dinah are just up the road if you need anything at all."

"Thanks. Have fun!" Courtney waved back.

"Fun? Didn't you tell her what we were doing?" Tobias lowered his brow as he turned to Everett.

"She knows. She's just rubbing salt in our wounds." Everett led the way to the small church on the river, which also served as the public transit stop. Since fuel was scarce, horse-drawn wagons served as the primary source of transportation in and around Batumi, Georgia. A series of such wagons made up the transit system and were funded by a five-percent sales tax on all goods and services.

They waited in front of the church where Gideon and Dinah had tied the knot two years earlier. Everett patted Tobias on the back. "What ever happened to Maya? I thought for sure you guys were going to get married."

"And leave Ali on his own?" Tobias tussled Ali's dark chin-length hair.

"We could have gotten him hitched also, if you weren't always around," Everett joked.

"Please." Ali crossed his arms tightly. "None of these Jewish girls would ever marry an Arab, Christian or not."

"Yeah, that's a little sad." Everett kicked the gravel beneath his feet. "A couple Arab girls live in Batumi. You go to town often enough."

Ali held one finger up. "Paul said the time is short, so that from now on even those who have wives should be as though they had none, those who weep as though they did not weep, those who rejoice as though they did not rejoice, those who buy as though they did not possess, and those who use this world as not misusing it. For the form of this world is passing away. But I want you to be without care. He who is unmarried cares for the things of the Lord—how he may please the Lord. But he who is married cares about the things of the world—how he may please his wife.

"I spent my whole life not knowing who is Jesus. We have only a few short months until we will see Him face to face. So, I will continue to study and do His will until He returns. I am happy, Everett. I do not feel like something is missing in my life."

Tobias nodded and stuck out his thumb toward Ali. "Yeah, what he said."

"Well!" Everett held his hands up. "If I ever had any doubt about whether you got a full dose of the Spirit, I guess you just put it to rest."

A wagon being pulled by a team of two horses stopped in front of the three men. "Hop on, gentlemen. Where are you headed."

Everett, Ali, and Tobias loaded onto the wagon. "The Knesset," Everett said.

They arrived at a Batumi government building less than half an hour later.

"Thank you for the lift." Everett waved at the man driving the wagon and led the way to the meeting with the Knesset.

Rabbi Herzog met Everett at the door. "Mr. Carroll. What a pleasure to see you again."

"Likewise, Rabbi." Everett shook hands with the man. "Is everyone here?"

"Almost. We have your maps and your whiteboard set up near the front. We have hot tea and cold water for you as well. If there is anything else I can get for you, don't hesitate to ask."

"A speedy approval for all of our recommendations would be great." Everett made his way to the front of the room.

"Ah, yes. We shall see." The rabbi laughed.

Ali and Tobias sat with Everett at the table which was facing the two rabbis and the twelve members of the Knesset.

Rabbi Weismann opened with the Shema and a quick prayer asking God and His Messiah to bless the meeting and guide it with His Spirit. He removed the tallit from his head and looked up. "Mr. Carroll, you may begin."

Everett stood up. "Thank you, Rabbi. As you all know, we have now been in Batumi, Georgia and the area in the surrounding mountains, which has come to be known as the Goshen Valley, since March three years ago. Or, to be more specific, 1,229 days."

Saul Stein, a member of the Knesset held up his hand. Saul was in his mid-fifties, tall, with an athletic build. "Mr. Carroll, we've heard your reasoning on this point before. We've all read Revelation 12:6. In fact, I'm sure most of us can quote the text. Then the woman, which we all believe to be the nation of Israel, fled into the wilderness, where she has a place prepared by God, that they should feed her there one thousand two hundred and sixty days."

Everett cut Saul off. "Then you should know you have exactly 31 days remaining."

Saul shook his head. "We didn't all get here on March 24th. We came in waves. You can't arbitrarily assign the day of your arrival as the day the clock started counting down the 1260 days. Most of the people in this room believe that HaShem will continue to provide for us here until the return of Messiah."

"Then you believe that in spite of what HaShem has written in the Holy Scriptures via His prophet, Daniel." Everett opened his Bible. "In Chapter 12, Daniel wrote, 'from the time that the daily sacrifice is taken away, and the abomination of desolation is set up, there shall be one thousand two hundred and ninety days. Blessed is he who waits, and comes to the one thousand three hundred and thirty-five days.'

"Angelo Luz put an end to the daily sacrifice and unveiled the Image in the Holy of Holies on March 22nd. In Matthew 24, Messiah instructed all of Israel to flee to the mountains immediately when that event happened. The fact that many of the Jews chose not to follow that directive in a timely fashion doesn't change the prophetic timeline."

Saul leaned back in his chair. "And what happens on the 1290th day?"

Rabbi Herzog, who was taking Everett's presentation much more seriously said, "Yom Teruah, the Feast of Trumpets. Why don't we let Mr. Carroll finish his presentation? I'm sure we'll have much to discuss afterward."

"Thank you, Rabbi." Everett began writing the coming judgments on the whiteboard, numbering the Vials of God's Wrath, one through seven. He spoke as he worked the dry-erase marker against the surface of the board. "The Vial Judgements begin with an outbreak of sores. This will only affect the worshipers of Luz.

"Next, the sea will turn to blood. I believe that includes all the seas and oceans on Earth. The smell isn't going to be very pleasant for those of you living around here, near the coast."

"The Third Vial—the rivers and springs turn to blood. This is really going to be a problem. Maybe we can store water and it won't turn, but the rivers aren't going to be available to us as a source of drinking water any longer.

"Fourth Vial." Everett wrote out the Roman numeral. "The Earth is scorched with searing heat from the sun. I don't know whether God will shield us from that plague or not.

"Fifth Vial—the kingdom of the Beast, or what we know as the Holy Luzian Empire, is plunged into darkness.

"Sixth, the Euphrates dries up and the kings of the east gather in the Valley of Megiddo for battle."

Everett paused from writing to face the Knesset and the rabbis. "But let's say God gets us through all of that. We still have to survive the Seventh Vial."

Everett turned back to the board and continued writing. "The final vial will bring the biggest quake in the history of the Earth. Bigger than the Great Quake. Revelation says every island fled away, and the mountains were not found."

He turned back to them. "In case you haven't noticed, we're surrounded by mountains. If they come down, we'll be crushed and buried beneath the rubble."

Everett continued writing. "Then, hailstones weighing a talent. Can anyone help me out on how much that is?"

Rabbi Weismann replied, "Depending on whether it is a Babylonian, Egyptian, or a Roman talent, it could be anywhere from sixty to seventy pounds."

"A gallon of water weighs just over eight pounds." Everett drew a large circle on the board. "We're talking about seven-gallon blocks of ice falling out of the sky. So roughly the size of this space on the whiteboard."

Everett put the cap on the pen and turned around. All the Knesset members and the two rabbis had grim looks on their faces.

Saul Stein crossed his legs, then his arms. "So, what do you propose?"

CHAPTER 2

And after that I looked, and, behold, the temple of the tabernacle of the testimony in heaven was opened: And the seven angels came out of the temple, having the seven plagues, clothed in pure and white linen, and having their breasts girded with golden girdles. And one of the four beasts gave unto the seven angels seven golden vials full of the wrath of God, who liveth for ever and ever. And the temple was filled with smoke from the glory of God, and from his power; and no man was able to enter into the temple, till the seven plagues of the seven angels were fulfilled.

Revelation 15:5-8

Everett introduced Ali to the Knesset and handed him the dry-erase marker.

Ali seemed nervous as he took the spotlight. "Yes, thank you for your attention." Ali looked at Everett as if he might endow him with the gift of confidence and an inherent knack for public speaking.

Everett offered a reassuring nod and a few simple words instead. "Go ahead. You'll do fine."

"As Everett mentioned. I am from Turkey. Tarsus to be exact, like Apostle Paul."

Saul Stein interrupted. "Except Paul wasn't an Arab."

Everett wasn't about to let that one slide. "Thanks for pointing that out for us, Saul. I'm sure everyone here is impressed by your astute faculty for observation, and we all owe you a great deal of gratitude for bringing such an insignificant factoid to our attention at the expense of the valuable information Ali was presenting."

Saul stood up, knocking his chair back with his legs, and pointing his index finger at Everett. "When you address the Knesset, you would be well advised to do so with the decorum expected by this assembly!"

Everett stood also. "If your behavior is indicative of the standard protocol, I should be well within the boundaries of Knesset etiquette. I might remind you, Mr. Stein, we are here at the request of the Chief Rabbinate Council. My group intends to act on the information we have put together, regardless of the decision made by this assembly. If you don't want to listen, I'll be more than content to shake the dust off my feet and move on."

"Enough!" Rabbi Weismann stood up. "Both of you!" The old rabbi scowled at Saul Stein. "Please, Saul, don't interrupt any of our distinguished guests. If you have questions, hold them until they have finished their presentation.

"Ali, on behalf of the Council and the Knesset, I apologize for the disruption. It won't happen again. Please proceed."

Ali took a deep breath. "Yes, sir." He nervously sketched out a rough contour of Turkey. "To north of where I am from is region of Cappadocia. One of big tourist attraction in region is underground city. The region has like two hundred underground city, but only few are open to public. Derinkuyu is bigger one. Derinkuyu can hold twenty thousand people. One other city that is open to public is Kaymakli. It can hold thirty-five hundred.

"My father took me to Derinkuyu when I was small boy. Originally, the city was build around 900 BC. Derinkuyu have many living space, storage space, stable for animal, larger meeting area, everything guys.

"Christians expanded the city during Roman persecution. They add many church. City continued to be use during Arab-Byzantine War, and by Christian during Ottoman rule.

"Ten-kilometer tunnel connect Kaymakli to Derinkuyu." Ali wrote the names of the underground cities that he could remember, listing the capacity of those he was most familiar with.

"Ozkonak is maybe like sixty kilometer from Derinkuyu. It is biggest underground city of all. Ozkonak hold sixty thousand people. Also is Mazi, Tatlarin, Gaziemir, other near Ağırnas. And new one just finded near to Kayseri is maybe bigger than Derinkuyu.

"Easily can be enough room for everyone in Goshen Valley plus room for dry good and many supply. That is all I have to share. Thank you very much." Ali held the dry-erase marker out for Tobias.

Tobias stood and took the marker. "Does anyone have questions about the underground cities before I begin my presentation on the logistical and security aspects of the move?"

Rabbi Weismann nodded. "Yes. How far are these cities from Batumi?"

Everett answered, "Roughly 550 miles, or about 900 kilometers."

Rabbi Herzog asked, "How safe are these cities? Isn't it possible that the coming earthquake could cause them to collapse?"

Again, Everett took this question. "We don't have any data about a quake the size of the one that's coming, but typically, the damage is only above ground. Body waves are transmitted through the earth's inner layers while surface waves are restricted to the uppermost layer of the Earth's surface, like ripples on the water. It's the surface waves that cause all the damage."

Another member of the Knesset, Morty Berkowitz, inquired, "What if the entrances were to collapse?"

"In the case of Derinkuyu, we have 600 entrances," Tobias said. "But even if we were to be buried, the material is porous volcanic rock. It's very easy to get through with simple chisels and mallets, which is why it was possible for these cities to be excavated on such a vast scale in the first place."

"If we decide to leave," Rabbi Herzog began, "we will take our provisions with us, I suppose."

"Yes, sir," Everett replied. "We've encouraged people to preserve as much meat and vegetables as possible via dehydration, which means it will be much lighter and easier to transport."

"Of course, the other side of that coin is that dehydrated food requires more water," Rabbi Weismann stated. "Do the underground cities have wells?"

"All have well." Ali nodded. "Actually, Derinkuyu mean deep well."

Murry Goldman was the Knesset member sitting to the right of Saul Stein. He asked, "How do we know the water in the underground cities won't turn to blood after the Third Vial? What if we leave the Goshen Valley where God has been providing for us to end up in a place where we have no water?"

Murry's concern seemed to spread like wildfire between the other members. They all began to whisper and speak amongst themselves.

Everett took a deep breath before responding. "We don't know. The water issue is out of our control. We'll have to step out in faith on that one. But I'm confident that God will provide. He's brought us this far."

"He's brought us this far in the Goshen Valley." Murry Goldman looked at the other members and the two rabbis. "To me, it makes no sense to leave the refuge HaShem has provided for us and run away in fear to some hole in the ground."

Rabbi Herzog spoke next. "HaShem provided Everett and his friends to lead us to this place. They brought us here safely. Perhaps it is also the Spirit of Adonai speaking through them to lead us to one last place of refuge."

Saul Stein crossed his arms. "Rabbi, respectfully, I want to remind you that Everett and his friends were acting under the direction of the prophets, Moses and Elijah, when they led us to this location."

Rabbi Herzog shook his head. "Moses and Elijah are not here. They are in Jerusalem. If Adonai is to lead us from this place it must be through someone else."

Morty Berkowitz said, "No offense to our distinguished guests, but I should think HaShem is more likely to lead us through the Chief Rabbinate Council and the wisdom of the Knesset before he would use an Arab and a Gentile."

Ali's eyes drooped. He didn't look angry about Berkowitz's statement. He looked heartbroken, as if he wanted to be the man's brother but knew he could not. He rebutted Morty's assertion gently. "Paul said you are all sons of God through faith in Christ Jesus. For as many of you as were baptized into Christ have put on Christ. There is neither Jew nor Greek, there is neither slave nor free, there is neither male nor female; for you are all one in

Christ Jesus. And if you are Christ's, then you are Abraham's seed, and heirs according to the promise.

"I am sorry you don't understand these things." Ali picked up the heavily worn folder with his notes about the underground cities and turned to Everett. "I will be waiting for you outside."

"This young man has spoken the truth. He is our brother and just as much a son of Abraham as anyone in this room." Rabbi Herzog stood to escort Ali to the door. "Perhaps even more so."

Everett gave Tobias a nod and the two of them also gathered their things.

Rabbi Weismann stood up to address Everett and Tobias. "Where are the two of you going? The assembly has not been adjourned. We're not finished."

Everett smiled at the man. "By all means, feel free to deliberate until the sun comes up, but we've finished our presentation and we're going home."

The heated discussion among the Knesset grew louder as Everett and Tobias exited the room. Once outside, they found Rabbi Herzog giving Ali a warm embrace.

The rabbi released Ali and turned his attention to Everett. "Thank you for coming. I'm sorry several of the members have been so difficult."

Everett shook the man's hand. "No apology necessary, at least not on your part. Our job was to provide the information. You've got the tough task of convincing them to do the right thing."

"Yes, well, do remember me in your prayers then." Rabbi Herzog chuckled as he shook hands with Tobias.

"I certainly will." Everett gave the man a smile and led his team toward the public transit stop where they would catch the last wagon home.

CHAPTER 3

And I heard a great voice out of the temple saying to the seven angels, Go your ways, and pour out the vials of the wrath of God upon the earth. And the first went, and poured out his vial upon the earth; and there fell a noisome and grievous sore upon the men which had the mark of the beast, and upon them which worshipped his image.

Revelation 16:1-2

Everett returned to the house Friday at sunset with a fresh catch of fish from the river. Courtney was on the couch watching television, which was powered by the small two-panel solar array Everett had put together. Between Ali's experience working with the Turkish mafia and Tobias' time with Mossad, the two of them had no trouble hacking the satellite signal to get basic TV service. Watch time was generally restricted to no more than twenty or thirty minutes as there were several other applications, like recharging batteries, which required the solar energy captured by the small photovoltaic system.

"Need a hand with dinner?" Courtney walked into the kitchen and greeted Everett with a kiss.

"I'm okay. Tobias and Ali are each bringing a dish. All I have to do is cook the fish."

Gideon and Dinah let themselves in the back door. Gideon was carrying a dish. "Tobias said there was a dinner party going on here. Do you have room for two more?"

Courtney gathered dishes to set the table. "Depends. What's in that casserole dish?"

Dinah smiled hopefully. "My famous squash casserole." Gideon's new wife had long black hair, fair skin, a prominent nose, and beautiful dark eyes.

"We'll make room, in that case." Everett opened the back door for Ali and Tobias who had just arrived.

"How did it go with the Knesset last night?" Gideon asked.

"Could have been worse," Ali said.

Tobias huffed. "It could have been better."

"Let me give you a hand with the dishes." Dinah grabbed some glasses and followed Courtney to the small dining space, which was in the same open area of the cottage as the living room.

Everett took the covered dishes from Ali and

Tobias and placed them on the counter. "Since the Council and the Knesset still keep the Sabbath, they won't meet this evening. They may get together on Sunday, but I doubt they'll be able to reach a conclusion."

Courtney called out from the dining area. "I wouldn't be so sure about that. You guys should get in here and see what's happening on television."

Everett led the way and the other three men quickly followed him to the living room.

GRBN Reporter Heather Smith handed a handkerchief to her co-anchor, Harrison Yates. "That bump on your head looks like it's weeping, Harrison. Here, take this. What did you do?"

Harrison took the handkerchief as if he didn't know what she was referring to. He pointed at Heather. "Your lip is swelling."

"What are you talking about?" The right side of her lower lip broke out into a boil as if she was having an allergic reaction. She seemed to feel the swelling and put the back of her hand on the boil.

Harrison located the pussing sore on his forehead, just above his left eye. He dabbed at it with the handkerchief. "What is happening? Where did this come from?"

Heather covered her mouth as she looked directly into the camera and mumbled loudly with her swollen lip. And waved wildly with her other hand. "Cut the feed! Go to break! Cut it now!"

The screen cut to a story from an earlier broadcast, about genetically-enhanced peacekeepers.

"Oh, it's that piece about the GR supersoldiers. We've seen it twice already." Everett picked up the remote and turned off the television. "That bump on Harrison's head looked like a rotten egg."

"Yeah," Courtney added. "And I guess Heather can skip her collagen injection this week. You couldn't ask for fuller lips than what she has."

"That was disgusting." Dinah peered through her fingers as if to make sure the grotesque image was gone from the surface of the television.

Tobias shifted his eyes to Courtney. "You think this will motivate the Knesset to act?"

"It's the First Vial. If it doesn't persuade them, I'm sure the next one will." She resumed setting the table.

"I don't know. We may not see much more television coverage of the sores breaking out on Luz's followers," Gideon said. "GRBN is slow to report on things the GR can't control. And since everyone around here believes that Yeshua is the true Messiah, I don't expect to see anyone in the Goshen Valley breaking out with boils."

Everett retrieved an extra chair from the desk by the window to make six seats at the table. "If the Black Sea turns to blood in the Second Vial, we won't need television coverage. We'll smell it all through the valley. The coastal areas in Batumi will probably be unlivable."

"Let's cook that fish and have dinner before I lose my appetite." Tobias headed back into the kitchen.

"You're right." Everett followed him. "We'll

have plenty of time to be miserable once the Second Vial is poured out."

Everett and Courtney spent the following week dehydrating vegetables and making beef jerky out of the meat they traded for fresh fish and excess crops from the garden. Even though they had only a small plot for growing, using fish heads and fish guts as fertilizer caused the little vegetable patch to yield an abundance of produce. Regardless of what the Knesset and the Chief Rabbinate Council decided about the relocation of the Jews, Everett and his group were in full preparation mode for the big move.

The following Friday, Everett's group scheduled another dinner together, but this time it would be hosted at Tobias and Ali's house.

Everett held hands with Courtney as they crossed the street. With her other hand, Courtney carried a big bag containing five loaves of homemade bread. Once they reached Tobias' house, Everett knocked.

"Come in my friends." Ali opened the door with a big smile.

"Good to see you, Ali." Everett walked in.

"Tobias is in his room listening to the Ham radio." Ali escorted them to the back of the house.

"Any news?" Courtney inquired of Tobias when they reached his room.

"Just lots of speculation about the sores. They've ruled out Bubonic Plague and don't think it's transmitted person to person. But it's much worse than what GRBN is letting on."

"GRBN didn't invent fake news, they just

perfected it." Courtney rolled her eyes.

Everett stood next to Tobias' desk. "We haven't seen a live reporter on GRBN since Yates and Smith signed off last week. That tells me everyone in the Holy Luzian Empire has sores on their face."

Someone knocked at the door. "That must be Dinah and Gideon. I will go let them in." Ali excused himself from the room.

"I don't mean to be rude, but I might have to eat and run tonight." Everett patted Tobias on the shoulder.

"Why is that?" he asked.

"I want to catch the last wagon down to the beach after sunset."

"He thinks the sea will turn to blood tonight," Courtney explained.

"Oh?" Tobias powered off the Ham radio. "Because Shabbat begins at sundown?"

Everett shrugged. "The First Vial began at sunset, last Friday. It could be a pattern."

"Gideon will lend you his horses. I'll ride with you unless Courtney was planning to go."

Everett turned to his wife. "She can ride behind me on the same horse if it's okay with Gideon for us to borrow them."

"We'll go right after supper." Tobias led the way to the table.

The meal consisted of fresh bread, roast beef, roasted potatoes, and summer squash. Ali asked God to bless the food and the six friends shared a wonderful meal. The conversation quickly turned to Everett's speculation about the Second Vial beginning at sunset.

"How long will you wait for the Knesset to decide?" Dinah asked.

Everett took a drink of water. "It depends. If the sea turns to blood tonight, that most likely means all the water will turn to blood next week. I'd like to be underground before that happens. The stench alone is going to be unbearable."

"If it's only the six of us, don't you think we'll be vulnerable during the trip?" Dinah moved her meat from side to side on her plate, as if she were apprehensive about the move.

"Less vulnerable than we will be to the seventy-pound hailstones. MOC fighters are a high probability between here and Cappadocia, but the massive quake and killer hailstones are a certainty." Everett looked up at her grimly. "I'm sorry. I wish we had better choices. But we've only got bad and worse."

"Will we be able to take the horses?" Dinah swallowed hard.

Gideon stroked his wife's back. "I found a trailer. We can hitch it to the Jeep. We'll take the horses."

"You are sure we have enough fuel?" Ali let his fork rest on the side of his plate.

Everett gave a slight nod. "The Golan is topped off with a mix of diesel, motor oil, and biofuel. That should get us there, as long as we don't make any wrong turns. We dumped as much fuel stabilizer as we could get into the Jeep. It's got a third tank of ethanol, which isn't optimal, but It should make the trip as well."

Tobias said, "We could take four more people with us, even with all of our supplies. That would give us a more substantial security force for the journey."

"We've got the capacity, but everyone I've talked to is waiting to see what the rabbis and the Knesset say." Everett took another bite of his potatoes.

Courtney sipped her water. "I bet they'll be lined up at the door wanting to go with us if you're right about the Second Vial being tonight."

"First come, first serve," Tobias said. "We'll take the first four people who voice an interest in coming with us. After that, they'll be responsible for providing their own fuel, provisions, and transportation."

"Do you know what day we will leave?" Ali waited for Everett to reply.

"Wednesday morning," he said. "It's only a one-day trip, but we're going in two vehicles that haven't been driven in years. We have to account for setbacks."

Gideon finished chewing. "Although, it's not like we're going in something we just pulled out of the junkyard. I fire up the engines once a week to keep the batteries charged and drive them up and down the driveway ever so often. I rub the tires with fish oil, lard or whatever I can find to keep them from dry rotting. If we had enough fuel for a leisurely Sunday drive, I'd take 'em out a little more often."

Ali smiled at Gideon. "You make good job taking care of vehicles."

"Thanks, Ali. I try." Gideon took another piece of bread from the center plate.

After dinner, Everett, Courtney, and Tobias took the two horses down to the beach. It took them just over half an hour to cover the ten-mile trek to the Black Sea. Everett let Courtney dismount first, then he stepped down onto the sand. He walked out to the edge of the water and bent down to let the wave wash up onto his hand. Immediately, he felt the water was thicker than it should be. He held his palm up to the light of the moon which was three-quarters full. It was red—blood red.

"Everett! Is that you, my friend?" A voice called out from the direction of the street.

Everett turned to see an old man and a slightly younger woman stepping onto the sand and heading his way. "Rabbi Herzog?"

"Yes. We saw you ride by us." The man hurried toward the edge of the water where Everett, Courtney, and Tobias stood with the horses. "This is Melinda Rosenbaum. She is a member of the Knesset."

"Yes, we've met. I would shake your hand but . . ." Everett held out his hand for the woman to see.

"Oh, have you cut yourself?"

"No. It's from the sea. This is my wife, Courtney. And I'm sure you remember Tobias."

Melinda Rosenbaum shook hands with Courtney. "It's a pleasure to meet you." She quickly shifted her attention back to Everett. "From the sea, you said. Is it . . ."

"The Second Vial. Yes, I'm afraid so." Everett

bent down to wipe the blood in the sand.

"This is not good." The rabbi shook his head as he looked out at the Black Sea.

"We're leaving on Wednesday to Cappadocia. You should come. We have room for both of you," Everett offered.

"I cannot leave. I must try to convince the Knesset to relocate the people."

Tobias asked, "What was the latest vote?"

"Three to nine. Rabbi Weismann is firmly entrenched on the side that wants to stay." Ms. Rosenbaum looked distressed.

"Yes, Rabbi Weismann follows the council of Saul Stein," Herzog said. "Saul was the president of the Israeli Diamond Exchange near Tel Aviv. Saul holds a lot of clout in the Knesset. Particularly with Morty Berkowitz. Saul and Morty go way back. Morty was one of the biggest diamond traders on the exchange. I'm afraid they still carry some residue of the pride from their former lives; especially Saul. And I'm sorry to say Rabbi Weismann is still influenced by that air of power, even though it means very little now."

Ms. Rosenbaum turned to Everett. "Although, this latest development may sway some opinions. When the sun rises and reveals a sea of blood, it will have quite a profound effect on anyone looking upon it. Everett, can't you stay just a while longer? I'm sure the Knesset will come around."

"We can't ma'am. We've done all we can do in presenting the truth. My responsibility now is to my wife and my friends who need no further convincing. We'll be leaving Wednesday morning,

Lord willing."

"I can't say that I blame you." Rabbi Herzog's head hung low.

"You should come, Rabbi," Tobias pleaded one last time. "Next week, if the pattern persists, the rivers and springs will also turn to blood. The journey will get much more difficult."

"I fear what you say is true. But the Messiah has assigned me to be a shepherd of His people, and I cannot abandon my post, no matter how stubborn the sheep may be."

"We should be going." Everett took Courtney's hand and led her toward the horse. "Let us know if you're able to convince them."

"I will, Everett." Rabbi Herzog waved.

Courtney waved to Ms. Rosenbaum. "It was a pleasure to meet you."

"Likewise," she replied.

CHAPTER 4

But God led the people about, through the way of the wilderness of the Red sea: and the children of Israel went up harnessed out of the land of Egypt.

Exodus 13:18

The following Tuesday evening, Everett took another load of supplies out of his cottage and packed them into the Golan military transport vehicle.

Gideon walked up the drive and met Everett as he finished placing his belongings in the Golan. "Good news."

Everett shook his friend's hand. "Oh, yeah?"

"Dinah's sister, Batya, and Batya's husband,

Levi, are coming with us. They both served in the IDF, so they'll round out our security team."

"Eight is better than six. We've got more room if they need to put some items in the Golan." Everett looked inside the vehicle.

Gideon shook his head. "We'll manage to get all of our belongings in the Jeep or on the cargo rack, up top."

"And they'll be ready to leave at first light?" Everett asked.

"First light." Gideon gave a short nod.

The sound of a moped coming up the road caused Everett to turn his attention away from Gideon. "Who could that be?"

"Gas-powered vehicles are a luxury to operate. Must be someone with resources." Gideon stood beside Everett, looking out at the road.

The motorized bike slowed and turned into Everett's drive and cut the engine.

"It's Rabbi Herzog." Everett walked down the gravel path to meet the man.

The rabbi removed a military-style helmet that was acting as a riding helmet. "Everett, I'm so glad you haven't left yet!"

"Are you coming with us? We've still got room." Everett smiled and embraced the rabbi.

Gideon shook hands with the rabbi. "We can take the horses to get your things if you want. There's plenty of space for your personal belongings."

"No, no. I have even better news." Herzog shook his head, his mouth grinning from ear to ear. "The Knesset has approved the move. Murry, Saul,

Morty, and even Rabbi Weissman have agreed to leave the valley and go to the underground cities in Turkey. All of us will be going."

"That's fantastic!" Everett exclaimed. "Why don't you come with us tomorrow? You can help us get the place aired out before the rest of them arrive."

The rabbi took Everett's hand with a firm grip. "Everett, we must all travel together, for safety."

"There is security in numbers, but you have nearly 150,000 people to mobilize. It will take you weeks to get them organized. There's no way they'll be ready to move tomorrow."

"No, but couldn't you delay your departure?" The rabbi looked at him with soft eyes. "I'm sure we can have everyone ready to leave by this time next week."

Everett shook his head and pulled his hand away from the rabbi's. "We can't. We've set tomorrow as our exit date for a reason. If our drinking water turns to blood this Friday night, the logistics of the trip are going to become much more complex. We gave plenty of notice and ample opportunity for the Knesset to reach a verdict in time for everyone in Goshen to leave with us. This isn't my problem."

"What can I say other than you are right." Herzog held his hands up as if to surrender. "But think of the people—God's people. You must consider your brothers and sisters." The rabbi clapped his hands together in a plea.

"I have, Rabbi. I've gone above and beyond, but I also have a wife and a mutual assistance group to think about. My first responsibility is to them."

"Moses, when he brought the children of Israel through the desert, had Arron to assist him. If you leave me here, I'll have no one." Herzog glanced at Gideon. "The former IDF soldiers look to Gideon and Tobias for leadership. And all of us look to you, Everett. Without the three of you, our security efforts will be very haphazard. We have lots of older folks, women, even a few babies. I might remind you, none of the children are older than six."

Gideon turned to Everett with a look that said he was about to cave in under the pressure of the rabbi.

Everett patted him on the back and gave Gideon's shoulder a squeeze. "I'm sure they'll all be just fine. We'll effectively be a reconnaissance team. If we hit any hot spots that you need to know about, we'll radio back and let you know."

The rabbi lowered his gaze. "No one can take your place. God has given the three of you a special gift. If you do not use it for the purpose he has given it, then the children of Israel will be very vulnerable." He looked back up, glancing from Everett's eyes to Gideon's. "I just don't want you to bear the guilt if something should happen that you could have prevented."

Everett tightened his jaw and nodded. This attempt at manipulating him through shame wasn't going to work. Not on Everett, anyways.

But Gideon, well—he was a different story. He turned to Everett with forlorn eyes. "Maybe we should just talk it over with Tobias—to make sure we're all on the same page."

Everett could feel the dam cracking. And once it lost its structural integrity, it was only a matter of time until the waters came crashing through, washing away any semblance of the barrier's prior fortitude and every one of Everett's hopes of leaving Batumi at first light. "Sure. We'll talk it over with Tobias."

The subsequent events played out in Everett's mind as if he'd seen them all in a crystal ball before they took place. He could predict the intonation of the rabbi's voice as he laid out his case to Tobias. He knew Herzog would manage to have Courtney and Dinah present so that Everett's rebuttals would have to be tempered with compassion so not to make him look like a soulless monster. Everett didn't even have to watch Tobias' affirming nods. He sensed with precision, the very moment that Tobias would cave in. Everett stared at the ceiling as he counted down the final seconds that his plan remained alive. *Six, five, four, three, two, one . . .*

"Maybe we could just hang around until Friday morning." Tobias turned to Everett. "We could advise the former IDF soldiers on a security plan, then head out at first light. We'd still be at Kaymakli before sunset Friday evening."

Everett dropped his head into his palms and mumbled through hands. "Okay. Whatever." There was nothing left to say. Rabbi Hertzog's years devoted to politics had given him a skill in persuasion that Everett simply couldn't contend with.

Ali patted Everett on the back. "You know I do whatever you say is best."

"Thanks, Ali." Everett took a deep breath.

"Can I make you some tea?" Courtney offered the rabbi.

To the victor go the spoils. Why shouldn't he want to drink in his triumph? Everett attempted to keep his bitterness over the matter concealed. After all, the man was still his friend, even if he'd just bested him.

"I'd be delighted, my dear." Herzog nodded with the smile of a child who'd just convinced Mommy to buy him that coveted box of sugary cereal.

The rabbi turned to Everett who had, for the most part, regained his composure. "Since the area we will be traveling through is heavily populated with MOC fighters, it would be good if we could acquire some heavy weaponry. Not to mention that it could come in handy if Luz decides to pursue us into Turkey."

Having lost his will to debate, Everett simply asked, "Okay, what do you have in mind?"

The rabbi held out his hand to Gideon and Tobias. "This is your area of expertise. I don't really know. Some rockets, anti-aircraft guns, fifty-caliber machine guns mounted in the back of vehicles."

Everett suddenly felt tired of discussing it all. He sighed. "Rabbi, you'll be doing good to scrape up enough fuel to just get everyone there. Now you're adding a shopping list of heavy weaponry. All this stuff takes time. Which, thanks to the slow-moving gears of bureaucracy, we don't have."

"Perhaps if money were no object, things might move a little faster?" The rabbi spoke cryptically.

"There is no money," Everett said plainly. "The

Mark system is the only access to the currency of the land, and none of us have it."

"No, but we have the next best thing." The rabbi took a black velvet pouch from his pocket. He reached inside and took out the largest diamond Everett had ever seen.

Courtney had just returned to the room from starting the tea. She gasped and covered her mouth. "Is that real?"

"Eight carats. We have several more. Not many eight carats, of course, but three to six carats." Hertzog poured the stones out into his hand. Most were white, but some were fancy yellow diamonds, and a few were pink or blue.

"Where did those come from?" Everett was mesmerized as he took the first giant round-cut stone.

"These constitute the lion's share from Saul and Morty's personal collections."

Everett passed the stone to Courtney who held her breath as she took it. Everett looked back to the rabbi. "It's a nice resource, but I don't have any idea how we could put them to use."

"Excuse me, Everett," Ali said softly.

"What is it? If you've got something to say, go ahead."

Ali looked at Hertzog, then back to Everett. "Perhaps Sadat can make some deal."

"Sadat?" Everett chuckled. "We don't even know if he's still alive."

"If he is, I am sure he is still at villa on Black Sea."

Everett shook his head. "Sadat wouldn't have

that kind of firepower."

"No," Ali said. "But Tariq have."

Tobias' eyes grew wide. "Tariq the Sheik?" Being from the intelligence community, this was a man he was all too familiar with.

"You have contacts with Tariq the Sheik?" Gideon was also obviously acquainted with the name.

"Not me, but Sadat."

Everett looked at Gideon. "Sadat was Ali's old boss. Turkish mafia."

The rabbi poured the stones back in the pouch and placed them firmly in Everett's hands. "If it is remotely possible, you must try to find this sheik."

Everett grunted as he tried to resist the responsibility of the gems. "Remotely possible, and unquestionably dangerous."

"Yes." Hertzog squeezed Everett's hands to let him know that it was too late and that the stones were already in his possession. "But you have the blessing and protection of Adonai."

Everett huffed in defeat. "We're going to need it."

CHAPTER 5

Then said he unto them, But now, he that hath a purse, let him take it, and likewise his scrip: and he that hath no sword, let him sell his garment, and buy one. For I say unto you, that this that is written must yet be accomplished in me, And he was reckoned among the transgressors: for the things concerning me have an end.

Luke 22:36-37

Everett inspected the map spread out on his dining-room table Wednesday morning. "So you don't know exactly where he lives."

Ali waved his hands. "I know when I see. It is between Rize and Trabzon. This road go along coast of Black Sea. Sadat house is on road directly off of road going by sea."

"You're talking about a fifty-mile stretch of road between Rize and Trabzon, according to this map." Everett was already perturbed about the change of plans. This issue of uncertainty wasn't helping.

"Yes, yes, but Sadat house almost in middle. So go twenty-five mile past Rize and be pretty close." Ali seemed to think his approach to the situation was sufficiently accurate.

Everett rolled his eyes and looked to Tobias. "Can you help me out here?"

"What landmarks do you remember about the house?" Tobias asked Ali.

"Like I say for Everett, road have no sign and have only one lane that go up into mountain. Sadat want villa to be off main road, away from people but still close to small town for shopping and restaurant."

Courtney stuck her hands in her pockets. "At least we don't have far to go. It's only about 100 miles from Batumi."

"We? There's no *we*. You're staying here with Dinah." Everett shook his head. "This is a quick trip. In and out. It's just me, Ali, Tobias, and Gideon."

Before Courtney had a chance to begin her protest, Ali said, "Everett, Sadat don't let Tobias and Gideon come to house. He don't know them. They cannot come."

"But Sadat knows me." Courtney crossed her arms. "Face it, you need me to come."

Everett turned toward Tobias. "It's only a

hundred miles, but it's a hundred miles through MOC-infested Turkey. What if we dropped you and Gideon off at the bottom of the hill and picked you back up when we left Sadat's place? Think you could keep your head down for half an hour or so?"

Tobias nodded. "You'll have to ask Gideon when he gets here, but that should be fine. As long as it's not in the parking lot of a Sunni mosque."

"No, no." Ali shook his head. "Road up mountain to Sadat house is all trees and bushes around. No building."

Gideon let himself in Everett's back door. "You guys ready to go?"

Everett put the sling of his HK rifle over his shoulder. "Not really."

Courtney dipped into the bedroom and came back out with her AR-15 and an assault pack over her shoulder. "Let's roll out."

Everett gritted his teeth. "You were already packed to go?"

She racked a round into the chamber of her rifle. "If Sadat thinks it's just you and Ali with all those diamonds, it might be too tempting for him to resist. I know he likes you and all, but an extra shooter might help keep an honest man honest."

"I'm not taking all the diamonds. Just enough to give him an idea of the quality we're dealing with." Nevertheless, Everett couldn't dismiss her logic. Tobias and Gideon would be nearby, but that wouldn't serve as a deterrent to Sadat who'd have no knowledge of their presence.

Gideon passed around branches from some type of herb to everyone gathered around Everett's dining-room table. "These are from Dinah."

Everett took one of the branches. "What is it?"

"Peppermint."

"Thanks," Courtney said. "What are we supposed to do with it."

"Crush a leaf or two between your fingers and rub it beneath your nose," Gideon replied.

Ali followed the instructions without question. "It is for good luck?"

Gideon laughed. "It's to cover up the stench. We'll be driving directly down the coast for 150 kilometers, then 150 kilometers back. The Black Sea turned to blood Friday at sunset which means all the fish have been dead nearly five days by now. They'll be about as ripe as they're ever going to get."

"Yuck." Courtney's nose crinkled.

"Not too late to back out." Everett offered a hopeful smile.

"Oh, please." She rolled her eyes as she pushed past him to the kitchen and out the back door.

"Good try." Tobias patted Everett on the shoulder as he followed Courtney.

"Okay, let's get this over with." Everett huffed as he picked up his assault pack, corralling Ali and Gideon out, and closing the door behind him.

The Jeep didn't provide enough protection and the Golan was too high-profile for the mission, so the team loaded into a black Mercedes Benz GL loaned to them by Saul Stein. Everett drove and Ali rode shotgun in hopes that he'd be able to identify the turn-off to Sadat's villa. Since the SUV had a third row of seats, Courtney sat behind Everett next to Tobias, who was behind Ali. Gideon took the rear seats to himself so he could watch for threats approaching from behind.

Despite keeping the windows rolled up and recirculating the cabin air, the rancid odor of rotting fish grew stronger as they approached the coast.

Everett retrieved a pinch of the peppermint leaves from his shirt pocket and rubbed them under his nose. "Gideon, remember to thank Dinah for me. The mint really helps with the smell."

"Sure thing," Gideon said from the back seat. "Hopefully the uninviting aroma will be too much for the Martyrs of the Caliphate, and we'll have an uneventful trip."

Everett nodded. "I guess I'll take a sea of decaying fish over a shootout."

The team continued along E70 which overlooked the Black Sea all the way from Batumi until their destination point. The gently rolling waves, which would have made the trip a scenic drive, were replaced by mile after mile of decomposing fish undulating in thick, blackish-red blood. Everett made a conscious effort to keep his head turned slightly to the left to avoid the gruesome view on the other side.

They eventually reached the town of Rize. It looked completely abandoned. Anyone with any means of escape would have no doubt gotten as far away from the morbid waters and the accompanying scent as possible. Everett wondered to himself if Sadat would still be at his villa when they arrived. "We must be pretty close, Ali. Do you see anything familiar?"

"Not yet. I come here only one time and coming from direction of Tarsus. Never this way."

Everett didn't feel reassured by Ali's statement but kept driving several more miles.

Suddenly, Ali pointed. "This bridge! I know this bridge. I see before!"

"Great!" Everett livened up. "So you know where we're at?"

"No, but close." Ali watched intently. "Very close."

Everett slowed down to allow Ali more time to study the surroundings. "Just let me know when you see the road."

They continued for what seemed like ten more miles, but Ali saw nothing else.

The sound of the paper map crinkling could be heard in the back as Tobias studied it. "We're more than halfway between Rize and Trabzon. Are you sure we didn't pass it?"

"I don't know." Ali sounded frustrated.

"Should I turn around?" Everett inquired.

"I said I don't know!" It was the closest thing to yelling Ali had ever done since Everett met him.

Everett kept driving.

"That is it! That is the road to Sadat house!" Ali pointed feverishly at the other side of the road.

"Roger that," Everett said optimistically. "Gideon, Tobias, I'll turn around and slow down right before we get to the road. You guys bail out and stay low unless you hear gunfire."

"You got it," Tobias said.

Gideon added, "Gunfire is the international language for trouble. If we hear shots, we'll be coming in hot, so get low."

Everett made the next available U-turn, then slowed down just enough for Gideon and Tobias to exit the vehicle and take cover in the brush.

Everett turned onto the single-lane road, which took a sharp turn to the right and had a steep incline up the hill.

"Go slow. Sadat have guard before you get to gate." Ali pointed up the winding path.

"Courtney, keep your rifle ready." Everett turned another sharp twist in the roadway.

Ali furrowed his brow. "Don't worry. We don't have problem."

Courtney replied, "You'll have to excuse us, Ali. We haven't known Sadat quite as long as you have."

Everett saw the first guard. "Do you recognize this guy?"

Ali shook his head. "No. Must be new guy."

"And that's why we operate with extreme caution." Everett's tone betrayed his lack of confidence about the situation. He rolled down his window as he reached the guard.

"Turn around. You cannot drive on this road," the guard said. A second guard held his rifle at low ready.

Ali lowered his window to speak with the guard. "Call to Sadat. Tell him Ali is here."

The second guard lifted a walkie-talkie with one hand but kept his finger on the trigger guard of his rifle with the other. Everett listened, but could not understand what he was saying over the radio.

Soon, the gate opened and four more gun-toting

guards emerged from the enclosed area. Two were humongous and bald. Even though they were in less formal attire than the last time he'd visited the Turkish gangster, Everett thought he recognized the sizeable men.

One of them approached the vehicle, Uzi pistol in hand. "Ali!"

"Doruk! Happy to see you, my friend," Ali said cheerfully.

"This is Americans that come to Sadat in Tarsus?" Doruk seemed to remember Everett and Courtney when he looked inside the vehicle.

"Yes. I stay with these guys since MOC take over Tarsus," Ali affirmed.

"Sadat will see you, but I don't know about Americans." Doruk looked the SUV over suspiciously.

"He like these guys. Call him. He will say okay," Ali assured Doruk.

Doruk walked back from the car and called on his radio. Minutes later he waved Everett through the gate.

As Everett expected, he, Courtney, and even Ali had to leave their weapons locked up in the Mercedes. Doruk and the other guard escorted them up several stairs that led to a three-story villa with a red tile roof. Magenta bougainvilleas flanked the white stucco walls of the structure that looked out over the black sea.

"I bet that was quite a view before the sea turned to blood," Courtney said to no one in particular.

Doruk winced as a breeze from the sea wafted the hideous fragrance of dead fish toward them.

"Now it is worst view in all of Turkey. When I open door, go inside fast. Sadat gets very angry if we let in the smell."

Everett nodded that he understood.

Doruk opened the door. "Go! Quickly!"

Everett led the way and continued through the entrance to make room for Courtney, Ali, and the two guards. The smell of cheap incense permeated the interior of the dwelling. The smoke from it was so thick that it formed a haze.

Courtney waved her hand in front of her face and coughed. "Wow. That will definitely cover up the fish smell. What is that, strawberry?"

"Cherry. The cheaper the incense, the better job it make of covering the smell," Doruk said unapologetically as he led the procession through a hallway, down a flight of stairs and into the finished basement.

Two much-younger girls sat on a large sectional couch on either side of Sadat as he drew a long toke from the stem of a smoking brass hookah. The girls were dressed in short dresses that looked cheaper than the cherry incense burning upstairs in the foyer.

Sadat wore an open robe, no shirt, and cargo shorts, with his bare feet propped up on an ottoman. He stood up and held out his arms. "Ali! It is so good to see you my friend. I always knew you were okay."

Ali rushed over and embraced the heavy-set bald man. "It is good to see you as well, Sadat. You remember Everett and Courtney."

"Yes, of course. And Sarah, where is Sarah?"

Sadat asked politely.

"She was killed by a MOC car bomb." Courtney swallowed hard.

Sadat's face lost its brightness. "I'm so sorry to hear this. These are troubling times indeed."

Everett nodded in agreement as he shook Sadat's hand. "Even so, it's good to see you again, sir."

"Please, sit down. Can I offer you a drink?" Sadat returned to his place on the couch.

"No thank you. We don't drink." Everett sat on the end of the sectional and motioned for Courtney to sit beside him.

"Cream soda then." Sadat waved at another girl who obviously functioned as a waitress.

"Cream soda? Where did you get that?" Courtney sounded surprised.

"I specialize in living the good life, even in the worst of times." Sadat laughed.

The girl returned and handed ice-cold bottles of cream soda to Everett, Courtney, and Ali.

Everett thanked the girl and retrieved the black velvet pouch from his pocket. "Then you'll be interested in what I have to offer."

"I'm sure I will be." Sadat held out his hand as Everett passed a six-carat, princess-cut, white diamond to him. He spoke to Doruk in Turkish.

Doruk left the room and quickly returned with Sadat's loop, placing it in the gangster's eager hand.

Sadat looked the stone over for several minutes. "I'm assuming you are looking for more than a vehicle and a place to sleep for the night in exchange for this one."

Everett poured out ten more stones, each one

over four carats, onto Sadat's coffee table. "Lots more."

Courtney said softly, "We need twenty up-armored vehicles with fifty-caliber machine guns and a hundred thousand rounds of fifty-caliber ammunition, three hundred shoulder-fired surface-to-surface missile systems, a thousand hand grenades, a thousand RPGs, and five anti-aircraft guns with ten thousand shells."

Sadat sat with his eyes wide open. "Anything else?"

"Oh, yes. I almost forgot. At least one thousand of the anti-aircraft shells should be tracer rounds."

Sadat looked at Everett as if he expected him to say that Courtney was only joking.

He didn't. Instead, Everett added, "We have more diamonds. These are just examples of our inventory."

Sadat turned to Ali to confirm.

He nodded. "It is true. I have seen one stone, eight-carat. Many stones like these, Sadat."

Sadat kissed the girl on his left. "Give us a minute. We need to talk business."

Both girls took their cocktails and left the couch.

Sadat turned to Ali and held up his hands. "You know I deal in the instruments of pleasure, not death. Why do you come to me about these things?"

"What about Sheik Tariq? You can make bargain for us. Anytime Tariq want drug or need make exchange for art or diamond, he come to you."

Sadat shook his head as he stared at the diamonds on the table. He didn't seem to want to step out of his normal scope of operations, but neither did he seem able to take his eyes off the glimmering gemstones. "I make no guarantee." Sadat picked up a five-carat stone and showed it to Everett. "I keep this for my trouble, regardless of whether I make a deal or not."

Courtney took the diamond out of Sadat's hand and replaced it with the smallest stone on the table. "That one is for your trouble. If you want any of these big boys, you'll have to make something happen for us."

Sadat grunted and squeezed the smaller rock in his hand. "I need a full inventory of the stones you'll be negotiating with. Carat, cut, color, and clarity. And don't play around with the appraisals. Get a real professional. If you overestimate the specifications and make me look like a fool to Tariq, I will take it as a personal insult."

Everett nodded slowly. "I think I might know a guy that can give a fair valuation."

"Good." Sadat wrote down a radio frequency on a piece of paper. "Call me back with the specifications of each stone as soon as you can."

"We'll call you tonight," Everett said.

"Okay. Then give me until Saturday night to speak with the sheik. That should give me time to put something together." Sadat wrote down code words for the weapons Courtney had requested. "I don't talk about guns on the airwaves. These are the words I will use instead of the items you want."

Everett took the paper, folded it, and tucked it in his pocket. "Thank you very much. We appreciate your efforts."

CHAPTER 6

And the third angel poured out his vial upon the rivers and fountains of waters; and they became blood. And I heard the angel of the waters say, Thou art righteous, O Lord, which art, and wast, and shalt be, because thou hast judged thus. For they have shed the blood of saints and prophets, and thou hast given them blood to drink; for they are worthy. And I heard another out of the altar say, Even so, Lord God Almighty, true and righteous are thy judgments.

Revelation 16:4-7

Everett gritted his teeth Friday evening as he

stood on the bank of the river waiting for sunset. Courtney held his hand. Next to her was Tobias and Ali. Gideon, Dinah, her sister Batya, and Batya's husband, Levi, were also present.

Ali looked at the water, then up at the sky. He turned to Everett. "Only a few more minutes."

Everett nodded. "Yep." He fought to not allow his anger to show on his face, but he was utterly disgusted with the situation. If everyone would have simply stuck to the plan, they'd all be safely underground right now, rather than standing on the shore of the Chorokhi River, waiting for it to run red with blood.

The light faded behind the mountains to the west, casting a crimson hue across the sky. Courtney looked down at the river. "I can't tell if the reflection of the sky is making the water look red, or if it's starting."

Everett and the others looked down at the water.

Dinah pointed at the confluence of the Acharistskali and Chorokhi Rivers. "Look!"

"The Acharistskali has turned to blood," Gideon pulled his wife close. "That's no optical effect from the sky."

Everett watched as the steady stream of blood flowed into the Chorokhi River, staining its waters scarlet as well. "I'm going to go check the stored water. I'll be back."

"I'm coming with you." Courtney clung to his hand and followed him up the bank, across the road and around the back of their small cottage.

Everett lifted the lid from one of the blue barrels. A clear water glass sat atop the adjacent barrel which had been pre-positioned for this particular test. He dipped the glass into the barrel and pulled it out.

Courtney tapped the tail cap of her flashlight, sending a beam of light through the glass. "It's clean. We should have enough drinking water for a while."

"Yeah, but not enough for bathing. Hygiene is a priority. Without any means of staying clean or washing dishes, disease won't be far off." Everett sipped the water as if it were the most precious commodity on the planet.

"Let's go tell the others that the stored water is still good." Courtney allowed Everett enough time to enjoy his water and replace the lid on their treasure, then led him back to the river's bank.

Tobias seemed anxious when Everett returned. "What's the verdict?"

"It's good." Everett offered an affirming nod.

"Praise be to Jehovah who has proven Himself to be faithful once again." Ali stretched his hands toward heaven.

"Yes, praise be to HaShem." Batya put her arm around Levi and looked skyward.

Dinah's eyes were downcast as she watched dead fish begin to float on the surface of the river in the fading light. "Too bad Moses isn't here to turn the blood to water."

Gideon let his hand slip from her back as he nodded in agreement. "Yeah, too bad."

Courtney pressed her lips together to echo Dinah's sentiment. Then, her brows knitted together. She turned to Everett as if trying to remember a distant dream.

"What?" he said.

"Do you remember what you told us when Sarah and I were trying to convince you that we had to bring Moses' staff back to him?"

"Not even remotely." Everett thought back. "Something about it being a crutch?"

"No, not that part."

"I can't remember. That was three years ago, and we've been through a lot since then."

She glared into his eyes. "You said that maybe he left it in the cave on purpose; for us."

Everett immediately caught on to what she was implying but dared not get his hopes up. "Don't say anything else. We try it out first. I don't want to disappoint everyone if it doesn't work."

"Okay, but we need to try it now," she said quietly.

"We'll be back." Everett waved to the others as he led Courtney back to the cottage.

She sprinted ahead to retrieve the staff from above the fireplace mantle and met Everett on the porch. She offered him the staff. "Do you want to do the honors?"

"It was your idea. Go ahead."

"Thanks!" She pulled the staff close to her body and grinned at him.

Everett held her hand to keep her from running ahead. "Let's temper our enthusiasm until we know."

"Right." She took a deep breath and slowed her pace.

When they returned, the others had dispersed and

were on their way back inside Tobias and Ali's house.

The remnants of daylight had grown too faint to see the color of the river. Everett directed the stream of light from his flashlight toward a spot near the edge. "Put it in right there."

Courtney sighed with eagerness. "Okay." She pierced the blood with the wooden stick, in the center of the beam from Everett's flashlight.

Everett watched as crystal clear water ran away from the location where the staff met the river.

"It's working!" Courtney exclaimed.

"I see!" He redirected the flashlight to inspect how far the clear water ran before it was completely diluted by the blood. "It runs clear for about ten feet."

Courtney took out her light and shined it in the other direction. "Look. The blood is turning to water upstream."

Everett followed the light with his eyes. Sure enough, the blood was clearing upstream. Only for about three feet, but it was growing. "Take out the staff and see if it stays clear."

Courtney lifted the stick out of the river. The flow of blood immediately polluted the clear water and the translucent liquid quickly melted back into the thick red river. "Gone. I wonder if we found the source of the river. Could we turn it back to water?"

Everett looked upstream. "Both the Chorokhi and the Acharistskali run for miles. It'd be easier to isolate the source of the creek behind our cottage. But not at night. We'll try it first thing tomorrow morning."

"Can we tell the others now?" Courtney asked enthusiastically.

"Sure. Let's get a bucket from the back of Tobias' house and do a little demonstration." Everett led the way to get a container for the exhibition.

"Great idea!" she exclaimed.

Before dawn Saturday morning, Everett awoke to the sound of a door knock. Groggily, he got up to answer it. "Ali? What time is it?"

"5:30. Everett, Sadat call on radio. He say Tariq the Sheik have samples ready. We are to go to Sadat house with half of diamonds. Be there by eight, then meet Tariq at eleven o'clock."

Everett needed caffeine before being bombarded with such a weighty matter. "Come in. Let me start some tea." Everett filled the tea kettle and took it out to the rocket stove on the back porch. "What does he mean by samples?"

"Probably like four or five vehicles that we ask for, some rocket, some grenade. I don't know."

Everett rubbed his eyes. "If he wants half the diamonds, we need half the merchandise."

Ali's forehead puckered. "No, Everett. That is not how these thing work. Always is fifty percent deposit for sample. If you like items, then everything else will be of similar quality. If you don't like, then Sheik try to make better product or say *no thank you* and everyone walk away. But always he need deposit to purchase items. If you make problem, then Sheik don't work with you, and Sadat don't work with you.

"I know you think these men are criminal, and probably you are correct. But, they have reputation because always they honor deal. You, on the other hand, have no reputation in this world. They only make business with you because of me."

Everett listened quietly.

Ali waved his hands. "I don't care more about these things. But if you don't make this deal, opportunity is gone. Sadat will not speak to either of us ever again. I hope so, by now, you trust what I tell you is true."

Everett waited for the kettle to whistle. "Okay. On your say-so, I'll give him half the diamonds for a sample of the goods."

"Good. I go get Tobias and Gideon. We must leave in half hour or we'll be late." Ali let himself out the back door.

Everett woke Courtney and offered to let her sit this one out. Of course, she declined.

"So much for our trek to find the source of the creek." She put her backup gun in an ankle holster before putting her boots on.

"I'm sure the bloody stream will still be there when we get back." Everett placed several magazines in his assault pack.

"Could we make a quick stop by the sea? I'm curious to see if Moses' staff will turn blood from the Black Sea back into salt water or if it might actually come back as fresh water."

"If we can get on the road before 6:00, we'll make a pit stop. Otherwise, it'll have to wait until we get back." The teapot whistled and Everett hurried to retrieve it from the rocket stove.

The team was loaded into the Mercedes SUV at 5:55. Gideon looked like he'd been awake less than five minutes.

"You ready, big guy?" Everett glanced at him in the rearview.

"For what?" Gideon had a bad case of bed head.

"To go buy some fireworks." Everett dangled the black velvet pouch in the rearview mirror as he put the vehicle in gear.

Remembering the previous trip, Everett had some idea of which parts of the roads were really bad and which parts were in good enough condition to drive a little faster. He made good time getting to the coast. He put the vehicle in park while he and Courtney bailed out. They ran to collect a sample of the blood from the Black Sea and hurried back to the SUV. Courtney retrieved the staff and stuck it in the one-gallon bucket containing the blood. Instantly, it turned to water.

"Now here's the real test." She put the bucket to her lips and sipped a small amount.

"What have we got?" Everett asked.

She passed the bucket to him. "Fresh water!"

Everett took a quick drink, then passed the bucket to Tobias. "Try this. It's the best water you've ever drank."

Everett closed the door behind Courtney, returned to the driver's seat, and continued toward Sadat's villa.

An hour and a half later, Ali pointed toward the coast. "There is fishing marina. We are nearly to

Rize. We should be to Sadat house on time."

"Is that a sanitation truck?" Tobias pointed at another vehicle on the road ahead.

"Wow," Everett commented. "I can't believe they have garbage service around here. I haven't seen any other signs of GR presence at all. I'd think trash pick-up would be toward the lower end of the priority scale."

Gideon called out from the back. "Something's not right. There's a delivery truck and a bus behind us. This is more traffic than we've seen in both trips put together."

Everett took his foot off the accelerator. "The garbage truck driver just stuck his vehicle sideways and blocked both lanes!"

"This is an ambush!" Tobias yelled. "Try to turn around and drive past the bus and the delivery truck!"

It was too late. Both vehicles were already behind Everett blocking any possible exit. "Lock and load!" Everett drew his rifle up to wait for the garbage truck driver to get out.

"Bad news," Gideon said. "I've already spotted six shooters on the rooftop of the apartment building to the left. No telling how many more are set up in sniper nests inside the windows."

Everett turned to Courtney. "Just stay down."

"No way! We're probably not going to walk away from this one Everett. I'm not going down without a fight."

His worst nightmare had come true. Unless God granted him the grace of catching a bullet before she did, there was a good chance Everett was going to have to watch his wife die a violent death. He took a deep breath and prepared to fight it out to the end.

A voice with a thick middle-eastern accent came over a megaphone, "Nobody want to die today. Just give us diamonds and you can leave. But don't try to keep any. We know exactly how many you have. Even we know size and color."

Everett turned to Ali. "Sadat set us up!"

"No! He never do this thing!" Ali protested strongly.

"Face it, Ali. He sold us out." Everett looked for shooters inside the windows of the apartment building on the side of the road. He saw many of the windows open and figured they weren't open for the fresh sea air since it smelled like rotten fish.

"What do we do here?" Everett looked at Tobias in the rearview.

Tobias shook his head in defeat. "I think we have to give them up."

"You think they'll really let us go?" Courtney asked.

"I don't know," Tobias replied. "But they'll get those diamonds one way or the other. We're massively outgunned here. If they don't let us through, we'll take as many of them as we can. But we've gotta try to get out of here without a firefight."

Everett rolled his window down just enough to hold the pouch out.

Gideon said, "We've got four armed men coming out of the bus behind us. They're approaching our vehicle. Tobias, get a bead on this guy. If they start shooting, we start shooting. Everybody get out of the SUV and make a run for the garbage truck. If we can kill the driver, we'll have the right side of the truck for cover from the snipers."

"Then what?" Ali asked nervously.

"Then we'll shoot it out until . . ."

"Until what?" Courtney inquired forcefully.

Gideon didn't answer directly. Instead, he said, "We weren't going to be around here all that much longer anyway."

Everett held the pouch steadily with one hand and kept the muzzle of his HK rifle trained in the direction of the approaching gunman with the other. They were dressed in solid black clothing with black face masks. Each one held an AK-47. One of the gunmen lowered his rifle just long enough to lunge toward Everett and snatch the black velvet pouch from his fingers.

The four gunmen backed away from the Mercedes cautiously and re-entered the bus.

Everett's heart pounded as he waited for the next event. Nothing happened for several minutes. Finally, the garbage truck's engine started and it pulled back into one lane.

The voice came back over the megaphone. "You may leave."

Everett stomped the accelerator to the floor and sped past the sanitation vehicle. He took a deep breath—angry that they'd been robbed, but immeasurably grateful that he'd not had to watch Courtney get shot.

"Now what?" Tobias asked.

"We go to Sadat's, gun down his guards and hold him hostage while we wait for his henchmen to show up with the stones." Everett clinched his jaw.

"No! Everett! I am telling you right now, Sadat don't do this!" Ali sounded furious.

"Then who did? Tariq?" Everett glanced over at him for only a moment.

"Tariq the Sheik don't make reputation by do these thing. They have code. I don't think so it was Tariq also."

Everett yelled in rage. "Then who, Ali? No one else knows we have the diamonds. You're in denial. You just have to accept the fact that Sadat set you up. He's not the same guy you knew three years ago. People change. And gangsters, when they change, it's for the worse."

"You make big mistake, Everett!" Ali shook his finger at Everett with his nose snarled and his eyebrows seized together in a knot. "Big, big, mistake!"

Gideon interjected. "Ali could be right."

"How could he possibly be right?" Everett snapped. The line of reasoning was simply insane.

"Our communications with Sadat could have been intercepted. We've been speaking openly over shortwave. If they strung everything together, they could have determined where we were coming from, where we were going, when we'd be here, and they'd have certainly known exactly what we were carrying."

Everett instantly realized that he'd completely overlooked this possibility in his fit of angst. He huffed. "An ex-CIA analyst was talking about millions of dollars' worth of diamonds on an open channel." Immediately, the guilt, shame, and humiliation hit him like a tsunami. He banged the steering wheel with his fist. "I can't believe it. I can't believe I was so stupid."

Courtney put her hand on his shoulder. "Don't be too hard on yourself. An ex-NSA analyst was right there beside you, and she said nothing."

Tobias' voice came from behind. "There may or may not have been two Mossad agents involved in the lapse of standard communications protocol. You certainly can't take all of the blame."

"The person who normally must be more cautious than all intelligence agent is the man who work for Turkish mafia. This type of mistake will get you killed in mob. I cannot let this go without I accept my portion of the responsibility." Ali looked sheepishly at Everett.

Everett quickly understood that while they'd lost the diamonds, he had something more precious; brothers and a sister in Christ who were in this thing with him no matter what. "Thanks, guys."

"So we need a new plan, that's all," Tobias said with an encouraging tone.

Everett turned to Ali. "Sorry I yelled at you. What do you recommend?"

"I raise also my voice. For this, I am the one who is sorry. I think so we should go to Sadat and say to him what happen. Still, we have other half of diamonds in Batumi. And we don't talk about when we come back over radio."

"You got that right." Everett continued racing toward Sadat's villa.

CHAPTER 7

Behold, I send you forth as sheep in the midst of wolves: be ye therefore wise as serpents, and harmless as doves.

Matthew 10:16

Everett lowered his eyes like the boy who'd sold the prize cow for a fist full of magic beans. "Obviously, we won't speak so openly over the radio again, sir."

Sadat threw his hands in the air and let them come back down on his face. "What am I supposed to do? I always make things fair, but this is not only me we talk about. Tariq the Sheik don't want to hear excuse. He make bargain. He fulfill his side. And he expect me to fulfill my side."

"We could race back to Batumi, pick up the

other half of the diamonds." Everett raised his eyebrows.

"Then what happen when it is time to settle for other half?" Sadat scolded Everett. "This is bad plan." Sadat looked at Ali. "I never work with these guys if not for you. I thought you understand how serious is this business."

"I do, Sadat. I am very sorry for disappoint you." Ali's head hung like a windsock with no breeze.

"What if we had something more valuable than diamonds?" Courtney stood with her arms crossed.

"No, no. You don't change deal one hour before we meet with Tariq. This is very bad." Sadat wagged his finger at her.

Courtney stood staring at Sadat silently as if she were waiting for a grouper to bite the shiny lure affixed to the end of her fishing pole.

Sadat rubbed his chin and glanced toward his bodyguard, Doruk, who was looking back at him as if he had something to say. "What?"

Doruk ever so subtly nodded toward Courtney.

Sadat caught the signal and turned back to her. He sighed. "Okay, tell me what is more valuable than diamond."

"Where are you planning to get water?" she asked.

"We will set up stills and distill the water from the blood." Sadat had obviously already come up with a plan before her inquiry.

"You're talking about a lot of resources. You'll burn every tree on this mountain just to distill enough water to keep you and your compound alive for six weeks."

"You have better plan I suppose?" Sadat seemed to be growing impatient.

"Can you have one of your guys fetch us a bucket of blood from the sea?"

"Why should I?" Sadat looked perplexed.

"Trust her, Sadat." Ali nodded. "You will want to see this."

"And pardon me. I need to get something from the SUV." Courtney turned to go back upstairs.

"I'll go with her." Everett followed his wife.

"Okay, but the two men who came with you stay outside with your vehicle," Sadat said. "Doruk, go with them. And have one of my men bring us bucket filled with blood. Tell them don't get it on the floor."

Once Everett and Courtney reached the Mercedes, Tobias asked, "How's it going in there?"

Doruk accompanied one of the other guards down the winding path to the sea.

"Could have been worse." Everett stood by as Courtney retrieved the staff.

"Let me guess, you're trying to renegotiate for water." Gideon leaned against the SUV.

"Diamonds won't do you any good if you die of thirst." She tucked the staff in the duffel bag and walked back to the house.

"I hope Sadat doesn't decide to liberate us from the staff." Everett nodded at the guard who opened the door as they walked back in the house.

"I don't think it will work for him," Courtney said softly.

"What makes you say that?"

"Just a gut feeling. I think it will only work for a

child of God."

"A gut feeling or is the Holy Spirit telling you that?"

She paused before going down the stairs. "The Spirit. I don't know how else to explain it, but I'm certain it won't work for anyone who isn't a child of God."

"Good enough." Everett continued down into Sadat's parlor.

Doruk arrived minutes later with a man carefully totting a five-gallon bucket half-filled with blood. Doruk placed a piece of cardboard on the floor for the other man to place the bucket on.

Courtney instructed Sadat, "Confirm that the bucket is filled with blood."

Sadat looked into the container. "Okay. Is blood."

She lowered the staff into the bucket and the blood turned to pure water. "Take a sip."

Sadat looked curiously into the bucket. "You go first."

Courtney cupped her hand and took a drink.

Sadat cautiously did the same. "Okay. Good magic trick. How do you do it?"

Everett stood nearby. "It's not magic. It's the power of God."

"You give me staff instead of diamonds?" Sadat inquired.

"Oh, no. It wouldn't work for you anyway unless you're ready to confess that Jesus is the Messiah and repent of your sins." Everett crossed his arms.

"Not just yet." Sadat laughed. "But you don't expect that I am going to take a few buckets of water instead of the diamonds."

"What if we can purify a permanent water source for you? A creek or a stream?" Courtney asked.

"Can you turn my well back to water?"

"I think so. If you can get me a shaft wide enough to lower the staff on a string and pull it back up," Courtney said confidently.

"You will need to provide a water source for Tariq the Sheik also. I think this plus other half of diamonds and we can still make deal work." Sadat stood up. "I will have men get drilling rig to drill out hole big enough to lower the staff. But first, to be sure this is not just some type of illusion, I would like to see you turn the creek behind my house to water. It will provide me and my people water for now, and it will go long way in repairing my trust."

Everett nodded, hoping that they would, indeed, be able to fulfill the request. "Can you show us the source of the creek?"

"It's further up mountain. Doruk will show to you."

Everett and Courtney followed Doruk, out of the house, through the small garden area and out a gate which provided access to the wooded hillside behind the villa.

"Here is creek." Doruk pointed. "It is not much of a stream."

Everett looked at the thin trickle of blood flowing over a channel of creek stone less than two feet wide. "Courtney, can I see the staff for a moment?"

She handed it to him.

Everett said a silent prayer beneath his breath

then thrust the wooden stick into the blood. Immediately, clear water ran down the creek from where the staff stood. Less quickly, the blood began to change into water upstream as well. Everett watched as the small stream converted back to water beyond the point where he could see.

"I don't believe it," Doruk said.

"But you had no problem believing when it turned to blood in the first place," Courtney said with the slightest note of sarcasm.

Doruk shook his head. "I didn't believe that either."

Everett held the staff for several minutes, hoping that the transformational power would eventually reach the source of the stream and permanently turn the blood to water. He lifted the staff from the unclouded brook and waited for several more minutes. "Why don't you go get Sadat. I think we've got it."

Doruk nodded. "Be right back."

Everett and Courtney quietly watched the water as they waited for Sadat.

He arrived minutes later. "You did it?"

"Seems as if we did. Actually, I can't take much credit for it." Everett passed Sadat a small New Testament from his back pocket.

"What is this?" Sadat slowly squatted by the brook.

"Living Water." Everett smiled.

Sadat took a drink with his hand from the stream and passed the small book back to Everett. "No thank you. I am Muslim."

"Pardon me for saying so, but you don't appear

to be all that—enthusiastic about practicing Islam."

"Then I probably would not make a good Christian either." Sadat smirked and headed back to the villa.

Courtney took the Bible from Everett. "How about I leave this on the table when we leave? You never know, you might want to know what's coming next. Every plague that's happened so far has been spelled out in the pages of this book."

"If you will leave me alone about it, you can put it on the table," Sadat conceded. "But for now, we must hurry. We will be late to meet with Tariq."

"Should we bring some blood from the sea to demonstrate the staff for Tariq?" Courtney asked.

"There will be plenty of blood where we are going." Sadat led the way through the gate. "But I would not do this demonstration for Tariq. He does not need to know how you are turning blood to water. Maybe he don't take your word that he cannot perform the miracle himself if he have the staff."

"Duly noted." Everett waited for Doruk and Courtney to walk through the gate, then pulled it shut.

"I'll insist that Everett and I be alone to pray over the blood for it to convert back into water." Courtney looked at Everett for approval of the improvised plan.

He gave a shallow nod. "That should work."

Sadat rode in a desert-tan Humvee with three of his guards. Everett and his team followed close behind in the Mercedes GL. Sadat's vehicle led them deep into the mountains, away from the Black Sea. The small village of Ispir, Turkey was nestled in the mountains, approximately 60 miles southeast of Sadat's villa. Ispir was located on a reservoir created by a dam on the Chorokhi River. Its secluded position and abundant supply of fresh water would have made it the ideal location for survival if the water had not turned to blood.

A few miles east along the reservoir was the dam. Just beyond that was a tunnel that took the modest two-lane road through the core of a mountain. On the other side of the mountain was a gravel clearing where five heavily armored Russian military vehicles sat next to a gold Bentley Bentayga SUV.

Sadat's Humvee pulled into the clearing. Everett followed. Sadat motioned for Everett and Courtney to join him as he exited the vehicle to greet a man wearing jeans, a tan blazer, and a black and tan shemagh draped high around his neck which partially obscured his bearded face. The man wore large wire-framed sunglasses and very short hair. He was nothing like the image of Sheik Tariq Everett had painted in his head.

Tobias, Ali, and Gideon remained in the vehicle.

"This is Tariq the Sheik," Sadat said, turning to Everett and Courtney.

"A pleasure to meet you." Everett shook the man's hand, introducing himself and Courtney.

Tariq wasted no time with pleasantries. He turned to the first three MRAPs. "These are Russian Typhoons. Each is mounted with remote-controlled 50-caliber machine gun turret. The other two are also Russian. They are called Patrol, manufactured by Asteys. They don't have turret, but the Patrols offer six hatches on top, which can provide six gunmen the ability to shoot from the top of the vehicle with their personal firearms or RPGs."

Sadat signaled for Tariq to take a break. "There has been a slight change in plans."

The sheik's expression soured instantaneously. "Sadat, how long do I work with you? You never try something like this before."

Sadat nodded affirmatively with his hands up. "Exactly, which is why you owe it to me to at least hear me out before you get upset."

Tariq glanced at the gold Rolex on his wrist. "Make it fast and make it good. I am very unhappy about having this sprung on me last minute."

"Okay. My clients were robbed coming through Rize. Evidently, they were overheard on the radio talking about the diamonds, and when they would be delivering them to me."

"Not my problem, Sadat!"

"Please—allow me to finish." Sadat's eyebrows lowered, becoming less apologetic and more demanding. "I had the same initial reaction as you are having. But, my guests soon convinced me that they had something far more valuable to offer than diamonds."

"There are few things more valuable, Sadat. So quit baiting me and tell me what you have to offer."

"It was their God, the God of the Jews and the Christians, who changed the water to blood."

"Then please remember to thank Him for me." Tariq pressed his lips together tightly as he glared at

Everett.

Sadat continued. "And their God has given them the power to change it back."

"I never suspected you to be a fool who would believe these childish superstitions, Sadat." Tariq began walking toward the Bentley and motioned for his men to get in the military vehicles. "Don't call me ever again. And thank whatever God you pray to that I am not going to kill you today for wasting my time."

Sadat evidently knew where Tariq's base of operations was. "You have to drive back by the reservoir. We'll go ahead. It will only take you a minute to stop and see if what I say is true. If I speak the truth to you, it would be you who is the fool for passing up such an opportunity."

Tariq turned and watched as Sadat motioned for Everett and Courtney to follow him in their SUV.

Everett jumped back in the driver's seat and turned to Courtney who was getting in behind him. "Find some string, quick!"

"What's the plan?" she asked as Everett sped away to keep up with Sadat who was already racing back through the tunnel.

"We've got one shot at convincing this guy. We're going to turn the reservoir back to water."

CHAPTER 8

So the waters were healed unto this day, according to the saying of Elisha which he spake.

2 King 2:22

Everett threw the shifter into park and jumped out of the vehicle leaving the motor running. He pulled a fifty-foot length of paracord from his assault pack.

Courtney got out of the vehicle with the staff. "It's going to take some time to turn that much blood to water! Tariq will be here any second!"

"Then we better move fast!" Everett exclaimed.

"What can we do to help?" Ali asked.

"You, Tobias, and Gideon line up by the ledge of the reservoir and start praying." Everett secured the paracord to the staff and began lowering it into the crimson pool below. "Heads bowed, eyes closed, and on your knees. Optics matter this time."

The three of them followed Everett's directive. Tobias knelt with his hands together in prayer by the guardrail overlooking the reservoir. He opened one eye and watched Everett. "If we turn the reservoir to water, Tariq has no reason to bargain with us."

"The Chorokhi is still pouring hundreds of gallons of blood into the reservoir every minute. It won't stay clear for more than an hour, once I pull the staff back out." Everett tied off the paracord at the base of the guardrail to allow the staff to wade freely in the reservoir below.

Courtney pointed at the water, several feet out from the edge where the staff was submerged. "It's working."

"I need more paracord!" Everett said.

Courtney raced to the Mercedes and retrieved the paracord from her pack. She brought it to Everett. "Here!"

The gold Bentley SUV pulled through the tunnel and parked next to Sadat's Humvee. Tariq got out and scowled at Sadat who was standing along the rail next to Doruk. "I feel like such an imbecile for even considering this."

"Not for long. Look. The reservoir has turned back to water." Sadat pointed at the body of water below.

Tariq said nothing as he stood near the rail shaking his head. "This cannot be. We drove by here less than thirty minutes ago. It was blood. I am sure of it." He looked on in unbelief at Tobias, Ali, and Gideon who were making a bigger show of their prayers than actually communing with the Father.

"Can you drink it?" Tariq's forehead was furrowed in distrust.

"Sure. I just need something to draw it up with. I have some cord." Everett presented the paracord to Tariq.

Tariq snatched the cord from his hand. "I'll draw it up, and you'll drink it. No more bait and switch today." Tariq walked to his golden Bentley and retrieve an empty water bottle. He tied a knot in the paracord around the neck of the bottle and picked up enough stones from the ground to weight the empty bottle so it would sink in the water. He lowered it over the rail. The bottle sank, and the sheik pulled it back up. He shoved the bottle into Everett's chest with a snarl. "Drink it all."

Everett took the bottle which was now filled with crystal clear water and still had the paracord tied around the neck. He tipped it back and chugged the entire liter, being careful not to let any of the pebbles wash into his mouth. He passed the bottle back to Tariq.

The sheik watched suspiciously, then took back the bottle, and tossed it over the rail to refill it. This time he handed it to Sadat. "Take a drink."

Sadat began to chug the bottle just as Everett had. Tariq snapped his fingers twice and held his hand out toward Sadat. "Give it back."

Sadat obliged. Tariq sipped from the bottle. He took a second drink; then a third drink, longer than the first two. He looked at the water, then up at Everett. "I do not know how you did. But you did it. I cannot deny it." He cocked one eye and pointed at Everett. "If this is some kind of trick, I will kill you. There is nowhere on earth you can hide from me. I have people everywhere. But, for now, I suppose we can renegotiate our arrangement. This reservoir, will it stay clear?"

"No." Everett shook his head. "Once we quit praying, the blood pouring into it from the Chorokhi will soon pollute it."

"What about a well? Can you make a well permanently turn to water?"

"Tell me about the well." Everett stuck his hands in his pockets.

"It is an old open well, from the fourteenth century. It has a stone wall around it, with a wooden frame and handle to lower and raise buckets for retrieving the water."

"I think we can. Without knowing if some other water source flows into it, I can't say for sure, but I will give you my word. If there is a problem with the well, we'll keep trying until we find an isolated water source for you."

Tariq crossed his arms and stood with his feet apart. "Can you do this now?"

"We need to be alone with the well to pray over it. No unbelievers can be present when we begin praying."

Tariq rolled his eyes. "You sound like MOC. Why can no unbeliever be present? I am here now while these guys pray."

"Yes, but when we began it was only us,"

Everett rebutted.

"Sadat was here." Tariq motioned toward his robust acquaintance.

"Sadat and Doruk waited reverently in the car until you arrived."

Tariq still seemed to detect that he wasn't getting the whole truth but appeared to be more anxious about getting his well converted than to continue pursuing the matter. "Okay, whatever. I'll go back and get my men. When we pass back through the tunnel, you'll follow us to my compound. No one ever comes to my home, so once you leave, never come back. Is that understood?"

"Perfectly." Everett watched the arrogant arms dealer walk back to his luxury SUV and drive back through the tunnel.

"All clear." Courtney immediately pulled the staff up out of the reservoir.

Everett untied the paracord from the rail. "Let's go!"

Everett's team loaded into the Mercedes, while Sadat and Doruk got in the Humvee.

Minutes later, Tariq the Sheik's convoy motored out the tunnel. Everett pulled in behind the last armored vehicle and followed it to the sheik's lair.

Tariq's convoy led them through the small village of Ispir, then continued past the town to where the pavement ended. The road became more coarse, jarring everyone in the cabin of the Mercedes as they maintained an adequate speed to keep up.

Everett kept a firm grip on the steering wheel. "I was wondering why anyone would want a Bentley

SUV."

"Now you have your answer," Tobias said from behind Everett.

"It's the only Bentley anyone is going to be driving on this road," Gideon added.

The convoy turned off the dirt road onto what looked like a path for a tractor. Two lines of dirt pierced an otherwise untouched area of grass and low shrubbery through a thick tree line.

"I guess this is the place." Everett stopped the vehicle behind the military vehicles and got out. The area was heavily wooded, probably to cover Tariq's activities from satellite and drone observation. Everett spotted at least a dozen guards wearing woodland camo patterns posted near various trees. He saw a dilapidated barn and another larger outbuilding with metal siding, but nothing that looked like the main dwelling structure for a rich-and-famous international arms dealer.

Tariq walked up to the Mercedes and motioned for Everett to get out. "Follow me."

Everett nodded and opened his door. He looked at his team. "We'll all go."

"Hold on!" Tariq held up his hand. "What is this? Why is everyone getting out of the vehicle?"

"We're all going to pray for your well," Everett answered as if the sheik's question was the silliest thing he'd ever heard.

"Only three of you were praying for the reservoir."

"We all prayed before you got there." Everett paused so not to upset the sheik. "Besides, the reservoir is going to turn back to blood. We want it to take the first time. I'd rather not have to come back. No offense to your fine property here, but it's a long drive for us."

That statement seemed to settle the matter for Tariq. He tossed his hands in the air. "Okay, fine. Do what you have to do." He pointed at the duffle bag which Courtney carried. "But no weapons. Leave the bag in the car."

She looked at Everett.

"It's not a weapon," Everett assured the sheik.

"Okay. Open it up. Let me see what it is." Tariq the Sheik walked toward Courtney.

Everett stepped between them. "Do you want your well to give you drinking water or do you want to continue to be a rather impolite host— molesting your female guest by invading her privacy and treating her suspiciously? Some people might take offense to such treatment and walk away."

Tariq glared at Everett for a moment, like the two of them were playing a game of chicken, seeing who would cave in first.

Everett wouldn't be the one to give. No way he was about to tip his hand about the staff after the warning Sadat gave him. If he had to, he'd put the team back in the car, and they'd figure out something else. They stood a better chance taking the Jews across Turkey without military vehicles than without water.

Tariq looked him up and down and must have sensed that Everett wouldn't budge. "Fine. Take your bag. And remember, for every guard you see, there's five more that you don't see. If you try something here, you'll die where you stand."

"Fair enough. Where's the well?"

Tariq motioned toward the barn. "Behind there. You'll see it. There is a one-meter stone wall around it with a red metal roof over the wooden frame."

Everett nodded and led his team to the barn. He spoke quietly. "When we get there, everyone gather around the draw well and pray. Pray that we pull this off and get out of here alive. Pray that none of his guards notice the staff and that Tariq doesn't rip us off."

"Yes, Everett. I am praying even now as we walk," Ali said.

"Good."

They reached the well and knelt around it. Everett subtly took the staff and tossed it over the side, holding firmly onto the paracord. "Lord, we pray that you'll turn this well to water, see us through this mission and bring us safely back to Batumi with the equipment we're purchasing here today."

"Amen," Courtney said.

Everett sat silently for a couple minutes, then reeled in the staff. "Ali, turn the crank to the draw rope. Let's see if we've got water."

Ali pulled the bucket to himself as it reached the top of the well. "Water! Praise God!"

"Praise God, indeed." Everett looked at Courtney. "Take the staff back to the SUV. Tobias, Gideon, escort her. Ali, you come with me to tell Tariq he's got fresh water."

When they arrived back to the area where the vehicles were parked, Everett gave Sadat a nod to let him know the water was good. He informed Tariq that they'd been successful and walked back with him to the well.

Tariq took a deep drink directly from the bucket, then passed Everett five sets of keys. "No more magic tricks. When you come for the balance of your merchandise, come with the diamonds or don't come at all."

Everett nodded. "I understand perfectly."

"You have couple cases of grenades, RPGs, and shoulder-fired missiles in the Typhoons. The rest of the items are going to be similar quality to these. If you don't like something, you tell Sadat by tomorrow. I should have everything ready by next Thursday."

"Can you push it to Wednesday? We're on a deadline." Everett figured the next judgment would be poured upon the Earth on the following Friday. He wanted to be settled underground well in advance of the scorching heat of the Fourth Vial.

Tariq said grimly, "I'll try."

"And we were supposed to have anti-aircraft guns."

"This is the thing holding me up. I am trying to find the right trailers for them. They need big tires because the guns are heavy and the roads are bad. Usually they are in the back of a pickup truck, but Sadat did not negotiate for this."

"Can I bring you ten pickup trucks? I can drop them here tomorrow."

"No, you cannot bring me pickup trucks. Either you wait until I can work it out or you take delivery without the antiaircraft guns. The price is the same either way."

"I'm not paying for something I'm not getting. Get the anti-aircraft guns here by Wednesday or I'll deduct it from the final payment."

Tariq seemed to be enjoying the art of the negotiation more than Everett. He looked like he might have been fighting back a smile. Haggling over price was a pastime that had never caught on in the west as much as the middle east. "Okay. I have everything here on Wednesday afternoon."

Everett shook the sheik's hand. "Nice doing business with you."

Tariq held his grip firmly. "If the well doesn't hold up, don't come back, because I will kill you."

Everett gripped the sheik's hand even tighter. "That wouldn't be wise. Then I wouldn't be able to fix it for you."

Tariq lost the battle over his smile. The corners of his mouth turned upwards as if he found Everett to be a worthy adversary. "I suppose this is true."

"I'll see you soon, Sheik." Everett made his way back to the vehicles, giving keys to Ali, Courtney, Tobias, and Gideon.

He shook hands with Sadat. "The Chorokhi, the river that runs into the reservoir, is the same river that runs past our house. I think we're going to take the back way home. I'm in no hurry to go back through Rize. Would you mind if Doruk drove the Mercedes back to your place? We can pick it up on our next visit."

"Actually, I've been wondering what it would be like to drive it. I will get it back for you." Sadat said with a smile which indicated he probably didn't intend on driving it slowly.

Everett wasn't about to stifle his fun. He passed him the keys. "Thanks. We'll be in touch. When I give you a day and time, subtract three from each. That will add a layer of security to our communications."

Sadat took the keys. "So, Thursday at 4:00 really means Monday at 1:00."

"Precisely." Everett waved and got into the driver's seat of the Patrol parked at the head of the convoy. "Take care."

CHAPTER 9

I would seek unto God, and unto God would I commit my cause: Which doeth great things and unsearchable; marvellous things without number: Who giveth rain upon the earth, and sendeth waters upon the fields.

Job 5:8-10

Everett waited impatiently Thursday afternoon by the Ham radio in Tobias' bedroom. "I can't believe this!"

Courtney sat on the floor in the corner of the room. "You can't believe a criminal arms dealer who supplies weapons to the Martyrs of the Caliphate failed to keep his commitment?"

Her articulation of the predicament made him

feel no better. Everett grunted. "I can't believe that we've managed to have nearly 150,000 people ready to mobilize but instead of moving them, we're stuck sitting here, essentially waiting on a phone call."

"If we haven't heard anything by sunset, we'll modify the plan to work with what we've got." Tobias stretched his hands behind his head.

"And cross desert with only five armor vehicle?" Ali's voice was anxious.

Gideon stuck his hands in his pockets and leaned his shoulder against the desk where the radio was set up. "Most of the Jews who will be traveling with us have served in the Israeli Defense Force. We have enough pistols and rifles for all of them to have a weapon. Even if we don't have the best armored vehicles, shoulder-fired weapons, or grenades, having that many shooters automatically makes us a hard target."

"But MOC have all these things. Some Mullahs in this part of Turkey may see this many Jews trying to pass through their territory as an invasion." Ali shook his head. "This is not good."

"Although, today was the day Tariq originally said he'd have everything ready, right?" Courtney stretched out her legs on the floor. "He's not exactly late."

Everett clinched his jaw. "I explained that we had a deadline and he agreed to have everything together by yesterday. When he accepted those terms, he obligated himself to have the goods to us on time."

The radio sprang to life. It was Sadat's voice.

"Meet me Sunday. Seven o'clock."

Everett jumped up from the foot of Tobias' bed and grabbed the mic. "Roger. See you then."

"Sunday at seven?" Gideon looked like he was about to blow a pressure seal.

Everett put up a hand to calm the man. "It's code. Sunday at seven means today at four. Go get the rest of the drivers. We need to be on the road in one hour."

"We can do that." Tobias tapped Gideon to ride with him. "Come on. Let's go get the guys."

"We'll be waiting for you when you get back." Everett helped Courtney up from the floor. "Let's grab our gear."

The two of them dashed across the street to get their assault packs and weapons. The additional ten drivers needed to get the armored vehicles back to Batumi lived nearby, so it wouldn't take Tobias and Gideon long to collect them in the big Typhoon-K which was designed to accommodate up to nineteen troops.

Forty-five minutes later, Everett heard the horn out front. "That's our ride."

Courtney stuffed the rest of a sandwich in her mouth, grabbed her gear, and followed Everett out the door.

Tobias drove the vehicle, Everett sat up front in the passenger's seat, and Gideon maned the remote control fifty-caliber machine gun. Even though this Mine Resistant Ambush Protected vehicle offered a much higher level of security than the Mercedes, Everett still insisted on taking the back way and avoiding Rize, the small Turkish town where they'd been attacked before.

"Sadat is going to meet us at a bridge, roughly ten miles north of Ispir." Everett looked his map over.

"Why is he coming?" Gideon asked.

Courtney dangled a black velvet bag filled with the remaining gemstones. "He's gotta take his cut for setting this whole thing up."

"A lifetime supply of drinking water isn't sufficient payment for introducing us to a gun dealer?" Gideon sounded annoyed.

"It's all a matter of perspective." Everett smiled. "Those diamonds won't be worth much in a few weeks from now anyway. Might as well put them to good use."

The rugged back roads added an additional hour and a half to the trip, but they finally arrived at the bridge which took D050, the main artery running alongside the Chorokhi, from one side of the river to the other. The black Mercedes SUV that Everett had left with Sadat was parked on the side of the road, next to the bank of the river. Tobias pulled off the road and cut the engine beside the Mercedes.

Everett looked through his binoculars at the cliffs above. Seeing no threats, he exited the vehicle. Courtney and Ali followed him over to Sadat.

Everett nodded at Doruk who was behind the wheel and Sadat who was in the passenger's seat. "I see you're taking a liking to the Mercedes."

"I am hoping you give to me for present." Sadat smiled.

Everett laughed. "And what do I get?"

"Already you get many things," the gangster replied.

"For which we're paying a high price." Courtney tossed the velvet pouch through the passenger's window and into Sadat's lap.

Sadat opened the pouch and stuck his loupe to his eye as he inspected several of the stones. "Water didn't cost you anything."

"It's not about what it costs. It's about what it's worth." Everett leaned on the top of Doruk's door and looked in the window. "Otherwise, I might say it didn't cost you anything to make our introduction to Tariq."

Sadat selected the five largest stones and dropped them into his shirt pocket before pulling the drawstring of the pouch. "You negotiate like a true Turk."

"I guess that's a compliment." Everett could only assume.

"Follow me. Tariq will be waiting." Sadat rolled up his window as Doruk put the Mercedes in gear.

Everett, Courtney, and Ali returned to the MRAP which followed Sadat's vehicle.

They weaved along the narrow road which snaked through dry mountains jetting up on both sides of the thoroughfare. They came to a stretch which had a wide enough shoulder to park several vehicles on, and that's exactly what the sheik had done. Everett could see the sheik's gold Bentley parked at the head of a long line of military vehicles. Everett counted fifteen vehicles but only three trailers pulling anti-aircraft guns. "Looks like we're gonna be renegotiating."

Once again, Everett checked the overlooking cliffs before getting out of the Typhoon. This time, he spotted no less than five snipers. "We've got more attendees than were on the guest list."

"Party crashers. How tacky." Courtney flipped off the safety of her AR-15.

"This is Tariq people," Ali said. "Always he have people to make secure."

Everett watched from the cab as Sadat got out and handed the black pouch to Tariq, then scanned the snipers on the cliff to watch what they would do. They didn't move, so Everett deduced that Ali might be right. He rolled down his window and pointed up at the snipers. "Are these your men, Sheik?"

Tariq made a shallow bow. "For your security."

"And yours, I'm sure," Everett replied.

"Tobias, keep the engine running. Courtney, stay on the fifty-cal in case we have trouble. Ali, Gideon, come with me." Everett took one last look at the snipers before stepping out of the truck.

Tariq passed Everett the keys to the vehicles. "All the weapons are in the back of the armored vehicles."

"We seem to be short two anti-aircraft guns."

"I told you those were going to be a problem."

"You told me getting the trailers was an issue."

"Yes, well, anyway, I threw in twenty fully-automatic AK-47s to make up the difference. I was sure you wouldn't mind."

"I do mind. Keep the AKs and give me back fifteen carats in diamonds." Everett held his hand out.

"No, my friend. It does not work like that."

"So how does it work? Because I'm not sitting back while you hand me the short end of the stick."

"I have Imam not 200 kilometers from here, in Erzurum, who will buy all of these things, no questions asked."

"And he's going to pay you with diamonds as good as those?" Everett gestured toward the black pouch in Tariq's hand.

The sheik tucked the pouch into the pocket of his jeans. "It doesn't matter. I already have the diamonds. The only question now is whether you will accept delivery of your merchandise."

"You think we'd just let you walk away with both?" Everett pulled his HK rifle hanging over his shoulder around to the front.

The sheik shook his finger. And looked up at the cliffs above. "You understand the concept of mutually assured destruction, I'm sure."

Everett looked up to see a glint of sunlight reflecting off the scope of a rifle pointed directly at him. "I guess we'll accept your altered arrangement without our prior consent."

"I thought you might." The sheik offered a sour smile.

Everett turned to the Typhoon and held up the keys to the other vehicles, signaling for the drivers to come out and take them.

Everyone but Tobias filed out of the MRAP they'd come in. Everett handed out keys which were on labeled key tags indicating which vehicle they belonged too. "I'll take the lead truck back to Batumi. Tobias will head up the rear. They should all have radios and everyone knows what channel to use, but don't break radio silence unless it's an emergency. If your radio doesn't work and you need to stop, blow your horn. That will stop the convoy."

"Thanks, boss." Courtney faked a salute as she took a set of keys.

Everett forced a smile. "You stay right behind me. I want to know where you're at."

He handed a set of keys to Ali. "You stay directly behind Courtney and keep an eye on her."

"Yes, Everett."

Once all the keys had been distributed, Everett walked over to the Mercedes where Tariq was saying his goodbyes to Sadat.

"Everything is acceptable, my friend?" Tariq asked.

"I guess it'll just have to be," Everett said with less than a smile. He quickly looked away from the sheik and directed his attention to Sadat. "We'll see you soon. Thank you for your help."

"Yes, Everett." Sadat smiled.

BOOM!

A blast from behind shoved Everett, face first, into the frame of the car door causing him to see stars. His ears were deaf and his nose throbbed like he'd been punched in the face. He regained his balance and looked around to assess what had just happened. "Courtney!" he yelled but he could barely hear himself.

He looked at the long line of military vehicles. The third vehicle away from him was gone. Only a smoldering pot hole remained. The vehicle behind it was missing the windshield, blown backward several feet into the next vehicle, and burning with fire. The MRAP in front of the missing vehicle lay on its side, with fuel running out of the tank and toward the flames coming from under the engine.

With his right hand, Everett pulled his rifle around front, and with his left, he grabbed the sheik by the collar of his sports coat. "You set us up!"

The sheik looked at Everett angrily. "Are you stupid, man? Do you think I would set off a bomb that close to myself?"

"Maybe it went off earlier than it was supposed to."

Tariq turned his head away from the barrel of Everett's rifle. "It was a Reaper."

Everett considered the possibility of what the sheik was saying.

Tariq pointed up. "It is probably recalculating right now and preparing to launch another Hellfire missile. We need to stop arguing and get inside the tunnel!"

His concern for Courtney forced Everett to let go of the sheik's jacket. "You better not be lying to me."

Everett turned and ran, "Courtney!"

He looked at the drivers of each vehicle until he saw her. She was jumping out of the truck with her rifle.

He pointed at the cab of her truck. "Get back in the vehicle and race to the tunnel. I think it was a drone attack."

She nodded and complied. Everett ran to the truck which corresponded to his key. He quickly set the radio frequency and picked up the mic. "We've got a Reaper overhead dropping Hellfire missiles. Everyone to the tunnel!"

He saw a brief flash of light fall from the sky in his rearview mirror right before a vehicle behind him exploded, disabling the MRAPs in front and back of it. He threw the Patrol in gear and pressed the accelerator to the floor, racing behind Courtney toward the tunnel. Once inside, he called her over the radio. "Keep going until you're at least a hundred yards inside the tunnel. We've gotta make sure the others have room to get in!"

Everett watched his rearview as five more of the Russian military vehicles followed him into the tunnel. He put the truck in neutral and put on the parking brake. He left the motor idling as he ran over to Courtney's vehicle. "Are you okay?"

"Yeah, I'm fine. Who got hit?"

Everett looked ahead to see Tariq's Bentley parked next to the Mercedes. He looked at the row of green trucks behind him but couldn't make out who the drivers were.

A third explosion from outside rattled the walls of the tunnel. Everett reached across Courtney's lap and called over the radio. "Tobias, are you in the tunnel?"

"Roger." His voice came back.

"Gideon, are you in?"

Tobias answered again. "Gideon was in the first truck that got hit."

Everett's stomach sank. He hurt for Gideon, and for his young widow, Dinah, who had no idea that her husband had just passed from this life to the next. Everett was consoled by the fact that the two would be reunited in a few short weeks.

"Ali! Are you inside?"

No answer came.

"Tobias, did you see Ali?"

"No. I'm going to do a count and see how many trucks are inside. I'll look for Ali also. I'll call you right back."

"Thanks." Everett passed the mic to Courtney and walked up to Sadat's vehicle. Tariq, his driver, and two guards were in the Bentley. Tariq was nursing a wound on his forehead with a paper towel.

Everett looked at Sadat. "Have you seen Ali since the blast? He's not responding to the radio call."

"No! Not Ali!" Sadat protested angrily.

Tariq yelled from his Bentley. "We're leaving."

"They've only fired three missiles. They probably have one more," Everett warned.

Tariq took the first-aid kit handed to him by one of his guards. "Reaper is probably carrying four Hellfire missiles and two Paveway laser-guided bombs. Paveway is 500-pound bomb. They can seal us in the tunnel with that. I'd rather take my chances outrunning one Hellfire than to be sealed in here like a corpse in a coffin."

Everett understood his reasoning but knew the convoy would never outmaneuver a Hellfire missile. Everett turned to Sadat. "What are you going to do?"

Sadat looked at Doruk. "I don't know."

"Take my advice, leave while you can." With that caveat, Tariq rolled up his window as his driver gunned the engine, propelling the gold Bentley toward the opposite side of the tunnel.

Half of a minute later, Everett heard a fourth explosion from the side Tariq had just exited. He doubted that the shiny easy-to-spot Bentley had been successful in its contest against the unmanned aerial vehicle above.

Seconds later, another blast rattled the ground beneath Everett's knees and nearly knocked him off his feet. The light from the far end of the tunnel dimmed.

BOOM! An identical explosion from the same direction cut off the last light from that side of the tunnel. Everett raced back to Courtney's truck. He picked up the mic. "Tobias! Any sign of Ali?"

"He was in the truck behind Gideon's"

Everett's heart stopped again. "Is he . . ."

"No. He's alive, but he's got some injuries. He just stumbled into the tunnel on foot."

Everett breathed a sigh of relief. "The Reaper has deployed all of its weapons. We need to get out of here."

Tobias came back over the radio. "We can't do that. We're in a convoy of slow-moving military trucks, in a remote location with no foliage for cover. This is the optimum environment for drones. Best case scenario, they'll launch another drone from Ankara, Turkey. It could be over us in an hour and a half. It'll take us three hours to get home. We'd lead them right to Batumi and end up dead anyway."

"Worst case scenario?" Everett asked.

"They've already got a backup drone in the

vicinity. It could be on us in fifteen minutes or less. We can't lose them on this road, Everett."

"If we sit here, the next Reaper will seal off the other end of the tunnel." Everett let go of the talk key on the mic and waited for Tobias' reply.

"We've got munitions. We can eventually blast our way out. Courtney has the staff, so we can get water from the river right now. We'll get enough to hunker down for a few days, then after they think we're dead, we'll blast our way out and go home."

Everett shook his head and pressed the talk key. "Bad plan. I hate it."

"What's your plan?"

Everett held the mic to his mouth, expecting words of wisdom to spill forth. They did not. He sighed, dropped his head, and let the mic dangle from its cord.

"Should we start looking for containers to store water?" Courtney put her hand on his shoulder.

"Yeah."

Everett walked back toward Tobias' location near the beginning of the tunnel.

Courtney retrieved the duffle bag containing Moses' staff and followed him.

Everett picked up his pace when he saw Ali sitting inside Tobias' truck with his head bandaged. "Ali! How are you?"

"Alive! Praise be to Jehovah." Ali's face and clothing were singed and covered with soot from the explosion.

Tobias handed a canteen of water to Ali, then looked at Everett. "What do you think?"

Everett walked to the edge of the tunnel entrance

and looked up at the sky. "The longer we wait, the better chance they have of getting a shot at us while we're collecting water."

Tobias followed him to the entrance. "Then we should get started."

Everett walked back to Tobias' truck and picked up the mic. "Everyone, find as many containers as you can that will hold water. We might be here for a long while."

Courtney stood near Everett. "What if we're unable to blast our way out?"

Everett didn't want to think about that. "Then this is where we die."

Ali looked up. "I hear more explosion."

Everett stood perfectly still and listened. "I heard it too, in the distance. It's too late. We'll have to ration the water we have. Get everyone back away from the tunnel entrance."

Tobias' voice sounded panicked. "We need the ordnance from the disabled vehicles outside! We may not have enough in these trucks to blow our way back out once the drone collapses the entrance!"

Everett grabbed Tobias by the back of his shirt to restrain him from walking toward the entrance. "Forget it. It's too late."

"Courtney, start this truck and move it deeper into the tunnel. It's still too close." Everett escorted Tobias away from the danger zone, and what could be their last hope of getting out of the tunnel alive.

Courtney drove the Typhoon another fifty feet inside the tunnel, parking it inches away from the bumper of the next to last vehicle.

Doruk and Sadat walked up from deeper in the tunnel. Sadat hugged Ali when he saw that he was alive.

The rumbling Everett had heard only moments ago got closer.

Sadat turned to him. "What is the plan?"

"You won't like it." Everett informed Sadat and Doruk of the situation and their likelihood of being buried alive.

"You're right. I don't like it," Sadat said grimly.

Yet another loud boom echoed from outside the tunnel. This one was even closer than before.

"What are they shooting at? It sounds like it's on the other side of the mountain." Courtney asked.

"Maybe Tariq's men came to look for him and the drones are bombing them." Sadat listened for more explosions.

It wasn't long until the next clamoring noise came. Everett listened with one of his eyebrows cocked higher than the other. "Wait a minute!"

"What?" Courtney asked curiously.

"Stay here for a second." Everett dashed toward the tunnel opening.

This time, Courtney did not follow his directive. Instead, she sprinted behind him. "What are you doing? Everett!"

Everett slowed his pace at the mouth of the tunnel with one finger in the air as a sign to be quiet. Yet another rumbling came. He turned to her with a look of hope. "I don't think those are explosions."

"Thunder?" she guessed.

A faint smile formed at the corners of Everett's

mouth and grew wider. "I think so."

She nodded—a slight grin manifesting on her face as well. "Reapers usually operate at an altitude above rain clouds. They'd have a very slim chance of locating and targeting us in inclement weather."

"One man's thunderstorm is another man's sunshine. Come on, let's go tell the others."

Fifteen minutes later, the wind was blowing and the first heavy drops of rain were falling. Everett led the convoy of military vehicles out of the tunnel, stopping long enough to load the salvageable weapons from the disabled vehicles into those which were still running. By the time that was finished, the rain was pouring. Drenched, Everett jumped into the cab of his MRAP and sped away. He pressed the talk key. "Everyone, drive as fast as you can but leave at least two truck lengths between yourself and the driver in front of you. We don't want to make it easy for them to take out two trucks with one missile, in case the weather clears up and they get a shot at us."

The heavy rain persisted for two and a half hours, only letting up slightly for the final leg of the journey back to Batumi.

CHAPTER 10

And the fourth angel poured out his vial upon the sun; and power was given unto him to scorch men with fire. And men were scorched with great heat, and blasphemed the name of God, which hath power over these plagues: and they repented not to give him glory.

Revelation 16:8-9

Friday afternoon, Everett and Courtney took a dish to Dinah, Gideon's widow. When they arrived at the house, Tobias and Ali were there. Dinah's sister and her husband were also present to console her.

"I'm sorry for your loss." Everett couldn't bring himself to look her in the eye when he offered his condolences. He felt responsible for the lives of everyone who accompanied him on the mission.

"Thank you." Dinah didn't look up anyway.

Everett felt sure Dinah blamed him in some small way. "Courtney made a casserole."

Dinah nodded and pointed to her sister. "That was very kind. You can give it to Batya."

Courtney handed off the dish and took a seat next to Dinah on the sofa. She put her arm around her and hugged her close.

They'd been unable to locate any recognizable remains at the attack site, so Dinah had only pictures of her husband over which to mourn.

Everett excused himself and walked out onto the porch. Tobias followed him.

"She's taking it hard." Everett looked out over the otherwise-scenic vista of the Chorokhi River running red with blood.

"She's tough. She'll mourn, then she'll do what needs to be done." Tobias took a seat in the wooden chair Gideon had often sat in.

Everett remained standing but leaned over putting his elbows on the rail of the porch. "What did the rabbis say about the move to the underground cities?"

"They agree with us. It's too dangerous to attempt unless we can figure out a way to evade detection by the drones."

Everett said nothing for a while. Finally, he glanced over his shoulder at Tobias. "Have you thought of anything?"

Tobias leaned back in the chair, putting it against the wall, with only two feet on the porch. "Not for such a massive movement of people."

Neither man said anything for several minutes. Tobias broke the silence. "We could move at night which would help some, but it won't hide us if there are drones looking for us. Rain is really the only thing that could possibly provide that much cover."

Everett stared blankly. "Rain in the central part of Turkey is nearly an unheard-of event in August. To get a storm that would cover our entire path would be nothing short of an act of God."

Tobias added, "Well, He has been fairly active in these last days, so there's always the chance of that."

Everett sighed. "Sure, but even if He sent a miraculous rainstorm, how would we know? We don't exactly have a weather radar that covers the five-hundred-mile stretch of road we'll be traveling."

"You've got a point."

Ali came outside to join them. "Tobias tell me that we might not be leaving after all."

Everett nodded. "I can't justify dragging all of these people out to the middle of nowhere only to watch them be blown-up by drones. It would be like shooting fish in a barrel."

"Moses did not hesitate to take the children of Israel through the wilderness even though he knew Pharaoh's army would pursue them."

Everett gritted his teeth. Ali's faith had a way of annoying him at times. "Moses isn't here. And from the looks of things, he won't be coming anytime soon. We turned on the television a few minutes before we left to come over. GRBN had some footage of Moses and Elijah on the Temple Mount. I guess Luz has finally had enough of them telling everyone that he's the devil. Luz sent a platoon of fifty peacekeepers to arrest the two of them and the entire platoon caught fire. It was like all fifty of them spontaneously combusted. The peacekeepers burned to ashes, in a matter of seconds.

"I couldn't believe the GRBN would even air the footage of it, but they're spinning it to make Elijah and Moses look like the bad guys. Luz is claiming this proves they're operating under the power of demons. I think it shows just the opposite. But then again, Luz's followers are deceived, by definition.

"All that to say, Moses has his hands full in Jerusalem. I don't think he'll be leading anyone else to the Promised Land."

"Perhaps it is you who are to lead the people, Everett. Do you not serve the same God who split the Red Sea for Moses? Are these not also the children of Israel?"

Everett clinched his jaw in expectation of Ali's next comment. He was sure Ali wouldn't be able to resist a statement about that stupid stick. *Wait for it*, he thought.

"Everett, do you not carry even the same staff that was given to Moses when he led those people through the sea on dry land?"

Everett wanted to lash out, to tell Ali how faith doesn't work like that, how you have to be practical about these matters. But he couldn't. In none of those stories about the Jews coming from Egypt did

Moses exercise practical wisdom or worldly rationale. Yet, in every one of those stories, Moses had stepped out in faith, doing things that only made sense because God had told him to do so. And Moses had done them because he possessed that same annoying faith, just like Ali's.

"You know what, Ali? Fine. You win!" Everett turned around with a half-scowling face. "If God speaks to me through a burning bush, and tells me to drag everyone out into the desert, I'll do it. But if He doesn't, you'll drop the subject. I already got Gideon killed. And look at you, you're all cut up from the explosion. Only by the grace of God, you escaped with your life."

"Exactly, by His grace." Ali was calm, unrattled by Everett's outburst. "I went yesterday because I believe God has chosen you as leader. Gideon went for same reason. And if he were here, he would tell you that he'd do it all over again."

Everett felt bad about being so harsh with Ali, but he wasn't ready to apologize yet. He turned toward the bloody river down the hill and across the road.

However, Ali wasn't finished talking. "You do not need a burning bush, Everett. You have the Holy Spirit of the living God. All you need is to be quiet and listen."

Everett kept his back toward Ali and Tobias as a wave of emotion washed over him and the tears streamed down his face.

Later that evening, Everett and Courtney sat at home, alone on their couch, listening to the GRBN radio to see if they'd announce anything to indicate that the Fourth Vial had been poured out. The radio offered additional analysis about the two evil men who were occupying the Temple Mount, but nothing hinted that the next wave of judgments had started.

Courtney held Everett's hand. "I guess if the Fourth Vial is scorching heat from the sun, it would be odd for it to start at sunset."

"Yeah, I suppose you're right." Everett rested his head, still contemplating the brotherly admonition he'd received from Ali earlier that day.

The next morning was a different story. Everett couldn't wait to turn on the radio when he woke up. Courtney was still sleeping so he carried it out to the back porch to listen as he heated water for his morning tea.

A female reporter with a middle-eastern accent spoke. "The Global Republic Ministry of Health has issued a warning for all citizens of the Holy Luzian Empire to stay indoors during daylight hours until further notice. GR scientists have identified a strange phenomenon with the sun. The sun's magnetic field is experiencing an unprecedented period of flux which is allowing its surface area to pulsate. Calculations estimate that this activity has allowed the sun's surface area to grow as much as two percent at certain periods, which scientist are calling solar engorgement."

Courtney walked out onto the porch. "Solar

engorgement. I wonder how long it took them to come up with that one?"

Everett held up his hand as a signal that he was trying to listen to the broadcast.

The reporter continued. "Typically, such an event would not have such a catastrophic effect on the Earth. But, two note-worthy occurrences have dramatically changed how this event will disturb our environment. First, our thermosphere was severely affected by the recent bombardment of space objects such as the Wormwood comet, the Apollyon comet, as well as the smaller asteroid fields we've encountered in the past seven years.

"The thermosphere is the Earth's first layer of protection against excessive heat from the sun. Until it regulates and heals, more of the heat that is normally filtered out will pass through to the surface of the Earth.

"Second, along with man-made climate change, the assault on our planet by the space objects just mentioned has devastated the ozone layer in the stratosphere. Without a proper amount of ozone to filter out harmful ultraviolet rays, people exposed to direct sunlight could potentially get first-degree sunburn in less than a minute under these conditions. Symptoms include reddening of the skin and increased sensitivity.

"Depending on complexion and skin type, three minutes of exposure may result in second-degree sunburn which can cause blistering of the skin and headaches.

"As little as five minutes of direct sunlight can

cause third-degree sunburn which will result in peeling skin and may send the victim into shock. More than that could cause death.

"It is unclear how long the phenomenon will last, but during this cycle, outside temperatures could reach 120 degrees today. However, the real threat is going to be from the intense ultraviolet rays.

"This is very serious and His High and Most Prepotent Majesty himself has urged all of his citizens to heed this warning. Do not, I repeat, do not venture outdoors during daylight hours for any reason."

"You should put out the fire and come in. The sun is coming over the mountains." Courtney gazed toward the east.

"Maybe I better." Everett covered the rocket stove and brought his teapot inside. "We should probably keep the blinds closed."

"The others might not know. I'll close the blinds, you call everyone that you can on the radio." Courtney pulled together the curtains over the kitchen window."

"Okay." Everett retrieved his small walkie-talkie and called Tobias, informing him of what was happening and asking him to put out an alert over the Ham radio which had much more reach than Everett's small handheld unit.

Once Courtney had finished closing the blinds, she asked, "You don't think this could damage our solar generator, do you?"

"I hope not." Everett peeked through two slats of the Venetian blinds. "We can't do anything about it now anyways. The sun is up."

Courtney watched over his shoulder as the sun edged over the mountains. "We were supposed to have a memorial for Gideon at the chapel today."

Everett pulled his fingers out from between the blinds. "It will have to wait until after dusk."

The next few days would be spent doing little more than sleeping, eating, reading the Bible, listening to GRBN radio reports, and waiting for the scorching power of the sun to cease.

Everett and Courtney watched through their front window as the sun set behind the mountains Wednesday evening. The ritual of waiting for the sun to retreat with its harmful rays became a daily custom repeated by everyone living in the Goshen Valley.

"All clear. Let's go." Everett opened the front door and led the way across the street to Tobias and Ali's house.

Courtney walked beside him. "You don't know what a blessing it is to go outside until you can't."

"I'm worried that I'm adjusting a little too well to staying up late and sleeping in all morning. It will be hard to get back to my normal routine when it's safe to go in the sun again."

"If," she said. "If it's ever safe to go in the sun again."

Everett knocked on the door when they arrived.

"Come in, come in." Ali held the door open and motioned for Everett and Courtney to enter.

"Thanks." Everett wiped his shoes on the mat. "Where's Tobias?"

"In his room listening to radio. New report is coming from GRBN. I think so is update about sun." Ali waved his hand for them to follow him. "Come on, maybe we can catch it."

Tobias raised his hand to greet Everett and Courtney when they walked in his room but did not turn his attention away from the radio.

A spokesman for the Global Republic Aeronautics and Space Administration was providing information about the agency's latest observations. "The good news about the event that GRASA scientist witnessed today is that we expect the massive flare will act to regulate the sun's magnetic field which should calm the solar engorgement phenomenon we've been monitoring over the past five days."

A female GRBN reporter was interviewing the man. "The way you made that last statement, it sounds as if I should expect a follow-up announcement. Are you about to issue some ominous caveat, Doctor Reynolds?"

The man laughed nervously. "Your journalistic instincts are well-honed, Miss Carter. I'm afraid there is some bad news that goes along with my analysis.

"Solar flares are graded in classes. A, B, C, M, and X. The classification system works something like the Richter scale. A C-class flare is ten times more powerful than a B-class. Obviously, we've had flares above X class before. Those are numbered to represent the magnitude. The strongest ever recorded was an X-28. The flare may have been larger, but the sensors cut out at X-28. What we saw today is so far beyond anything we've ever watched, GRASA has categorized it as an Omega-Class flare."

Carter quizzed, "Couldn't you have assigned a numeric value to the X-class? Let's say an X-1000. Did this event really warrant a completely new class?"

The doctor continued, "No. It was that magnificent."

"I have a feeling this isn't going to be good," Carter said.

Reynolds proceeded to tell of what was to come. "Large solar flares, or Coronal Mass Ejections, are popping off all the time, but they generally are just projected out into space. Regretfully, this one exploded in the general direction of our planet. Lucky for us, it is not a direct hit, but it will be close enough to cause massive disruption to electrical services, computers, and most electronic devices."

"Oh, no. We'll lose power?"

"Yes, but the Global Republic has already begun making preparations to mitigate the effects of the Coronal Mass Ejection. We'll be taking power grids down this afternoon to try to isolate critical components from the power lines, which will act as conductors to the violent pulse from the CME. This action will greatly reduce the time and resources necessary to restart the grid, once the threat has passed.

"We expect the effects to hit the Earth Friday evening. The electromagnetic wave generated by the CME is so large, the planet could be immersed in it for up to three days."

The GRBN reporter asked, "Is there anything we can do to protect our own electronics?"

"I'm glad you asked. The best thing you can do is unplug everything, disconnect your antennas or retract telescoping antennas, and remove power cords from anything that has a removable cord. (The wavelength of a CME is rather long, so it needs a significant length of conductive material to couple into.) Household electronics typically won't be affected, as long as they're unplugged."

"Will my Mark still work?"

"Yes and no," the doctor answered. "The components in your Mark won't be affected by the CME, but the infrastructure with which your Mark uses to connect with Dragon will have to be temporarily taken offline. We recommend that people stock up with a minimum of three days' worth of supplies."

Tobias chuckled. "Three days. Like they'll be able to just flip a switch and turn everything back on in three days."

Courtney gave Everett's arm a squeeze. "This is our chance. We can relocate to the underground cities when they take Dragon down for the CME."

Everett nodded. "The Fifth Vial begins Friday at sunset. We'll leave at dusk."

CHAPTER 11

And the fifth angel poured out his vial upon the seat of the beast; and his kingdom was full of darkness; and they gnawed their tongues for pain, And blasphemed the God of heaven because of their pains and their sores, and repented not of their deeds.

Revelation 16:10-11

Everett and Courtney checked their gear Friday evening as the sun sank low in the sky. They would be driving one of the Russian Typhoons at the front of the convoy traveling across the Turkish mountains to the underground cities in the Cappadocia region, roughly 500 miles from their location in Batumi, Georgia.

Everett opted to keep his HK G36C for his primary battle rifle, even though its magazines were not compatible with the rest of his team. Its short, compact design made it easy to maneuver from the driver's seat of the vehicle. He stuffed as many magazines as he could into the pouches on his load-carrying vest. He wore his Sig pistol on a drop-leg holster. A tactical sling hung around his left side, holding five hand grenades. An open crate of additional grenades sat between the driver's seat and front passenger's seat of the Typhoon he'd be driving.

Everett's team would be the tip of the spear for this perilous journey. The convoy's route would take them directly through MOC territory. While the imminent CME would reign down technological darkness on the Holy Luzian Empire and crippling the Anti-Christ's ability to launch drone attacks, the Martyrs of the Caliphate would be nearly unaffected.

Everything except last-minute supplies had been loaded into the vehicles at sundown the previous day. Due to lack of fuel, many of the civilian vehicles in the convoy had not been driven much in the three years prior. Most of the automobiles were in poor repair, and much of what little fuel they had was stale. If the children of Israel made it across this stretch of remote, barren, and hostile terrain, it would be no less of a miracle than the journey of the Jews out of Egypt so many thousands of years before.

Everett and Courtney were well-rested for the mission at hand. Everett took his wife's hand.

"Let's pray before we head out."

She kissed him. "Good idea." She bowed her head.

Everett closed his eyes and made a conscious effort to clear out the anxiety and fear from his mind. "Lord, you have carried us this far. We've seen miracle after miracle. We've watched you pour out your Spirit on your sons and daughters as you promised you would do. We've seen the thing that the prophets before us only dreamed about and we've been honored to be a part of the most exciting period in the history of your creation.

"We know our redemption is close, the time when we will see you face to face. We pray only for courage and strength in these final hours of this age, and that we might honor you in all we say and do.

"I pray that you will watch over my precious bride and grant us success on this mission. Thank you for all you have done for us, especially salvation. Amen."

Everett looked up, but Courtney did not.

She added, "And protect my husband, God. Don't leave me here without him. Amen."

Everett hugged her. "Are you ready?"

She smiled and ran the back of her finger along his cheek. "I'm ready."

The two of them grabbed the last of their things and headed for the Typhoon parked across the street at Tobias and Ali's.

Rabbi Hertzog stood by a black Russian Patrol MRAP speaking with some of the former IDF soldiers who would be part of the security element.

Courtney handed him the green duffle bag

containing Moses' staff. "You're in charge of the water. No matter what, you have to get through with the staff. Otherwise, we're just jumping out of the frying pan and into the fire."

The rabbi nodded graciously. "I will protect it with my life."

Everett repositioned the straps of his various pieces of battle gear. "We'll get to Kayseri first. When we arrive, you should enter the underground city right away and transform the water supply there. Kaymakli will be the next underground city, then Derinkuyu after that. All three of them are fairly close together so we'll focus on getting water for them first. Then, once we're settled, we can go around to the remaining cities."

Rabbi Hertzog gave Everett's arm a squeeze. "I will do just as you have recommended. Thank you for your help."

"It's my honor to serve the children of Israel." Everett smiled.

Ali patted Everett on the back. "I need you come in house for a moment if you please. We have some last-minute detail to cover."

Everett waved at the rabbi, then he and Courtney followed Ali into the house. A large map of the area they'd be traveling through was spread out on the dining-room table. Tobias and the IDF team leaders were gathered around.

Tobias nodded at Everett. "Ali is pointing out the suspected MOC hotspots."

Ali put his index finger at a position on the map. "All area from Ankara to Van is heavy MOC territory."

"No way around it?" Everett asked.

"We cannot," Ali replied. "Barely we have fuel for trip straight through. Go around can be one day more of travel. And still does not guarantee we don't see Martyrs. Only way is through."

Everett looked at Tobias. "You know MOC is going to look at the blackout as an opportunity to raise havoc."

Tobias shrugged as he looked at the map. "Maybe they'll focus on attacking GR outposts and leave us alone."

"Ignore 150 thousand Jews crossing through their territory?" Everett looked at Tobias as if he were a bit naive. "That's wishful thinking."

Levi pulled his rifle close to his chest. "We've gotta do what we've gotta do."

"Okay, so let's do it." Everett looked around the room, sizing up the resolve in the eyes of each man. He turned back to Ali. "What have we got?"

Ali tapped a location on the map. "This is Imranli. We must go through it. It is small town. Maybe 500 people. Probably we have fight but we can do it."

Everett nodded. "Great. We'll just go in expecting to fight. We'll roll in hot and heavy with 2000 troops and kill anything that moves. What's next?"

"Next thing is Zara. Also is small town. Good thing is that highway go outside town—don't go through it."

Everett looked at the map. "That's great, but what are the odds they won't call up all their fighters to come hit the weaker section of the convoy after the primary security component has passed by?"

"Probably not good. Also probably going to be MOC person go from Imranli to tell them we coming," Ali added.

"Then we should probably just roll on in and subdue all military-age men in the town." Everett looked up.

"How do you intend to do that?" Tobias asked.

"We've got a bullhorn on our Typhoon. I'll drive up and tell them they've got thirty seconds to come out in the street with their hand over their heads."

Levi laughed. "You watched too many John Wayne movies as a kid. What are you going to do when they start shooting before they even let you finish your sentence?"

"Shock and awe. We've got enough RPGs and surface-to-surface munitions to level a small village."

Tobias crossed his arms and looked at Levi. "I don't like the idea of announcing our arrival over the bullhorn, but you can't argue with the effectiveness of shock and awe."

Ali continued, "Next is Hafik. Same thing like Zara. Maybe 500 people, maybe less."

Levi looked at Everett. "More shock and awe?"

"More shock, more awe." Everett glanced up from the map to look at Tobias. "But no bullhorn."

Tobias smiled to let him know he appreciated that Everett was following his advice.

"Then is coming Sivas. Major city. Talking like 300 thousand before Great Tribulation start."

Everett's confidence began to fade. "So how

many do you think are still alive?"

"Probably 100 thousand."

Everett nodded. "Figure half of them are men, and three-quarters of the men are capable of engaging us in a firefight. What's that—like 40 thousand potential shooters?"

Ali shook his head. "Anyone still living is probably shooter. All weak people have been taken out by judgments. Those still around are toughest of the tough."

Everett huffed. "That's reassuring."

"What's the plan?" Tobias asked.

Everett didn't have one. "Any chance they'd let us pass through in exchange for drinking water?"

Ali nodded. "Sure. Then they slit your throat the minute they have water. Al-taqiyya is Islam doctrine of lying. Muslim can say anything to unbeliever to make deal then go back on their word without consequence from Allah."

Everett lifted his eyebrows. "Scratch that idea." He looked up at the other team leaders. "Anyone else has a suggestion?"

Courtney examined the map. "What if we cleared the three smaller towns, then pushed in with our entire security force and lined the highway all the way from one side of the city to the other?

"We don't have to take and hold the city. We just need to secure a corridor to get us from one side of the city to the other. It looks like most of the population is concentrated on the north side of the highway. We could put two soldiers on the north side of the highway for every one soldier we assign to the south."

Everett considered her plan. "Theoretically, that would work, but when the enemy hits you, they center all of their energy on one location. We'd be spread too thin to resist a concentrated attack."

She looked at the map. "So we have pre-positioned platoons every half mile that can provide backup when someone gets hit. It's only four miles through town. We've got more than enough soldiers for eight platoons."

"We'll be operating without radios. We can't even turn them on. They'd be fried by the CME." Everett shook his head.

"What about flares?" she asked.

Tobias looked at Ali. "You've got those fireworks you were saving for a special occasion."

"Probably they are too old. Might not even work."

"Go get some and try them out."

Ali shuffled off to his room and returned with three large boxes of mortars. "I have many more."

"Where did you get those?" Everett asked curiously.

"Someone in town found them in basement when we first got here. I traded for some fish I catched in the river." Ali stood holding the colorful boxes.

"Why didn't we ever shoot them off? New Year's Eve, your birthday, anything," Everett asked.

Courtney said, ("Maybe he was saving them for such a time as this.")

Ali smiled revealing his big white teeth. "Perhaps this is why, Courtney."

Everett led the way outside. "Well, let's see if they still work." He selected three mortar shells, one from each box as a test sample. Everett dropped the shell in the tube provided, lit the wick dangling out the edge of the tube, and stepped back.

Poof! POP! The shell shot out of the launch tube, soared upwards and exploded in a shower of red and white sparks. He ignited the wick of the next one. Thoop! Likewise, it went airborne. POW! A dazzling display of golden embers radiated out from the center of the pyrotechnic burst. The third shell also took flight. BANG! It provided a shimmering ball of white and blue light in the evening sky.

Everett unboxed the remaining mortars. "I guess they're still good. We'll do the math and figure out how far apart we need to spread our security forces to line the entire four-mile stretch of road through Sivas. We can allocate one shell to every tenth man who will be assigned as a signalman."

Levi nodded. "It's a good plan, but you've only got one launch tube per box of mortars."

Everett looked around. "Do we have some PVC pipe roughly the same diameter as the launch tubes? It doesn't have to be exact as long as it's not too tight."

Tobias nodded. "We've got some under the crawl space of the house."

"Great. Can you and Ali work on cutting one-foot sections of pipe?"

"Yes, but it will have no base to hold it up," Ali said.

Everett replied, "It's mostly sand all through that region. The signalmen can just stick the launch tube in the ground. Even if they have to hold it with their hand and look away while the mortar exits the tube, it won't kill them."

Courtney wrinkled her nose. "Sounds dangerous."

"Less so than being attacked and not being able to call for backup. Safety is relative in times like these." Everett put his arm around her.

The finishing touches were put on the battle plan over the next hour and teams were assigned for the various objectives. Six MRAPs, including Everett's, would storm each of the small towns, with large cleanup teams coming in behind them to eliminate or detain any additional threats. The assault squads would engage and destroy hostiles while the motorcade passed through the smaller towns, then the assault squads will fall in behind to form a rear guard.

If they weren't pursued by the jihadists, the rear guard would retreat from the small villages behind the caravan. If they were, the assault teams would be armed with sufficient force to leave the towns without anyone alive who was capable of firing a weapon.

They would soften up Imranli first, then Everett's armored squad would proceed past Zara, and straight to Hafik. A second wave of former IDF troops would secure a path through Zara while the motorcade drove through then meet up with Everett's team in Hafik.

They would fend off any hostiles while the caravan passed through Hafik, then escort the convoy to a remote area of farmland about halfway between Hafik and Sivas. The countryside would be used as a staging area before moving on to the major city of Sivas. Once all the vehicles in the convoy were progressing steadily toward the city, Everett's group would lead the charge through Sivas and serve as one of the reinforcement teams to assist any portion of the defense line that came under fire by locals.

Everett and Courtney loaded their remaining supplies into the Typhoon.

Courtney paused to look up at the sky. "I've never seen the Aurora Borealis before."

The remnants of daylight vanished behind the mountains, revealing ribbons of emerald green light floating in the night sky like the wake of a glowing phantom. Everett had never witnessed the phenomenon either. He stared up at the glowing bands above him. For a moment, he forgot about the mission at hand, about the trouble that waited for him just up the road, and about the remaining hardships he'd have to endure to make it through these final days.

Tobias patted him on the shoulder. "Come on, the entire convoy is waiting on you. If this CME is as bad as it's supposed to be, you'll be able to look at those lights for our entire trip."

Everett kept his eyes on the sky as he stepped into the cab and closed the driver's side door. "Even with all the stuff I've been a witness to in the Great Tribulation, all the things the prophets couldn't even describe, I've never seen anything as magnificent as this."

Everett continued to look at the spectacle of the Aurora Borealis as he started the engine. Even though the lights would be above him for the entire trip, his mind would have to focus on the conflict around the corner. Once they left Batumi, he'd have to think about killing and dying; his mind would be marred by death, haunted by violence. There'd be little room left for the stunning beauty of God's creation.

CHAPTER 12

Though the Lord be high, yet hath he respect unto the lowly: but the proud he knoweth afar off. Though I walk in the midst of trouble, thou wilt revive me: thou shalt stretch forth thine hand against the wrath of mine enemies, and thy right hand shall save me. The Lord will perfect that which concerneth me: thy mercy, O Lord, endureth for ever: forsake not the works of thine own hands.

Psalm 138:6-8

Everett led the convoy along the coastal route as far as possible. Both because the four-lane highway allowed the caravan of nearly 30 thousand vehicles to flow more steadily, and because it avoided many of the radical Islamic strongholds in the interior of the country. Of course, this choice took them directly through Rize, the city where they'd been ambushed only two weeks earlier, but the band of petty criminals that pulled off the heist wouldn't stand a chance against the heavily-armed motorcade of Israeli expatriates.

The convoy progressed under the cascading luminescence of the aurora all the way to the seaside town of Trabzon without incident. From there, Everett turned southwest, leading the Jews away from the Black Sea through the mountains. The highway from Trabzon was also a four-lane road in moderate repair. Since there was very little oncoming traffic, the caravan used both the north and southbound lanes for their journey, forcing the occasional passing vehicle to drive on the shoulder until the colossal motorcade had passed by.

Nine hours into the journey, Everett pulled to the side of the road, halting the front end of the motorcade to give the rear a chance to catch up. Everett addressed all of the security personnel in the Typhoon with them. "We'll wait for thirty minutes. That will give everyone in the caravan a chance to move around or do what they need to do. Then, we've only got another twenty minutes of drive time before we hit Imranli."

Courtney swung her door open. "Great. I'm going to stretch my legs."

Ali opened the rear door. "Me, too."

Tobias, Levi, and the other three former IDF

soldiers also got out of the vehicle.

Everett addressed the female IDF soldier riding with them in the Typhoon. "Tonya, why don't you and Courtney stay together. I'd rather no one get off by themselves. You never know who might be lurking out here in the countryside."

"Yes, sir." Tonya saluted him, even though there was no formal military organization, ranks, or any other requirement to do so.

Everett walked back to speak with the driver of the Typhoon behind his. "Tell everyone to do a last-minute weapons check. We'll be rolling into enemy territory when we leave here. Inform all of your men, then have them pass it on to the vehicle behind them and so on."

"Sure thing." The driver also gave Everett a salute.

"Thank you." Everett patted him on the shoulder and returned to his vehicle. He checked the time on his watch and started the vehicle precisely thirty minutes after they'd stopped. They had less than an hour before sunrise, and Everett was determined to hit Imranli before daylight.

An old gas station which showed signs of it being used as a trading post in the absence of regular fuel supplies stood as a testament to the changes the planet had undergone over the previous seven years. Everett watched the structure closely for movement as they passed. He saw no one there nor in the next two farmhouses he passed. They reached the edge of the village where houses were closer together. Everett watched the windows as light appeared inside the various dwellings.

"They know we're here," he announced to his team in the vehicle. "Be ready for anything."

Pow! TINK! The sound of the first rifle round striking the side of the heavily armored Typhoon rang inside the vehicle. Everett pulled to the shoulder of the road, allowing the MRAPs behind him to take positions further up the road. "I saw a muzzle flash from that two-story house with the rusted tin roof. Levi, can you take it out with an RPG?"

"Yes, sir." Levi unlocked the hatch on the roof.

Everett turned to face his crew. "Tobias, can you give him some cover fire with the fifty?"

"I'm on it." Tobias let out a volley of rounds via the remote-controlled turret sitting atop the Typhoon.

SHOOWF! The RPG flew straight and level into the upstairs window of the house. BOOM! It exploded inside lifting three sheets of the flimsy metal roof from the house.

The next wave of hostile fire came from an apartment building seventy-five yards up the road on the left. "Everyone hang on, I'm going to take it to these guys. Tobias, you want to let them know we're here?"

"Roger." Tobias began peppering the building with fifty-caliber rounds while Everett brought the vehicle in closer.

More small-arms fire came from the right, and the MRAP behind Everett's addressed the threat with additional RPGs.

Everett glanced at the radio. "It would be nice to have communications with the rest of our team so we'd know what's going on behind us."

Courtney watched her rearview. "The enemy doesn't have comms either. At least it's a level playing field. I saw a vehicle leave one of the houses back there. Looks like he's heading west."

"He's probably going for back up. We'll try to catch him before that happens." Everett turned to Levi. "Can you pop out of the hatch and motion for the MRAP behind us to follow me?"

"Yep."

"And don't spend any more time out there than you have to." Everett put the truck in gear and began rolling toward the vehicle Courtney had spotted.

The hatch door slammed behind Levi. "Unit two saw me. They're on our tail."

"Good." Everett kept up with the small pickup truck racing west on the side road which ran parallel to the main highway.

"I bet he's heading to that mosque up ahead. He'll probably use the minaret to put out a call to arms." Courtney pointed straight in front of the vehicle.

"I can cancel that plan if you want," Levi said.

"You'll need more than an RPG," Everett replied. "Hit it with one of those Vampirs."

"Technically, it's still an RPG," Levi replied.

"The PG-29V rocket in that thing is nearly three-feet long. Call it whatever you want. It's got a lot more kick than what you've been shooting." Everett kept a steady path toward the mosque.

Ali crouched low between the two front seats and looked out the front windshield. "Something telling me this apartments will be big problem."

"Why?" Courtney turned to him.

"Can be that jihadis have been relocated to be near to mosque."

"We're in for a fight either way. It would actually be easier for us if they were concentrated around a central location." Everett slowed the truck and turned back to Levi. "Is this close enough?"

"Perfect." Levi pushed the hatch open and David, one of the other IDF fighters, helped him get the cumbersome launch tube up through the opening in the roof of the vehicle. At six-feet long, the Vampir Soviet missile system was much more awkward to operate than the shorter, standard RPGs.

"Hit the minaret near the base. Maybe you can bring it down." Everett turned toward the rear of the vehicle.

Boooowf! The rocket left the tube. Everett watched the minaret with anticipation. POW! The warhead struck the minaret roughly two-thirds of the way from the top on the left-hand side, leaving a gaping hole, but the structure still stood.

"Should I hit it again?" Levi asked.

Everett waited for the smoke to clear. "No. That guy isn't going to be in a hurry to climb that tower. Besides, you probably took out a section of stairs inside. I doubt he can even make it past the breach."

Ali pointed at the minaret. "Look. It is leaning. I think it will fall!"

Everett's mood improved as he studied the tower. Sure enough, it was lurching toward the dome on top of the mosque. The tower leaned slowly at first, then suddenly collapsed, falling on the roof and splitting the qubba wide open. Everett turned to look at Levi. "Great shot!"

Small-arms fire rang out from the three apartment buildings adjacent to the mosque. Tobias directed the remote-controlled fifty-caliber machine gun toward the center building and systematically sent rounds through all of the windows.

"We'll have to get out of the truck to engage them," Courtney said with a tone of urgency.

Everett pointed at her to add emphasis to his statement. "No way. You help Tobias reload the fifty. That's our most critical asset right now. The rest of us will engage from top hatches."

Everett stepped out of his seat and made his way to the back of the truck. He held his hand out to Levi. "Hand me an RPG launcher and a couple of grenades."

Levi passed him one of the smaller launchers with a grenade already mounted. "You should come back inside the vehicle to reload. You'll be drawing fire the second you pop out of the hatch."

Everett nodded to let him know he would heed the warning. "Thanks." Everett pulled the latch handle and pushed the hatch door open. Fully automatic AK-47 fire peppered the hatch door. Everett turned away for a moment, took a deep breath, and jumped up through the hole with the weapon. He quickly identified a target in the building closest to them and pulled the trigger of the RPG. The grenade launched toward the window where the rifle fire was originating. BOOM!

Everett dropped back down and loaded another

grenade into the launcher. The three IDF soldiers worked together, taking turns shooting their AR-15s out of one of the hatches. Ali used another hatch to shoot an additional grenade at the building. When Everett came back up out of the hatch for the second shot, he noticed that five more MRAPs from his convoy had arrived and were now actively engaged in the skirmish. Everett located another window with a hostile shooting at him and pulled the trigger, sending the grenade barreling at his enemy. BOOM!

Everett rapidly transitioned to his HK rifle and shot three men working their way on foot toward the vehicle. As soon as they were eliminated, he felt someone inside the MRAP pulling him down by his belt. He let himself drop back into the Typhoon to see that it had been Courtney pulling him down.

"What are you doing?" she yelled. "Pop up, take a shot and get back down. Do you want to get killed? The sun is up and your head makes an easy target sticking out up there."

He couldn't take time to explain. "Courtney, I'm doing what I have to do."

"You're their leader. You have to stay alive to lead. That's what you have to do."

Everett ignored her as he loaded another grenade. He emerged from the hatch, RPG in hand and launched the projectile toward the same building, but a different window where yet another shooter was firing at them. The grenade exploded inside the apartment. The flash lit up the interior, revealing several other armed men who had been in the same room.

More trucks from Everett's convoy arrived, and the hostiles in the apartments were soon suppressed. Everett made his way back to the driver's seat and addressed his crew. "We'll let the clean-up team handle it from here. I want to keep the convoy moving."

The team acknowledged Everett and locked the top hatch. Everett started the engine and honked his horn to signal for the rest of the advance team vehicles to follow. "Next stop, Hafik."

Everett's advance team would roll right past the small village of Zara unless they were engaged, but since the highway didn't go through the center of town, that was unlikely. A secondary defense team of heavily armored vehicles would provide security while the convoy drove by Zara.

It took just under forty minutes to reach the outskirts of Zara. Everett saw very little activity while driving by. He checked the rearview mirror, making sure none of the other vehicles in the advance team took fire. If they did, the motorcade would stop and engage the enemy until the secondary team arrived. "All clear?" Everett asked Tobias who was scanning the area via the remote camera on the machine gun turret.

"I don't see any activity," Tobias replied.

Everett kept driving on to Hafik. He arrived thirty minutes later, completely undetected. If it were only Everett and his team, they could have easily slipped right by the tiny Turkish town without being noticed. But it wasn't just them. Ali had assured Everett that the men of Hafik would attack the convoy, leaving him no choice but to start a fight. Everett scanned the skyline for a minaret. He looked to the north. "There's the mosque. I guess that's where we should go."

"It's at least five blocks off the main road. Maybe we should just sit here and wait for them," Courtney said.

Everett shook his head. "We can't. If Ali's reasoning holds true, once we're spotted, they'll rally at the mosque, formulate an attack plan and come hit us with a much more cohesive force than if we go kick over their hornets' nest."

Ali leaned forward between the two front seats. "I think so Everett is correct."

"Then let's get it over with," Tobias said from the remote-control turret seat behind them.

Everett slowed down and waited for the other five MRAPs to turn off onto the dirt road that led back into the neighborhood. "Is everybody ready?"

"Ready!" Tonya said.

"Locked and loaded." Levi sat beneath a hatch with an RPG in hand.

David called out, "I'm ready, sir."

Everett pressed his foot on the accelerator and drove straight toward certain trouble.

CHAPTER 13

Behold, I send an Angel before thee, to keep thee in the way, and to bring thee into the place which I have prepared. Beware of him, and obey his voice, provoke him not; for he will not pardon your transgressions: for my name is in him. But if thou shalt indeed obey his voice, and do all that I speak; then I will be an enemy unto thine enemies, and an adversary unto thine adversaries. For mine Angel shall go before thee, and bring thee in unto the Amorites, and the Hittites, and the Perizzites, and the Canaanites, the Hivites, and the Jebusites: and I will cut them off.

Exodus 23:20-23

The armored vehicles of the advanced team roared down the dry dirt road kicking up a cloud of dust in their wake. They quickly arrived at the five-story mosque with the shiny silver dome. Two minarets flanked each side of the mosque like missiles ready to launch. Each was topped with glistening silver cones, which matched the metallic dome.

Levi prepared to deploy one of the PG-29V rockets. "Should I take out one of the minarets?"

"Take them both," Everett replied. "We're not here to win hearts and minds."

Levi slapped the latch and pushed open the hatch. David assisted him with getting the six-foot launch tube through the roof.

"Shooters on the roof!" TA, TA, TA, TA TAT! Tobias began hammering the adjacent building with fifty-caliber machine-gunfire.

Shwooof! Everett watched from the driver's seat as the first rocket flew toward the minaret on the right. BOOM! A direct hit in the center of the tower caused it to topple, raining debris onto the dome of the mosque and the surrounding sidewalk below.

A window opening in the grey concrete building to the right of the mosque caught Everett's eye. "Gun!" Everett instantly jumped up from his seat, released the clasp on the hatch above the front cab, and stuck his HK out the opening. He wasted no time before unleashing a volley of bullets toward the open window.

Levi had just reappeared with his second rocket,

ready to launch. He flinched at the surprise of seeing Everett spring up through the roof of the Typhoon and sent the rocket careening off course. BLAM!

Everett turned to see what the projectile had hit. A gaping hole in the center dome of the mosque billowed smoke and ash into the morning sky. He turned to Levi with a grin. "Not a complete waste. Go ahead and give that minaret one more try. I've got you covered."

"Yes, sir." Levi dropped back into the MRAP.

Everett watched the grey concrete building through his reflex sight. Gunfire rang out from behind him and he spun around to see local jihadis charging toward the other vehicles in his advance team. Everett emptied his magazine in their general direction, then dropped back into the cab to change mags.

Courtney was pulling another belt of fifty caliber ammunition out of a box and assisting Tobias with reloading. "Everett! Stay in the cab!"

"I'm just taking a few pot shots. I have to cover Levi." He slapped the fresh mag into the well of the HK and jumped back up through the hatch.

Levi leveled the launch tube.

Everett scanned the windows and roofs of the surrounding buildings while the approaching hostiles kept themselves busy attacking the other MRAPs. "You're all clear, Levi. Just keep it steady."

SHWOOFP! Everett felt the heat of the rocket as it left the tube. BLOOOM! The second minaret dropped with a mighty crash on top of the already decimated mosque. "Good shot!" Everett saw another window open on the grey building. He took aim and began firing, cutting down two armed men inside before they could get a shot off.

"What's next?" Levi lowered the tube into the vehicle.

Everett signaled for Levi to drop down into the Typhoon, then lowered himself as well. Once inside, he addressed the team. "The buildings on each side of the mosque are crawling with MOC fighters. Let's soften them up with some regular RPGs. If you see any activity inside a doorway or window, light them up. Two-man teams. David, you're with Levi. Ali, with me. Tonya and Silas, you're a team. One person fires, the other reloads the RPG launcher. Tobias and Courtney, you two are responsible for keeping that fifty rolling."

Tonya furrowed her brow. "How do we know they're hostiles if we can only see a figure through a window?"

"Non-combatants are probably going to be running out the back door or hiding under a bed. Anyone going toward a window after all the noise we've been making has to assume they're taking their life into their own hands." Everett loaded a grenade into a launcher and climbed up through the hatch over the cab. He saw movement through the window on the lower left-hand side of the concrete building. He swiftly took aim and pulled the trigger. Shoooowf! Boom! The grenade hit, blowing out the window and part of the wall.

As he lowered back into the cab, Ali took the launcher and loaded it. "I take this shot please."

"Go ahead." Everett handed off the launcher to Ali and looked at Courtney who was giving him a disapproving look.

BOOM! A loud blast shook the Typhoon, rocking it so hard that Everett was thrown from his seat. He instantly turned to Courtney who had also been knocked to the floor. His ears were ringing from the noise so he yelled at her. "Are you okay?"

She nodded with a concerned look and pointed to Ali who was lowering himself down from the open hatch above the cab.

Everett looked up. Ali's eyes were open wide in shock and blood was coming from his mouth.

"Are you hit?"

Ali wiped the blood from his lip and looked at it for a brief moment before answering Everett. "No. The explosion made me bang my face on edge of hatch. I think I cut my lip."

Everett nodded and surveyed the other crew members. His eyes met Tobias'. "Any idea what that was?"

Tobias repositioned himself to operate the big gun. "We're not the only ones who brought RPGs to this party. You need to get this bus moving before we take another hit."

Everett gave a short nod, spun around to the steering wheel, released the brake, and threw the shifter into gear. He gunned the engine and drove the Typhoon toward the back of the mosque, hoping the other vehicles would follow his lead. "Check the rearview. Is everyone else behind us?"

Courtney studied her side view mirror. "Looks like we've got four vehicles behind us."

Everett growled. "There should be five. I hate this. We need radios!"

"Shoot, move, and communicate. That's the three things you have to do in the battlefield," Tobias said from behind. "With no comms, it's like we're sitting on a two-legged stool."

"That's not good," Courtney added as she kept her eyes on the mirror.

Everett barked, "What?"

"Three Toyota technicals with machine guns mounted in the rear just cut in behind the fourth vehicle."

Everett tried to concentrate on his driving despite the noise of battle all around him. Steady machine gunfire from varying distances was regularly drowned out by loud explosions. "We've got to get back around to the front of the mosque. The last vehicle in our convoy is cut off from the pack and probably being picked apart by MOC."

Everett pulled the steering wheel hard to the left, slinging the crew around in the rear of the truck and catching the hip of a MOC fighter with his front bumper. "Ali, Levi, get some RPGs ready and make sure your hatches are unlocked. As soon as we get back to the front, it's gonna be show time."

"I am ready, Everett." Ali held to the back of Everett's chair with one hand and gripped the RPG launcher in the other.

Everett rounded the corner past a dozen other jihadis on foot armed with AK-47s. He craned his neck to get a visual on the other vehicle as soon as possible. The lone MRAP came into his view just as an RPG struck the left front tire of the isolated

138

Patrol. The grenade detonated sending the front end of the truck up into the air several feet, then dropping it back down to the dirt road with a thud.

Everett grunted as he watched the MRAP try to back out of its volatile position while dragging a mangled front wheel rim with no tire. "They're dead in the water. We've got to get them out of that truck and into ours. Tobias, keep that fifty running. Split it up and try to keep all the hostiles off their game. Ali, Levi, concentrate on those two technicals coming toward us."

As Everett sped to maneuver the Typhoon up to the door of the disabled MRAP, his crew went to work fending off the combatants that were trying to close in on the inoperable Patrol vehicle.

Everett stopped the nose of the Typhoon inches away from the rear bumper of the Patrol. "Courtney, make sure Tobias has a fresh belt of ammo, then kick open the side door and tell the crew of the Patrol to get in here. Have them bring all their guns and ammo. We're going to need it!"

"Yes, sir." Courtney had never acknowledged his directives like that before.

But the proud feeling of being spoken to with such a level of respect was lost on Everett. He felt that everything happening to them was his fault. He mumbled in a low voice just above a whisper, "I never should have led these people into this quagmire, especially without radio communications. What was I thinking?"

Gunfire and grenade explosions rang all around while the fighting raged on. Everett watched as the five crew members of the Patrol boarded the

Typhoon. "David, Silas, help them transfer as much weaponry as you can. We've got to get out of here before we get stuck."

The two former IDF troops hustled to help the crew of the Patrol. The Typhoon accommodated up to nineteen troops, but with all the supplies and additional gear, the five extra passengers made for tight quarters. The munitions and weapons from the Patrol were loaded in less than four minutes. Courtney slammed the door of the Typhoon shut. "Everyone is in! Go! Go! Go!"

Everett sped away from the stagnate location, careening into a small, dirty Toyota Tacoma carrying six MOC fighters in the bed of the truck. The Typhoon easily pushed past the comparatively tiny vehicle, flipping it on its side and spilling jihadis all over the dirt road like a jar of moldy jelly beans. Everett only had to fight his smile for a moment as the gravity of their dire circumstances quickly overruled any notion of mirth.

The man who'd been the last to board the Typhoon from the incapacitated Patrol stuck his head between Everett and Courtney's seats. Like most of the other former IDF troops, he wore his old Israeli Defense Force uniform. "Mr. Carroll, thank you for coming for us. You saved the lives of my crew."

Everett didn't feel like a hero. In his mind, it was he who'd put their lives in jeopardy in the first place. "You can call me Everett." He swung the truck around the corner and raced to rejoin the rest of the convoy who was taking heavy fire from all directions. "And trust me, it was the least I could do."

"Nevertheless, we owe you our gratitude. My name is Abram." Two men and two women, all wearing IDF uniforms, pressed in behind Abram. "With me are Avigail, Daliah, Seth, and Micha."

"Welcome aboard." Everett had to focus on the road, so he couldn't take time to match names with faces. He'd apologize for his poor manners later—if they survived.

The crew of the Patrol made their way to the rear of the vehicle, leaving Everett to concentrate on driving. He caught up with the rest of the pack who were heavily engrossed in a firefight with the Martyrs of the Caliphate. Everett shouted orders to his crew, "Keep engaging! We can't give these guys five seconds to think about putting a plan together. Pop up through the hatch, shoot a five-round burst, then drop back into the vehicle. Take turns and always use a different hatch than the last guy. Hopefully, our whack-a-mole strategy will keep anyone from getting hit."

Everett drove near the front of the oncoming MRAP. He motioned backward with his thumb over his shoulder and then held up five fingers. The driver nodded. Everett hoped the driver understood that he meant to fall back in five minutes. Everett maneuvered the Typhoon so that he could make eye contact with the driver of the next vehicle from his convoy. He made the same motions but got a very dissimilar response. The driver shrugged and shook his head. Everett waved at the man and headed to the next vehicle, hoping that the drivers who were less adept at this critical game of charades would catch on once the convoy began moving out.

Everett swung the vehicle around to face the next MRAP. The third driver nodded as if he understood when Everett signaled with his hands once more. He moved on to the fourth truck whose driver seemed less sure of the intended message than the last.

Everett called out to the crew in his MRAP, "Keep them occupied for two more minutes, then we're all going to fall back."

"Roger!" Tobias kept the remote-controlled fifty-caliber rolling, pausing only for Courtney to help him reload.

Everett eyed his watch, waiting until the five minutes were up. Everett's convoy managed to kill dozens of MOC fighters and destroy more than ten MOC vehicles which consisted mostly of civilian pickup trucks, some armed with large weapons in the beds. "Five minutes are up! Everyone in your seats, we're moving out."

Everett raced back toward the main road. All four of the remaining MRAPs followed him. He glanced at his side view mirror from time to time to see if the Martyrs were going to give chase. He hoped that the attack had created enough fires and damage to keep them busy for at least a few minutes. Everett pulled onto the main road and turned the Typhoon around to face the village. He then stood up and opened the hatch above him, signaling for the other four drivers to do the same.

Everett looked up the road to see the first vehicles of the main convoy heading toward them. He called out, "We're going to have to go back in there before the civilian motorcade passes by, I just wanted to pull back long enough for us to put together a better plan since we can't communicate."

"What's the plan?" a driver yelled out from the top hatch of the MRAP parked next to Everett's.

Everett looked up the road again. "We should have some reinforcements in the front of this group of vehicles. When they get here, we'll divvy up into two elements, Team Alpha and Team Bravo. Alpha will roll straight back into the square and start raising havoc. The second element can cut around to the east and slide in quietly from the side. Snipers can shoot from up the road toward the jihadis running around us trying to take us out."

"Sounds great, but the snipers will be shooting straight at us," the man replied.

"We'll stay inside, hatches closed. We'll only operate the remote-controlled fifty-cals. As long as Bravo's snipers don't take a direct shot at the center of the windshield or take out a tire, their fire won't hurt us. The enemy, on the other hand, doesn't have any heavy armor that we've encountered so far." Everett looked at the other drivers. "What do you guys say?"

All four nodded in agreement. The man closest said, "Considering we've got no radios, I guess it's the best play we've got."

Four more MRAPs soon arrived from the front of the main convoy. Everett briefed the drivers on what they'd just been through, then brought them up to speed on the latest plan. Everett gave the signal and all nine vehicles rolled toward the small but irascible village.

The four newcomers split off from Everett's convoy and went east. Everett's team rolled back into the square they'd left minutes earlier and begun peppering the buildings with their fifty-caliber machine guns.

Tobias looked for targets while Everett drove. "How long do we have to keep this up?" Tobias asked.

"Until they decide we're too big of a force to take head-on and crawl into a hole to hide." Everett intentionally rammed the back of a pickup truck full of MOC fighters, sending the vehicle through the front window of a shop, on the bottom floor of the building next to the mosque.

Tobias unleashed a volley of bullets on the concrete building as they passed it. "I hope that's soon because we're eating up a lot of rounds. If the little town of Hafik is this tough, we're going to need a lot of ammo for Sivas."

"You don't have to hit anything. Just keep them busy until the convoy can get through. Team Bravo's snipers will take kill shots when the opportunity presents itself." Everett rammed an abandoned truck which was still burning from an RPG earlier, pushing it up against the building. He hoped it would ignite the structure and give the jihadis another problem to worry about besides the civilian convoy trying to pass by on the main road just blocks away.

Courtney watched through the passenger's window. "It looks like your plan is working. I think the enemy combatants are taking cover inside."

"Probably they think we will invade house to

house," Ali said. "I think so they are preparing for fight soldier if we come into building."

"As long as they don't hit the main convoy, we're doing our job," Everett replied.

The armored vehicles kept up the assault, and one by one, the MOC fighters slowly pulled back from the fight. An hour had passed when Everett signaled to the other drivers of Team Alpha to keep circling the mosque while he drove back to the main road. When he arrived, he saw the convoy progressing at a steady pace, roughly forty miles an hour, but the back end of the convoy still stretched farther than Everett could see. The main convoy used both the eastbound lanes and the westbound lanes, leaving the shoulders for security teams to travel on.

Courtney looked through her binoculars. "Is that the end of the motorcade?"

"Can I see the field glasses?" Everett held out his hand and Courtney passed them to him. Sure enough, the convoy was nearly through the area of Hafik. Everett breathed a sigh of relief. "We did it! Let's go tell the others it's time to roll out."

CHAPTER 14

Keep me as the apple of the eye, hide me under the shadow of thy wings, From the wicked that oppress me, from my deadly enemies, who compass me about. They are inclosed in their own fat: with their mouth they speak proudly. They have now compassed us in our steps: they have set their eyes bowing down to the earth; Like as a lion that is greedy of his prey, and as it were a young lion lurking in secret places.

Psalm 17:8-12

Once the word to withdraw from the town square of Hafik had been given, Everett's team zoomed past the main convoy leaving Team Bravo behind as the rear guard. Everett's vehicle and the four remaining MRAP's from the advanced team raced to the front of the motorcade on the shoulder of the road. When they reached the staging area outside of Sivas, Rabbi Hertzog was there waiting for them. Everett pulled close to the black 6X6 Patrol armored vehicle in which the rabbi had been riding.

"Rabbi!" Everett stepped out of the Typhoon.

Hertzog stood beside several troops in IDF uniforms. They were studying a map which was spread out on the hood of a Jeep Wrangler. The rabbi turned his attention to Everett. "My friend! How are you?"

"We're good, praise God. We lost one vehicle in the assault against Hafik, but none of our people were killed."

Courtney walked up behind Everett. "Not even any injuries."

"Almost no injury." Ali tenderly touched his swollen lip with the back of his hand. It was no longer bleeding, but the swelling was sufficient to impair his speech slightly.

The rabbi hugged Ali with one arm. "If that's the worst thing that happened, we must give all the glory to HaShem."

"Indeed. All glory to Jehovah." Ali smiled carefully with one side of his mouth.

The rabbi turned his attention back to the map. "My security detail tells me we are roughly five miles out from Sivas."

Everett nodded. "Our team will escort you and your security force through Sivas. Once you're through, we'll act as one of the response teams in case the perimeter line along the main highway is attacked. You're in a Patrol which is a very secure vehicle, plus you'll have the heavily armored Golan, which we brought from Israel, as part of your escort. That's in addition to the civilian vehicles in your security motorcade. I'm confident that they'll be able to provide you with enough protection to get you to the underground cities, once you've cleared Sivas."

Hertzog put one finger high in the air. "And I will be hidden in the shadow of the wings of Adonai!"

Everett smiled, grateful for the reminder that the fate of Israel did not rest solely upon his own shoulders. "Yes, and the covering of the Almighty."

"But I do so appreciate your efforts, Everett." Rabbi Hertzog squeezed Everett's hand, then turned to Courtney, Ali, and Tobias. "And the bravery of your friends."

"It is an honor to serve you and the people of God," Ali said.

Everett looked at the long line of cars parked bumper to bumper in all four lanes of the highway. "The most dangerous part of our journey lies just ahead. We should be going."

The rabbi looked at the soldiers around him and nodded. "Then let us be on our way."

"Remember, you have the staff. Nothing is more important than getting that staff to the underground cities. Without it, the subterranean dwellings are just pre-dug graves."

"Yes, Everett. I will do all that I can." Hertzog

shook Everett's hand and walked to his armored vehicle.

Everett addressed the drivers around him. "I'll take point. Truck Two and Truck Three from my team will follow me. The rabbi's Patrol will be behind them, with the Golan following the rabbi. The remaining two trucks from my team will be behind the Golan."

The driver of the Golan asked, "Wouldn't it be better if we boxed the rabbi in?"

"That would be as good as painting a sign that says 'this is the most important vehicle in our convoy'. At least this way, we keep them guessing. And keep three vehicle lengths between you and the next vehicle so they can't take out two of us with one shot."

The driver of the Golan looked at some of the other soldiers as if he didn't trust Everett's decision.

Tobias stepped forward. "He's right about not boxing in the rabbi. We'll be traveling at top speed. We'll need to be single file so we have both lanes in which to maneuver."

The driver of the Golan nodded. "Okay. I'll follow your lead."

"Let's roll out!" Everett whispered to Tobias on the way back to the Typhoon, "Thanks for that. It seems some folks would just rather hear things from a fellow Jew."

"And I apologize for that. We can be a stubborn people at times."

Everett patted him on the back as they loaded into the Typhoon. "That's not always a bad thing. I'm sure it's part of what has kept you alive as a race for over four thousand years."

The convoy was soon on their way. They covered the short stretch of road to Sivas in less than four minutes. If they could keep up their current rate of travel, they'd have the rabbi through the danger zone in another four minutes. Everett took a deep breath, hoping, praying for a clear, open path, wanting so badly to at least get Hertzog past the city before they were detected.

"Watch out!" Courtney yelled.

Everett slammed the brakes with his eyes as wide as biscuit cutters. In the westbound lane of the highway sat a tank. Not only was the heavy weapon pointed right at them, it was flanked by no less than ten armored vehicles. Most looked to be American military vehicles which had been re-appropriated by ISIS in Iraq years earlier. A dozen technicals were interspersed among the heavily-armored military vehicles. Everett called out to the rear of the truck. "Bad news, guys. We've got a welcoming committee and the designated chairman is a T-72 Iraqi tank. Ali, Levi, I need you guys to hit this thing hard with the Vampirs. Try to stick a rocket in the turret ring. It might not disable the tank altogether, but if we can keep the turret from turning, we can keep them from aiming."

"And then what?" Ali was already opening the top hatch.

"Hit the treads. Even if the turret won't swing, they can still point left and right if the treads are operational."

The first shell fired out of the 125-millimeter

main gun of the tank, hitting the asphalt, behind Everett and right beside Rabbi Hertzog's Patrol.

"You're gonna have to shoot on the move, guys. We can't sit still, nor can we have the good folks behind us sitting still. Tobias, hit these guys with all you've got. Our only choice is to try to drive straight through this mess. It ain't like we can just turn around and go back home."

Courtney looked at Everett like he was crazy but said nothing.

He forced a smile at her. "Help Tobias stay loaded. We're gonna need it."

The second 125-millimeter shell shot out of the giant gun. This one didn't miss. It exploded in the grill of the Golan, leaving the vehicle in scraps of metal too small to tell they had ever belonged to an armored vehicle. The fireball from the truck mushroomed into the sky and Everett's heart broke for the brave soldiers who'd been inside. Still, he had his mission, and it was to get the rabbi to the other side of the city.

Everett drove straight at the tank as he watched the turret spin in his direction. The gun lowered and he saw the flash of light. He closed his eyes, gritted his teeth, and prayed that it would miss them.

"Direct hit!" Ali called out from behind.

Everett opened his eyes to see smoke rolling out from the right side of the turret ring. The flash he'd seen was the explosion of the PG-29V rocket that Ali and Levi had fired at the tank. "Great shot. Let's see if you can do that one more time!"

A barrage of machine gunfire hit the hood and cracked the heavy glass windshield of the Typhoon as Everett drove straight toward the line of battle delineated by the armada of war machines only yards away. RPGs flew by like fireflies on a summer night.

BOOM! Everett looked in his side view mirror to see yet another of Hertzog's security team taken out. This time it was the Jeep Wrangler.

POW! Everett saw flames shoot out from the tread of the tank. "Great job, guys!"

He heard a commotion in the rear of the vehicle. "What's happening?"

Tonya called out, "Levi has been hit?"

"Is it bad?"

"Headshot," David replied.

"I'll take his place," Abram said. "I'll help Ali with the rockets."

"Thank you." Everett hated putting them in harm's way, but he had no other choice. "Everyone stay in your seats for a few seconds. I'm going to have to go off road to get around this mess."

The bullets rained down on the Typhoon as Everett smashed into the front of a large pick-up which was blocking his path. He quickly pushed it off the road and drove onto the grass. The Typhoon sped across the berm which separated the highway from the parking lot of an apartment community. Everett split his attention between the threats lined up in front of him and the other vehicles in his convoy.

BOOM! He looked in his side view to see the Typhoon directly behind his turned on its side. As badly as he wanted to stop and help, he had to get Hertzog beyond the roadblock. The other vehicles were still following him through the parking lot of the apartment complex.

"Ali, Abram, see what you can do to take out any of the vehicles closing in on the disabled Typhoon behind us!"

"We will do it!" Ali shouted.

"I'm giving them cover as well!" Tobias swung the fifty-caliber around and began firing.

BOOM! Everett's Typhoon lifted up from the ground and dropped back down. "Is everyone okay?" He looked at Courtney first.

She looked rattled by the explosion, but she wasn't bleeding, and she was alive. "We're fine, just get us out of here!"

Everett had to work the gears to get the truck moving again. Hertzog's Patrol and another Patrol from Everett's team raced by his Typhoon. Soon, he was rolling again. Hertzog had gotten around the roadblock, but they still had two more miles to escape from Sivas, and there was no promise that the danger was over.

BOOM! Everett looked in his side view mirror just as a rocket hit another MRAP from his convoy. Fire and smoke poured from the rear wheel well and the vehicle sat motionless, demobilized from the blast. "God, protect them." He shot up a quick prayer, then addressed his crew. "It's a bumpy ride, but if any of you think you can get a couple of shots off from the hatches, it would be much appreciated. Tobias is doing all he can with the fifty-cal."

"I can do it." Ali volunteered yet again.

David said, "I'll assist Ali."

"Silas and myself will form a second team," said

Abram.

"Thanks, guys," Everett acknowledged. "Stick with simple RPGs. It's going to be too rough of a ride to try to get those huge launch tubes up and aimed for the PG-29Vs."

Everett checked his side view yet again. The rest of his convoy and the remaining vehicles in Hertzog's security element had been cut off. They were now being pursued furiously by a huge desert tan MAXX PRO, two US Military Humvees, and a swarm of technicals. All were armed with fifty-caliber machine guns, and the technicals each had at least one MOC fighter operating some form of shoulder-fired weapon from the beds of the pick-ups. "Focus your fire on the technicals!" Everett shouted toward the rear. "Let's get the low-hanging fruit first, then worry about the heavily-armored trucks once we've picked off the ankle biters."

Everett drove hard to keep up with Rabbi Hertzog's Patrol and the other MRAP between them. However, he did not attempt to pass them. Everett intentionally maintained his position at the rear of the three-truck convoy, putting himself—and his wife—in between an arsenal of destructive weaponry and the rabbi's vehicle.

BOOM! Another blast rocked the Typhoon, slinging Everett against the shoulder strap of his seat belt. The truck was still rolling, so he did not let off the accelerator. "Are you okay?"

Courtney lay on her side, between the two front seats. She wasn't strapped in because she'd been assisting Tobias with keeping the hungry fifty-caliber machine gun fed. Groggily, and bleeding from her forehead, she said, "I'm okay."

"We lost the remote-controlled machine gun," Tobias reported.

Tonya cried out from the back, "David and Silas are dead."

Everett sighed with grief. "As much as I hate to say this, we have to keep fighting. We've lost our primary means of defense and we must continue laying down fire from the hatches."

"I'll take Silas' place," Tonya said.

Ali worked his way to the front of the cab. "I can put cover fire with AK-47 from front hatch. It will help to make up for not have fifty-cal."

"I'll form a new RPG team to take the place of David and Ali's." Tobias threw open a hatch in the rear of the vehicle.

"I'm with you," Courtney tried to get up from her position.

"No!" Everett's scream was panicked. "I need you to help me navigate."

"I have to be in the fight, Everett." She continued to move toward the back.

With his right hand, he caught her belt. "The windshield is cracked. I can barely see. I'm just aiming the truck at the Patrol in front of me. I need you to watch out for road hazards, or we'll all be dead!" His plea was that of a desperate man, and that of a husband that was not going to take no for an answer.

"I will assist Tobias," said Micha.

Reluctantly, she turned around, scowled at Everett, and took her seat.

Everett tried to disguise his relief.

BOOM! BOOM! BOOM! "Our team just eliminated three technicals!" Courtney reported as she checked her side view mirror.

"Praise God!" Everett pressed hard, trying to stay ahead of the pursuing threat, yet keeping his distance from the Patrol in front of him.

He glanced at his side view to see one of the Humvees advancing on the driver's side. "Watch this guy on the left!"

TA, TA, TA, TA, TAT! The Hummer peppered the side of the Typhoon as it raced past him. Just then, an RPG from an enemy vehicle struck near the passenger's side front wheel causing Everett to swerve off the road and nearly flip the Typhoon. He slammed on the brakes to regain control and get the giant MRAP back onto the pavement.

Ali dropped down from the hatch to change magazines in his AK. "Abram is dead. The fifty-caliber shoot him as it passing by."

Everett took a deep breath as he glanced at Ali who was still staring at him. "What else, Ali? You're not telling me something."

Ali's eyes welled up with tears. "They also shoot Tobias."

"No!" Courtney screamed and crawled to the back toward Tobias.

"Is it fatal?" Everett kept his eyes on the road.

"Headshot." Ali wiped his eyes and stood back up, putting his rifle through the hatch first.

Seth and Daliah filled the positions vacated by their fallen friends.

From the corner of his eye, Everett watched the side view as his team took out the remaining technicals from behind him. BOOM! Again, Everett had to swerve in order to miss the Patrol from his convoy as a massive explosion flipped it on its side, causing it to skid to a stop right in front of him. A large shoulder-fired rocket shot by a jihadi in the Humvee which just passed him had taken out the Patrol.

The contest was now down to five remaining vehicles. The rabbi's Patrol was still in the lead, but the enemy Humvee was between him and Everett. The MAXX PRO and the other Hummer trailed close behind Everett.

"We have to focus our fire on the Humvee in front of us. The entirety of the Jewish nation is depending on Rabbi Hertzog to get through with Moses' staff. Otherwise, all we have lost will be in vain." Everett's words were not only intended to be a morale booster, they were the brutal truth—economically encapsulating the grave reality in which the team was immersed.

CHAPTER 15

When thou passest through the waters, I will be with thee; and through the rivers, they shall not overflow thee: when thou walkest through the fire, thou shalt not be burned; neither shall the flame kindle upon thee. For I am the Lord thy God, the Holy One of Israel, thy Saviour: I gave Egypt for thy ransom, Ethiopia and Seba for thee. Since thou wast precious in my sight, thou hast been honourable, and I have loved thee: therefore will I give men for thee, and people for thy life. Fear not: for I am with thee: I will bring thy seed from the east, and gather thee from the west; I will say to the north, Give up; and to the south, Keep not back: bring my sons from far, and my daughters from the ends of the earth; Even every one that is called by my name: for I have created him for my glory, I have formed him; yea, I have made him.

Isaiah 43:2-7

BOOM! Another rocket hit the center of Rabbi Hertzog's Patrol near the bottom of the truck. The blast caused the MRAP to flip off the road and roll onto the grass, coming to a stop and resting perfectly upside down.

Instinctively, Everett slowed down and brought the Typhoon to a complete stop, with the side door positioned feet away from the door of the inverted Patrol. "Courtney, I need you and Ali to get the bodies of the fallen out of our truck."

"Everett, we can't just leave them," she pleaded.

"We have to make room for the living. I'm sorry." He hated issuing such a morbid directive. "Daliah, Avigail, get into the rabbi's Patrol. Get the rabbi and Moses' staff first. Then get the wounded from the Patrol into the Typhoon. Everyone else, fight like you've never fought in your lives!" Everett opened the latch on the side door and kicked it open. "Tonya and Micha, keep RPGs going in all directions. Focus on the fifty-cals. Seth, you're with me. We've got to cover the door while the girls get the rabbi!"

Everett used the large metal door for cover as he

took aim at the driver of the Humvee, firing at him with his HK rifle. Everett got down on one knee to lower his profile and his odds of catching a bullet. He peered beneath the Typhoon to see the other Humvee circling around so he could get a shot between the two vehicles. Everett reached into his tactical sling hanging at his side and retrieved a hand grenade. He pulled the pin and waited until he saw the bumper of the Humvee. He lobbed the grenade, which arched perfectly into the rear of the Hummer. POW! The detonation of the grenade tossed the gunner of the fifty-cal out of the vehicle and dropped his mangled corpse in the path of the MAXX PRO which was right behind the Humvee. Crunch! The MAXX PRO slowed as it came into view of Everett and Seth.

"Get down!" Everett yelled as he rolled under the Typhoon.

The machine gun mounted on top of the MAXX PRO peppered the slim corridor between the Typhoon and the upended Patrol, cutting Seth down. Multiple rounds ripped through Seth's body, and he fell to the ground with his hollow, lifeless eyes facing Everett.

BOOM! A shower of sparks rained down from the vicinity of the MAXX PRO's machine gun. Everett hoped his team had hit it with a rocket, but he couldn't see the source of the explosion from his position. What he did know was that the heavy gun had ceased its insatiable barking—for now.

Everett rolled back out from beneath the Typhoon and yelled to Tonya inside the truck. "Toss me an RPG!"

"Here!" She quickly complied.

Everett took the launcher and ran out from the corridor between the vehicles. He had to draw the fire away from the doors so the girls could get the rabbi and Moses' staff. Everett ran in front of the Typhoon, waiting for the MAXX PRO to come back around. He dropped to one knee and fired. Shwooofp! The grenade took flight, streaking toward the grill of the giant vehicle. The grenade exploded, but the truck continued hurtling toward Everett. Everett bounded out of the way, retreating beneath the Typhoon and crawling back toward the open side-door in the corridor created by the two vehicles. Everett looked in the truck. "Is the rabbi inside?"

"I'm here, Everett!" Hertzog was banged up, nursing a massive cut on his leg.

"And the staff?"

Tonya handed the first aid kit to the rabbi. "Avigail and Daliah went back into the Patrol to look for it."

"Are there any other survivors in the Patrol?" Everett asked.

"The driver and one other guard, they're in pretty bad condition, but still breathing," Tonya replied.

"There were two other security personnel with you. They didn't survive the crash?" Everett's eyebrows drooped as he turned to Rabbi Hertzog.

The rabbi lowered his head. "No. I'm afraid not."

Everett tightened his jaw. "Okay. Tonya, hand me a couple more grenades for the RPG."

She passed him two projectiles. The first, he loaded into the launcher. The second, he tucked inside of his load-carrying vest. Everett dashed back out into harm's way. The MAXX PRO came around again. Everett noticed a steady flow of white steam spraying from beneath the hood. His previous assault had not stopped the beast of a vehicle in its tracks, but the radiator was cracked, and it wouldn't be a threat much longer. Everett watched for the next Humvee. It came around from the back side of the Patrol, and Everett sent a grenade on course for a head-on collision with the Hummer. KABOOM! The front end of the vehicle lifted off the ground and the vehicle flipped onto its side. Immediately, Everett rushed toward the wreckage, transitioning to his HK rifle, enabling him to eliminate the survivors of the crash. The MAXX PRO finally came to a sputtering halt, and the MOC fighters from inside flooded out, AK-47s firing as they exited.

Everett turned, facing what was to be his end. Outgunned by the jihadis, his time was up. Not being one to roll over and die without a fight, he shot the last man struggling to leave the wrecked Humvee, then directed his fire at the massive wave of assailants who were charging right for him.

Everett took one final breath from this realm and squeezed the trigger. PA, PA, PA, PA, POW!

Miraculously, the MOC fighters were falling dead as soon as they could get out of the stalled MAXX PRO. Everett kept shooting, unable to see the source of the enemy's demise.

"Everett!" Courtney called out from the cover of the Typhoon as she lowered her weapon.

Stunned to still be breathing, Everett rushed to her position where he found that it was she and Ali who had neutralized the sword of death swinging for Everett's head.

TA, TA, TA, TAT! BOOM! Machine gunfire and RPGs still fell like hail as the team continued to be bombarded by the last remaining Humvee.

"Did we get the staff?"

Avigail emerged from the upside-down Patrol, holding the wooden stick triumphantly in the air. "Got it!"

Everett smiled. "Great, let's go!"

TA, TA, TAT! Three bullets ripped through Avigail's body from the direction of the Humvee.

"Avi!" Daliah screamed, covering her mouth in horror.

Everett grabbed the staff from the fallen girl, pushing his wife, Ali, and Daliah into the Typhoon. His stomach soured and he fought back the urge to vomit. As much as he hated to lose men in battle, ten times more did he loathe the disgusting feeling of losing a woman under his command. It just didn't seem right. Perhaps he thought soft beautiful creatures like Avigail didn't belong in such a grotesque arena as the theatre of war. Or perhaps it was too much of a painful reminder of Courtney's mortality. Maybe it was a little bit of both. But there was no time for philosophical reflection at the moment. He had to get Courtney, Moses' staff, and the rabbi away from the relentless massacre at hand, or they would all surely perish.

Once back in the vehicle, Everett shoved the gear stick and pressed the accelerator propelling the Typhoon back onto the road. "Ali, I need you and Tonya to take out this Humvee. Micah, Daliah, you have to provide cover fire for Ali and Tonya so they can get the Vampir launch tube through the hatch and aim. I know what I'm asking you is dangerous, but if we don't get rid of this Hummer, none of us will survive. We have to protect Moses' staff with our lives. It's the most critical element to our entire plan."

Without asking, Courtney stood up and flung open the top hatch over the cab. She fed her rifle through the opening and began firing to cover Ali and Tonya's effort with the rocket launcher.

He shouted, "No, Courtney!" But it was no use. She probably couldn't hear him from outside the hatch. And even if she could, she obviously wasn't going to comply.

Everett pushed the heavy Typhoon as fast as it could go, but it was no match for the much-smaller, much-lighter, and much-faster Humvee.

Ting, Ting, Tink! Everett could hear the bullets from the Hummer striking the side of the Typhoon. He tensed up as he heard the impacts get close to the front of the vehicle and closer to Courtney, whose head and upper torso were exposed to the gunfire.

Everett saw the Humvee creeping up beside him. "Even if I'm slower, there's still one advantage to being bigger." Everett cut the wheel hard to the left, swerving into the Hummer, sending it careening into the median, and across the road to the other side. He pulled back to the center of the road and watched the Humvee as its driver fought to regain control. The driver could not and the Humvee hit the steep drainage grade past the shoulder of the road, flipping several times before coming to a complete stop in an inverted position.

Everett hit the brakes and brought the Typhoon to a halt before driving it over the median and turning it around.

"You did it!" Courtney dropped into the cab and closed the hatch.

"Great job, Everett!" Ali exclaimed as he and Tonya retreated to the inside of the vehicle.

"Why are we turning around? We still have to get the rabbi and the staff to the underground cities!" Courtney exclaimed.

"We'll have to make two trips. First, we can drop the rabbi off at Kayseri, then come back to Sivas. The convoy will never make it through without our help. There are too many MOC fighters and they are too well armed," Everett replied.

"Still, Kayseri is the other way," Courtney said.

"I know, but I need to check that Humvee for fuel. We'll never make it back with what we have in the tank." Everett slowed as he reached the wrecked Hummer. "Tonya, Daliah." He reluctantly turned to his wife. "And Courtney, we need you to cover us from the top hatches. Ali, Micha and myself will eliminate possible survivors and retrieve any fuel we can find."

"You got it!" Courtney unlatched the metal door on the ceiling of the Typhoon once again and climbed up through it.

Everett led Ali and Micha out the side door of the MRAP with their weapons drawn. They shot each body they saw twice in the head before moving on to the next. Once they were certain no survivors remained, Everett retrieved a five-gallon bucket of dry storage food from the Typhoon. He emptied the contents onto the floor of the truck and brought the bucket to the Hummer, placing it beneath the fuel cap. Since the vehicle was upended, fuel was already leaking out of the cap. "We need a water bottle or something to transfer the fuel from the bucket to the Typhoon."

"I've got one!" Micha sprinted back to the Typhoon and returned with his bottle. He finished the last sip and passed the receptacle to Everett.

Ali pointed back toward the road. "Look! Five-gallon metal fuel can. Probably fell off from Humvee when it went rolling!"

"Great! See if there's anything in it and put it in the tank if there is." Everett poured the first liter of fuel from the bucket into his MRAP.

Micha found another bottle and assisted Everett with the slow process of relaying the fuel from the upside-down Humvee to the Typhoon's tank. The tan metal can Ali located was indeed filled with fuel and would go a long way in helping them on the return trip from Kayseri.

Everett's hands smelled like diesel when he returned to the Typhoon, but it was a relatively small problem in light of the events which had transpired on this fateful day.

CHAPTER 16

And not only so, but we glory in tribulations also: knowing that tribulation worketh patience; And patience, experience; and experience, hope: And hope maketh not ashamed; because the love of God is shed abroad in our hearts by the Holy Ghost which is given unto us.

Romans 5:3-5

Two and a half hours later, they reached the underground city of Kayseri. Everett stopped the vehicle just long enough to let out the rabbi and the two injured soldiers from his vehicle. "Daliah, Tonya, Courtney, you three help the rabbi and the injured men. You'll stay here with them to take care of their wounds. We'll be back soon."

Daliah and Tonya assisted the rabbi, whose leg was severely injured from the wreck. Courtney, however, did not get out of her seat. "I'm not getting separated from you, Everett."

Everett knew what she was going to say before she said it. He nodded. "Okay. Can you just hand the staff to one of the girls?"

Courtney did so, careful not to step out of the vehicle as if she thought Everett might take off without her.

Ali and Micha helped the other two men out of the vehicle, then unloaded the dry storage food and other provisions which had been brought along in the Typhoon.

"We'll be back soon. Get down into the city and find the well. Turn it to water and be waiting for us. We'll still have to purify the wells of the other cities when we return," Everett said.

"We'll be ready when you arrive." Tonya waved with her free hand.

As Everett put the truck in gear, Ali stuck his head between the seats. "You should let me drive, Everett. You need rest. Take nap for couple hours. I wake you when we get close to Sivas."

"What about you? You've got to be exhausted also." Everett looked at his friend.

"I sleeped on way here. It help me so much."

Everett nodded. "Maybe I will. But wake me when we're like twenty miles out, or if you see any signs that the convoy broke through the hostiles in Sivas."

"I will do it." Ali switched places with Everett who went to the rear of the truck and made himself comfortable. Courtney also moved to the back, sat down, and put her head on Everett's shoulder.

Everett was awoken from his slumber by Micha. "Mr. Carroll, Ali said to get you up."

"Are we almost there?"

"Yes, sir."

"Thanks, and you can call me Everett." He waited for Courtney to become fully conscious and take the weight of her head off him before he stood up and made his way to the cab.

"It does not look good." Ali's face was troubled.

Everett peered through the cracked windshield of the Typhoon to see plumes of smoke rising from Sivas in the distance. "I hate that we had to leave the others behind, but we had no choice. If the staff hadn't made it through, nothing else would matter."

"You are correct. Please, do not blame yourself for leaving." Ali stayed on course.

"Do you want to stay at the wheel?"

"I can drive. Many times I drive in dangerous situation for Sadat."

"I'll get some RPGs loaded and make sure MOC knows we're back." Everett returned to the rear of the vehicle.

Courtney, Micha, and Everett prepared their weaponry for the battle that was before them.

Minutes later, Ali called out to the team, "We are coming in from behind the Martyrs of the Caliphate. It looks like our people pushed them back while we were gone."

Everett nodded. "Our guys are still fighting, so we still have a chance. Stop when we're about 300 yards out. I'll focus the PG-29V rockets on their heavy equipment until we're spotted. Once they see us, get us out of there. Try to find a side road that will take us back around to the Israeli side of the fighting."

"Okay. I will do it," Ali said.

"Micha, cover me with your rifle. Courtney, keep feeding me new rockets. Once we're spotted and Ali initiates our retreat, I'll transition to the regular RPGs since they'll be easier to deploy from a fast-moving vehicle."

"Got it!" Courtney began organizing the various projectiles that she would be handing off to Everett once the assault began.

"You can count on me, sir." Micha checked the magazines in the front of his load-carrying vest.

When the Typhoon began to slow down, Everett hoisted the six-foot launch tube through the hatch. He found his first target, an unsuspecting desert-tan Cougar MRAP, which had probably been stolen from Iraqi forces by ISIS years ago. Everett aimed at the rear bumper of the vehicle, hoping to either damage the transmission or the rear tires. The Cougar was heavily-armored and even a direct hit from an ordnance as large as the PG-29V was not guaranteed to take it out unless he could hit it at just the right spot. SWOOEESH! The rocket left the tube. KABOOM! The back end of the cougar lifted several feet from the ground and descended hard when it came down. Flames licked the back of the vehicle while smoke trickled out from beneath. The rear door opened and MOC fighters began fleeing the vehicle.

"Rocket." Everett reached down through the hatch and took another projectile from Courtney.

"Good shot, sir." Micha watched from the hatch adjacent to Everett's with his rifle ready to fire.

"Thanks." Everett loaded the next rocket, aimed toward a Humvee closer to the front of the MOC firing line, and pulled the trigger. SHROOOFP! BOOOM! A ball of flame and smoke billowed up from the vehicle into the air.

Micha took aim. "I think they've identified us as the source of the assault, sir."

Everett nodded. "One more before we go!" He took the next rocket from Courtney, quickly loaded it into the tube and fired at a technical, also near the front of the MOC line. BLOOOM! The truck exploded like a grenade, sending fire and shrapnel in every direction.

TINK! TING! The first bullets from the enraged jihadis began hitting the armored plates of the Typhoon.

KA, KA, KA, KA! Micha's rifle spit out a steady stream of cover fire in return.

"Give me a grenade launcher and tell Ali to get us out of here!" Everett let the launch tube of the Vampir roll off the side of the roof. Since he had two more launch tubes in the vehicle, it was more expendable than the precious moments needed to transition to the smaller RPG.

"Here!" Courtney passed him the rocket-propelled grenade as the Typhoon turned to make its retreat.

Everett lifted it up through the hatch, took aim at a truck filled with MOC fighters and fired. BOOM! The truck swerved to miss the projectile but lost control in so doing, and ran off the road. It hit a telephone pole, which ended the pursuit.

"Grenade!" Everett held out his hand for another projectile from below.

Micha fired at the next pick-up truck racing toward them while Everett armed the launcher and fired. Shweeoooo! Away it went, smashing into the windshield of their assailants, exploding and leaving nothing but a burning hull of a truck.

Everett took the next grenade from Courtney. "We're clear for now, but more are coming. Tell Ali to look for a turn-off!"

Everett loaded the new projectile onto the launcher and held tightly to the frame of the hatch as Ali slung the vehicle hard on a sharp left turn. Once the vehicle leveled out, Everett resumed his firing position, waiting to see if they'd be pursued by more MOC fighters. As soon as Everett was sure they weren't followed, he dropped into the Typhoon and walked toward the cab. He held onto the back of Ali's chair for balance. "Are we going to be able to meet back up with the Israelis?"

Ali pointed straight ahead. "This bridge is Red River. Should be we can follow river east for little while, then return to main road where is Israelis—if road not blocked by MOC."

"I hope the IDF troops recognize our vehicle when we get there. I'd hate to survive everything we've been through only to be taken out by friendly fire." Everett worked his way over to the passenger's seat.

Courtney squatted between the two front seats. "We've yet to run into any MOC fighters with Russian vehicles. Hopefully, it won't be a problem, but I'll find something to make a white flag with, just to be safe."

Everett nodded. "If you find something, tie it to your rifle and stick it through the top hatch. Don't let yourself be exposed to gunfire. Everybody is in condition black and that's when mistakes happen."

"Okay." She brushed her hand against his shoulder briefly, then returned to the back of the vehicle.

Ali reached the bridge and turned east onto the dirt road. He followed the river for two miles, then took another left. "This should be far enough to put us behind the Israeli line."

Everett looked through the binoculars to see a watchman from their side looking back at him. "They see us. He's lighting off one of your mortar rounds to signal for back up. He thinks we're trying to attack from the side road. Courtney, get that flag up!"

"Got it!" Her voice preceded the sound of one of the rear top hatches being opened.

Everett watched as a Range Rover, a school bus, and a Volvo wagon arrived at the intersection. "Here come his reinforcements. It's good to know our signaling system is functional." Troops wearing IDF uniforms poured out of the three vehicles and took aim at the Typhoon.

"They are going to shoot us!" Ali exclaimed. "What do I do?"

"Slow down." Everett watched the soldiers through the field glasses. "They're lowering their weapons. I think they saw the flag. Just keep creeping toward the main road. I'll stick my head out and explain who we are once we're within earshot."

Ali cautiously continued driving toward the line.

"That's close enough, Ali. Stick the shifter in neutral and put the parking brake on." Everett unlocked the hatch above the cab and gently opened the cover. He stuck both hands out first, then his head.

"Mr. Carroll!" The soldier at the center of the line lowered his rifle completely.

Everett had never been so glad to hear his own name. "Hey."

Everett instructed the soldiers to get back to their positions and asked the man who'd recognized him to hang back so he could fill Everett in on what was happening.

Micha opened the side door of the vehicle and let the soldier in.

"I'm Josiah. It's an honor to meet you, sir. I've heard you speak more than once at various assemblies in Batumi." The man who looked to be a few years older than Everett offered his hand.

"Nice to meet you, Josiah. We had to get Rabbi Hertzog and the staff through to the underground cities. We just got back. What's going on?"

"It's a mess, sir." Josiah's forehead puckered. "We've lost most of the armored vehicles and we're down to civilian cars and trucks. We've been engaged in a prolonged firefight for more than five hours. The non-combatant section of the convoy is stopped about two miles back. They're waiting on us to provide a secured corridor for them to pass through."

"Is anyone watching that section of the convoy? What if they're attacked?" Everett was concerned about the women and elderly up the road from the fighting.

Josiah nodded confidently. "When you're talking about Israeli Jews, the term non-combatant is relative. They're all armed and ready to fight. Those who are capable of firing a weapon are in battle formation and watching for potential trouble. Additionally, they have mortars that they can send up if they're attacked. I believe we have you to thank for that idea."

Everett shook his head. "That was my wife's idea, and those were Ali's fireworks. I can't take credit for that.

"What's the enemy's situation? Do they still have armored vehicles? Tanks? What are they working with?"

Josiah replied, "I think they've been reduced to pickup trucks. A few are outfitted with machine guns, but I think all the big toys have been taken out."

"So now we're just killing each other, man to man and gun to gun."

Josiah nodded. "We're doing more killing than they are, sir. Few of the remaining MOC fighters appear to not have any military experience at all. Some look like this is their first time actually shooting guns."

Everett looked at Josiah's rank insignia. "Staff Sergeant, given your knowledge of the battlefield, how would you utilize this Typhoon, since it's one of the few remaining armored vehicles?"

"It's probably the last, sir. I'd drive hard into the enemy line. I'd ram the jihadis with the truck, which would break their line and force those not hit by the vehicle to fall back. I'd stick the Typhoon sideways, which would provide the Israelis a secured barrier to fight from behind."

Everett turned to Ali. "Then that's what we'll do."

"I'd be honored to fight beside you, sir. May I request to stay in the vehicle with your team?"

"We'd love to have you." Everett put his hand on Josiah's shoulder and quickly introduced him to the team.

Everett assigned roles for each of them. Once the Typhoon came to a stop, he and Micha would fire RPGs at the enemy while Ali and Josiah provided cover fire. Courtney would keep Everett and Micha supplied with rocket-propelled grenades for their launchers.

Once he confirmed that everyone understood the strategy, Everett slapped the back of the driver's seat. "Okay, Ali—let's wrap this thing up!"

The Typhoon barreled through the grass, several feet off the main road's shoulder. Everett and the others stayed seated with their seat belts fastened until Ali had smashed through the front line of the MOC jihadis. From the passenger's seat, Everett pointed through the windshield. "If you can hit that technical with the fifty mounted in the back, it would help our cause immensely."

Ali's face seemed unsure regarding what he was about to do. "If you say so, Everett."

"You've got this, Ali. We'll be just fine."

Ali focused on his path, weaving past burned-out vehicles strewn about like the toys of an adolescent pyromaniac. "Tell for everybody to hang on!"

"Brace for impact!" Everett yelled out to the passengers in the rear of the truck.

Ali snapped the wheel to the left, aiming the giant machine right for the MOC firing line. SMAAASHHH! The Typhoon collided into the Toyota Tundra with the fifty-caliber machine gun mounted in the bed, just as Everett had directed. Everett's body jerked forward into the shoulder strap of his seat belt with such velocity that he saw stars momentarily.

The Typhoon knocked the Tundra out of the way like a bulldozer snapping over a two-year-old cedar-tree sapling. The MRAP plowed through the second and third vehicles, sending them spinning off on either side of the monster armored vehicle. The Russian military truck finally came to a complete stop.

Outside of Everett's side window, a Toyota Tacoma sat turned on its side with flames coming from the engine and fuel leaking from the tank. He released his seat belt. "Everybody okay back there?"

"We're all good." Courtney's voice blended with the sound of seat belts clicking and soldiers scrambling to prepare for battle.

Everett retrieved the RPG launcher from beside

his foot and looked at Ali. "You good?"

"Considering I was just in very bad car crash," Ali was visibly shaken. "Yes. I am pretty good."

BOOM! A rocket hit the front end of the Typhoon, shaking everyone inside. Smoke poured from the engine compartment.

"They've incapacitated our truck. Retreat is no longer an option. We've got to fight like we've never fought in our lives." Everett shouted out the mandate.

With his AK in hand, Ali shoved the hatch door open above the cab and prepared to provide cover fire.

Everett made his way to one of the center hatches. Micha would use the other center hatch so Courtney would be equidistant from each of them and ready to hand off the next grenade to whoever needed it.

"Let's go!" Everett popped his hatch, sprung up and took aim at yet another pickup truck falling back to form a second battle line from which the jihadis could defend their position. SWOOOOfff! The grenade glided over the heads of several fleeing MOC fighters, finally finding its intended target. BOOOOM! Fire, ash, and metal exploded in all directions. BOOM! Micha's first grenade struck a second target, an off-white Land Cruiser, which was also reduced to a heap of black billowing smoke and flame.

TA, TA, TA, TA, Ta! Machine gunfire rang out from all around. Everett and his team had proven themselves to be the biggest threat on the road, but in so doing they'd also marked themselves as the most high-valued target.

"Cover me!" Everett took another grenade and loaded it into the launcher. He took aim at a box truck parked diagonally in the road which was being used as cover for multiple hostiles who were directing their fire toward Everett and his team. Shwoooofp! The grenade hit the truck. BOOM! He watched several of the jihadis fall behind the box truck, but one was still crawling around.

"Courtney, quick! I need another grenade!"

She passed another warhead to him which he expeditiously loaded and aimed toward the single man crawling beneath the frame of the smoldering box truck. The jihadi made his way to the edge of the truck and took aim at Everett.

Everett pulled the trigger, sending the grenade toward the man. BOOM! Everett felt a sharp pain burn like a hot iron inside his right arm. The heat so intense, the torment so unbearable, he could not even make a sound. He gasped for air as his reflexes caused him to drop his launcher. He knew what had happened. The man had gotten off one last shot before the grenade sent him to find out that eternity held something quite different for him than the seventy-two virgins he'd been promised.

Blood flowed freely from two adjacent holes in Everett's right forearm. One was just above his wrist, the other slightly below his elbow. The exit wound was only slightly larger than the entry, which gave Everett hope that it had been a full-metal jacket rather than a hollow point. Nevertheless, he was done shooting RPGs for the day. Everett quickly brought up his HK rifle, which he could operate with his left hand in a pinch. And indeed, this situation was the dictionary definition of a pinch.

Everett called out to Ali. "Switch functions with me. You take over the RPGs. I'll lay down cover fire."

Ali's face wrinkled in horror as he looked at Everett's arm.

Everett held a finger to his lips and shook his head, signaling for Ali to say nothing of the matter. The last thing any of them needed was Courtney losing focus because of her concern over Everett's arm. She'd have plenty of time to console him later—if they survived the battle.

Ali retreated inside the vehicle and popped back up through the hatch with a loaded RPG launcher. Everett nodded with a smile and continued to shoot at jihadis as he had opportunity.

Suddenly, a wave of MOC fighters came running from behind their various positions of cover, shooting AK-47s, RPGs, and various other pistols and rifles. The barrage of lead and munitions pounded the side of the Typhoon as Everett sprayed bullets into the charge, Tink! Ting, tink, TINK, TING! A second bullet hit Everett's right shoulder but he continued to fire until his magazine ran empty. He then pulled his tactical sling off of his injured shoulder with his left hand and pulled out the remaining fragmentation grenades. He pulled the pins with his teeth and pitched them to the oncoming crowd of jihadis with his left hand. One after the other, the frag grenades detonated taking out significant swaths of the mob, but they kept coming en masse.

Ali cried out, "Everett! Get in the truck. Micha and Josiah are dead!"

Everett was glad to hear Ali's voice but sorry for the news it conveyed. With the hail of bullets and shrapnel, he was surprised any of them was still alive. Everett had no intention of giving up the fight, but he was unable to change magazines with one hand, and he was out of grenades. When he felt Ali pulling him from below, he let himself be taken into the truck.

Courtney slammed the hatch door behind him, then turned her attention to his wounds. "You're hit!"

"Don't worry about me right now. We have to come up with a solution. Sooner or later, one of those RPGs will take out the front windshield. When that happens, they'll come pouring through. Ali, reload my HK for me."

Disregarding his command, Courtney already had two pouches of QuikClot opened and was unpackaging an Israeli Battle Dressing.

Ali reloaded Everett's HK as well as his own rifle while Courtney applied the hemostatic pouches to each of Everett's shoulder wounds, then secured them to the injuries with the sterile bandage.

"Thank you, but I need you to get your rifle and prepare to fight when they breach the vehicle." He looked at his beautiful wife compassionately, wishing she didn't have to be here for what was about to happen.

She fought back a tear and nodded. "Okay." She bit her lower lip and grabbed her AR-15.

"The windshield is their only way in." Everett could hear the jihadis beating on the roof of the Typhoon while other continued to shoot and beat on the windshield.

"It has been such an honor to know you both. I look forward to many good years in the kingdom of heaven with you." Ali forced a smile.

Everett returned the artificial expression. "Same here, Ali."

Courtney also seemed to resign herself to the inevitable fate. "I love you both." She choked. "Especially you, Everett."

Explosions and gunfire rang out from all around. BOOM! A grenade from under the Typhoon rocked the vehicle violently. BOOM! Another grenade hit the center of the windshield, sending debris, smoke, and shrapnel into the cab of the truck.

Everett raised his rifle, ready to make his final defense. He watched for the army of jihadis to come rushing through the breach to finish them off. He stood in front of Courtney in case the last assault would come in the form of another RPG or fragmentation grenade.

But none of those things happened. The bullets pounding the side of the Typhoon slowed. The pounding on the roof of the truck ceased. Nothing and no one came through the pierced windshield, yet Everett continued to wait.

"The fighting. It is moving away from us," Ali said softly.

Everett listened to confirm what Ali told him. He signaled with his left hand for Courtney to stay seated in the rear of the vehicle. He picked up his

HK and slowly worked his way to the front. He looked through the missing section of windshield to see multiple civilian vehicles racing past them. Armed troops wearing Israeli uniforms ran by on foot, advancing in the direction the jihadis had been only minutes earlier. "The IDF soldiers have MOC on the run!" Everett shouted with glee.

Ali laughed and hurried to Everett's location, giving him a gentle hug.

Courtney also jogged to the front of the truck. She kissed him on the mouth, then said, "Let's get that arm dressed."

He grinned from ear to ear. "Okay." Everett looked her in the eye, glad to be alive, and thankful that God had spared her as well. He held out his forearm for her to clean while she rifled through the contents of the first-aid kit.

CHAPTER 17

It is of the Lord's mercies that we are not consumed, because his compassions fail not. They are new every morning: great is thy faithfulness.

Lamentations 3:22-23

Sitting on the bumper of the Typhoon near the entrance to the underground city in Kayseri, Everett looked at his watch. "Midnight."

"That's the last of the convoy. All the children of Israel have arrived." Rabbi Hertzog carefully maneuvered his crutches and leaned on the bumper next to Everett.

"We still have to get them moved to the other cities." Everett adjusted the sling around his neck, which held his right arm.

"Let's get some rest. The people can sleep in their vehicles or on a blanket on the ground for one night. Everyone is tired. Tomorrow is a new day, and we will all feel much better after a few hours of sleep."

The physician who had been attending to Everett and the rabbi's injuries came by. "Mr. Carroll, I need to give you another shot of antibiotics."

"You gave me the pills," Everett replied.

"I know, but you've sustained major tissue damage in multiple locations. On top of everything else, your wounds were open for an extended period of time in battlefield conditions. An infection would seriously hamper your ability to heal. It is imperative that we do all we can to keep one from setting in."

Everett pulled the collar of his shirt down to expose his bare shoulder and turned away from the needle. He winced for a moment while the doctor gave him the injection. Once it was over, he said, "Thank you for looking after us."

"I'm the one who should be thanking you, Mr. Carroll." The man replaced the cap on the syringe. "Are you both certain that I can't give you something for the pain?"

"The nurse gave me some ibuprofen." Everett pulled his shirt back over his shoulder.

"Considering what you've been through, I think your injuries warrant something a little stronger." The physician stuck his hands in the pockets of his white lab coat.

"Some of these other guys need it a lot more than

I do. Besides, I have to keep my wits about me. This mission isn't over until we have everyone settled in. Tomorrow is going to be another long day."

The doctor smiled at Everett. "Exactly, and you'll need some rest."

"I won't have any trouble sleeping." Everett nodded confidently.

"And you, Rabbi? Your leg is in pretty bad shape."

"No, thank you." Hertzog held up a hand. "Likewise, the nurse gave me some ibuprofen."

"Suit yourselves. But both of you, get some rest." The man waved as he walked away. "Doctor's orders."

"Thanks." Everett held up his left hand to bid the man goodnight.

Courtney and Ali arrived carrying hot food prepared by some of the non-combatants. Courtney asked, "What did the doctor say?"

"I needed another shot of antibiotics," Everett replied.

She said, "If you're going to be in this situation anyways, I suppose it's nice to be in it with a race of people who are disproportionately high regarding their involvement in the medical field."

Hertzog lifted his index finger. "This is true."

"Both of you, come on inside the truck and sit down to eat. Ali and I brought food for all of us."

"Thank you. After that, I'll be ready for a good long sleep." Everett pushed off the bumper with his left hand, then offered it to the rabbi, helping him to get his weight back onto his crutches.

The first light of the sun beamed through the broken windshield of the Typhoon Sunday morning, rousing Everett from his slumber. He'd slept on the floor with only a camping mat and a sleeping bag for padding. He'd been forced to sleep solely on his left side because of his gunshot wounds. Between the injuries, the stagnate sleeping position, and the stress of battle from the day before, his body was stiff and sore all over. The pain served as an adrenaline booster in the stead of his usual morning tea. He sat up and leaned forward, stretching to reach his toes with his good hand.

Courtney rolled over beside him. "Good morning. How did you sleep?"

"Like a rock on a rock."

"That's a fairly accurate description of my night. I was out, but I wasn't exactly comfortable."

He kissed her forehead. "Maybe our accommodations will be a little better tonight."

"Have you decided which city we'll settle in?" She stretched her neck as if she were trying to work out a crick.

"Kaymakli. It's one of the smallest, but it's also connected by a tunnel to Derinkuyu, which is one of the largest. With only 2,500 other people, we won't feel so claustrophobic, but we'll have options in case we're overrun and have to escape to Derinkuyu."

"Overrun? I thought we were done fighting. Who would attack the underground cities?"

Everett shrugged, forgetting about the gaping hole in his shoulder until he'd already made the gesture. He gritted his teeth and closed his eyes until the pain from the ill-thought-out movement passed. He took a deep breath. "I don't know who might attack it. But this is the Apocalypse, and trouble is never far away."

Courtney pulled her boots on her feet. "Do you need help getting dressed?"

"No, I'll be fine." Everett soon regretted his answer as he tried to slip his own boots on.

Courtney didn't wait for him to admit he required assistance. She gracefully loosened the laces, shoved a boot on each of his feet and tied them tight.

"Good morning, Everett and Courtney!" Ali was entirely too chipper for such a short night's sleep. Both of his eyes were black from the impact of his face into the door of the hatch during the prior day's battle. His nose was swollen which added to the drastic contrast between his beat-up appearance and his upbeat smile.

"Good morning, Ali. You sure are in a good mood." Courtney seemed to have contracted the infectious grin, although her expression wasn't quite as vibrant as Ali's.

"This is the day that the Lord has made! I will rejoice and be glad in it!" Ali laced up his boots and strapped on his pistol belt.

Everett also caught the bug. Soon he had an expression of gratitude and the corners of his mouth turned up. Yes, he'd had a rough day, but much less so than many of the other soldiers who'd either died in the battle or sustained incapacitating injuries.

Members of the Knesset assigned living quarters

to the people in the convoy based on the capacity of the individual underground cities and the amount of fuel remaining in the tanks of a given traveler's vehicle.

Everett was given the task of assigning security teams to the cities. He regretted having the task, not because he found the work to be arduous, but because he felt it should have been Tobias or Gideon who had the honor. But they were no longer among the living, so he discharged his duty with a level of integrity and humanity that he felt his fallen brothers-in-arms and brothers-in-Christ would have approved of.

Everett went out of his way to make sure troops were assigned to secure cities where their families were going. He studied the numbers and attempted to keep an even allocation of troops which was commensurate with the populations.

Once that task was complete, Everett, Courtney, Ali, and Rabbi Hertzog began their grand tour of all the underground cities. They traveled from city to city, locating the water supply, and turning the blood to water. In most cases, the rabbi stayed in the vehicle. Traversing the many stairs carved into the soft rock to reach the lower levels of the cities where the wells were located was an undertaking which did not bode well for a person incumbered by crutches.

Everett looked at his watch as Ali cut the engine of the Typhoon outside the entrances to the Kaymakli underground city. "Midnight again."

"We're home. You can sleep in tomorrow

morning." Courtney grabbed her duffle bag and Moses' staff as she opened the side door of the vehicle.

"We still have to locate the well and change it before we can get settled in." Everett slung his duffle bag over his good shoulder.

"You look for well. Courtney can help rabbi downstairs and find good place for live. I will bring in food and gear from truck." Ali's glowing tone gave Everett the extra push he needed to finish the task at hand.

"Thank you, Ali. I think that's an excellent division of labor." Everett took the staff from Courtney as she helped the rabbi out of the MRAP.

Everett and Ali followed Courtney and the rabbi down to the first level. They quickly located quarters in close proximity to each other. Everett's group would stay on the first level, not only because of the rabbi's leg, but because they were part of the security force that would defend Kaymakli in case of an attack.

"This looks like a good place." Courtney looked around at three individual spaces which were all adjoined by a single passageway.

It looked like the inside of a beehive or a giant colony of ants to Everett. "Fine with me."

"I think it is wonderful." Ali placed the duffel bags he'd brought in from the truck near one of the doorways. "I will get another load from Typhoon."

"I'll go find the well and meet you all back here," Everett said.

"We'll be waiting." Courtney helped the rabbi to take a seat on a bench that had been carved into the wall.

Everett carried a hand-drawn schematic, which had been copied from a map posted near the entrance to the underground city. He worked his way from the first level to the eighth, following tunnels and narrow stairwells, which were crowded with other Jews from the convoy who would be making Kaymakli their home for the next several weeks.

Everett considered all the various places he'd called home since he was a child. But ever since his parents' divorce, nothing had ever felt like a real home to him. Sure, he and Courtney had made a home in the little cottage by the river back in Batumi. Likewise, they'd enjoyed their time in John Jones' cabin back in the mountains of Virginia. They'd even made the best of a bad situation while living in the cave with Kevin and Sarah, Elijah, Sox and Danger, even Elijah's two goats, Samson and Delilah. But none of those places, and certainly not this one, really felt like a permanent home.

However, he knew the real thing, a permanent dwelling, his final home was just around the corner. He took a deep breath as he wondered what his last abode would look like. What would it smell like? Would it have the same types of food as Earth? And what about furnishings? Obviously, they wouldn't need to sleep, so would there be beds or couches? He'd read so many times about the Wedding Feast of the Lamb. Evidently there would be tables and chairs. But what would they eat from? Would the plates and serving instruments be similar to those of the mortal realm?

As Everett descended to the lowest level where the well was located, he wondered what heaven would be like. He felt like a child who'd never been to Disneyland, one who'd never even seen a picture of the place but had heard stories about its magnificence, its vivacity, and its grandeur.

He finally arrived at the well and using a length of paracord, lowered Moses' staff down in. He confirmed that the blood had been turned to water and reeled the staff back in. Having finished his formidable list of duties for the day, Everett felt worn and weary. He climbed back up to the first level where Courtney had already spread out his sleeping bag in a cozy corner next to hers. After a few minutes of bedtime chitchat and some assistance from his wife removing his boots, Everett closed his eyes knowing there'd be no morning sun in the subterranean dwelling to awaken him tomorrow. Soon, he lost consciousness and slept harder than he had in years.

The days passed and the inhabitants of Kaymakli began to develop a routine. Most everyone was pretty good about pitching in and doing their fair share. Life in the underground city necessitated a higher level of communal living than what they'd all grown accustomed to back in Batumi, Georgia. Some prepared meals, some cleaned; Everett, Ali, and Courtney took regular shifts in the security rotation.

Rabbi Hertzog moved to the second tier of the city as the church was situated on that level. He offered a daily devotional teaching in the chapel area. Every service was packed to capacity.

On the Thursday evening following the Jews' exodus from Batumi, Everett made his way to the surface. It had become a ritual where he, like a groundhog coming up from beneath the earth to check for his shadow, would emerge nightly to check the status of the Aurora Borealis. The night sky on the evening prior presented only faint wisps of green light, like a phantom fading back to the ghostly realm from which it had originated. Everett walked out into the crisp night air. He breathed in the freshness after having spent most of the day within the walls of the subsurface labyrinth. He looked up at the clear sky above. The stars shimmered brightly against the utter blackness of space. "Nothing. Not even a trace of the lights."

Quickly, he descended back to his quarters to find Courtney and Ali. The two were sitting on the floor of Everett's room playing a hand of cards.

"The aurora has stopped!" he announced.

Ali turned as if he were having trouble thinking about anything other than his hand and his perfect strategy for defeating Courtney in this present contest, which required more skill than luck. "That's . . . good."

"It's great, Ali!" It means we can pull an antenna to the surface; maybe try to pick up some Ham signals or a radio broadcast. It means we can hook up the small solar generator and use our walkie-talkies to coordinate our security teams. We might even be able to stay in contact with the other underground cities."

Courtney caught the excitement, dropping her cards. "Wow. I'd almost forgotten that an entire world exists outside. I guess I adjusted to being cut off from everything better than I thought I would. Can we try the radio now?"

Everett located the crate with the electronics. "Yeah, let's just take it to the surface for now. We'll run a wire for an antenna tomorrow morning, first thing."

Ali carefully placed his cards in his upper shirt pocket. "Courtney, you should pick up your cards and keep them with you. I do not want you to say that I win because I cheated."

"There's no risk of that." Courtney followed Everett up the carved-out staircase.

Ali trailed close behind them. "Of me cheating?"

"No," she quipped. "Of you winning."

"Oh no, I must inform you that I am now holding the hand that is to turn the direction of this game!" Ali shook his handful of cards in protest as he scurried along behind her.

Once they arrived topside, Everett briskly extended the telescoping antenna of the portable radio. He took a seat on the grass, turned the receiver on and searched through the AM and FM channels.

Courtney and Ali ceased their bickering over the game and listened closely as Everett moved the dial across various sounds and degrees of static. Finally, he stumbled across a channel.

"This is the Global Republic Broadcasting Network."

CHAPTER 18

And the sixth angel poured out his vial upon the great river Euphrates; and the water thereof was dried up, that the way of the kings of the east might be prepared. And I saw three unclean spirits like frogs come out of the mouth of the dragon, and out of the mouth of the beast, and out of the mouth of the false prophet. For they are the spirits of devils, working miracles, which go forth unto the kings of the earth and of the whole world, to gather them to the battle of that great day of God Almighty. Behold, I come as a thief. Blessed is he that watcheth, and keepeth his garments, lest he walk naked, and they see his shame. And he gathered them together into a place called in the Hebrew tongue Armageddon.

Revelation 16:12-16

For Everett's group, the Friday evening meal consisted of MREs, some canned vegetable soup, which Courtney had made while in Batumi, and dehydrated apples. Like everything they'd eaten since their arrival in Kaymakli, the soup was served cold. The inhabitants of the underground city had no sustainable fuel source, so they made the best of what was available.

Rabbi Hertzog joined them for dinner in Everett's living quarters. Courtney and Ali had helped him up the stairs so he could listen along to the radio broadcast with them while they ate. It proved to be easier to bring the rabbi up a flight of stairs than to run the radio antenna another flight lower.

The rabbi blessed the food, then they began eating.

Having waited for the rabbi to pray, Everett powered on the receiver and adjusted the volume.

"Tonight will begin the Sixth Seal?" Ali tore open his MRE.

"We shall see." Everett checked his watch. "The sun set about half an hour ago."

"Shabbat has begun." Hertzog took a hand full of dried apples, put them on a paper towel, then passed the jar to Everett.

Everett placed the jar in the center of the circle formed by the four of them sitting on the floor with their legs crossed. He was more interested in the radio than his food at the moment.

The first voice was an Indian woman. It was a repeat broadcast of what they'd heard the night before. "The entire power grid has been restored to Jerusalem and the Ministry of Energy is working tirelessly to get electric service turned back on in major metropolitan cities. Paris, London, Istanbul, Madrid, and Rome are the current priorities and are slated to have power for emergency services and essential infrastructure by the end of the month.

"The Ministry of Health is advising those who were relying on electrical power to distill water from blood to try using, propane, wood fires, or any available fuel while you wait for service to be reinstated. Those who have no other alternative fuel sources can construct a solar still from glass, aluminum foil, or any materials available.

"The Ministry of Health also recommends setting up rain catchment systems to collect rain water from roofs in case the rains should return.

"More than eighty percent of the Holy Luzian Empire has been in drought conditions and has seen no rain whatsoever in the past six months. GRBN has recorded footage of the Two Troublers of Jerusalem claiming that they are responsible for the prolonged period with zero precipitation.

"In a statement earlier this week, Pope Peter condemned the two curious old men as being workers of evil and masters of a dark form of witchcraft practiced by an archaic radical sect of Christianity. The Pope assured subjects of the Holy Luzian Empire that the two men calling themselves Moses and Elijah have no connection to his brand of Christianity nor should their dark magic be confused with Wiccan, Druidic, Satanic, or other Pagan arts, which are approved by the Ministry of Religion.

"His Majesty himself has pledged to find a permanent solution to the Two Troublers by week's end. Hopefully, when the two old men are finally disposed of, the rains will return and bring much-needed relief to those who are in perilous and desperate need of water. The loss of life due to dehydration has been growing exponentially ever since the phenomenon of water turning to blood occurred.

"In other water-related news, a tremendous sinkhole has mysteriously appeared below the dam on the southeastern side of Lake Assad in Syria. All of the blood flowing past the dam which would normally feed into the Euphrates is falling into the sinkhole. Global Republic geologists are speculating that recent events like the asteroid strikes and earthquakes have loosened barrier rocks which were separating the river from a humongous underground cavern system.

"GR geologists are unsure how deep the cavern system could be but hope that it will drain off much of the blood so that when the rains return, the river will flow unpolluted more quickly than if the rains had to wash away the blood little by little."

Everett picked at his food as he listened. Even though he'd heard it all the night before, he paid close attention for anything he might have missed.

A different GRBN reporter, a man with a British accent, began a new broadcast. "This is Archibald Cromwell for the Global Republic Broadcasting Network, and this is a breaking news alert. His High and Most Prepotent Majesty Angelo Luz has issued an emergency call to arms. The Holy Luzian Empire's Ministry of Defense is in need of all able-bodied citizens to report to the nearest Peacekeeping station to register for service. Stations will be equipped to begin accepting volunteers at six o'clock tomorrow morning, local time.

"In case you're just tuning in and are not yet aware of this urgent need, I will review this morning's developments. As you know, the empire had to take all terrestrial and celestial surveillance systems off-line to preserve the hardware while the Earth passed through the electromagnetic waves of the unprecedented Coronal Mass Ejection from last week's colossal solar flare.

"The Chinese-Russian Alliance used the blackout as an opportunity to move their military forces across Global Republic borders. Surveillance drones launched last night and satellite images transmitted this morning show a large build-up of Alliance troops, vehicles, and equipment positioned in Eastern Syria, Western Iraq, and in Turkey along the northern border of Syria.

"I'm glad we didn't run into all of that on our

way here!" Courtney paused from eating with her eyes wide open.

Ali shook his head. "Probably they moved forces down through Azerbaijan. Maybe even sending down cargo ship with many troop and equipments on Black Sea. This is much easier than go through Georgia. Too many mountain."

Everett snapped his fingers. "I wouldn't be surprised if we find out that the Martyrs of the Caliphate have formed some type of coalition with the Chinese-Russian Alliance."

Rabbi Hertzog raised his eyebrows. "That would explain why the jihadis in Sivas seemed to be in such a high state of military readiness."

Everett looked at the rabbi. "Yep. We probably threw a wrench in their plan."

"So this is it." Courtney stared at the radio as if her mind were wandering off to another place. "Armageddon."

Everett nodded slowly. "This is it. This is the war to end all wars."

"I hope we can ride it out here. I have no desire to have a front row seat for this one." Rabbi Hertzog seemed apprehensive and didn't eat much more after the announcement.

Everett turned the radio up slightly to hear the rest of the broadcast.

The reporter continued, "Thousands of tanks, armored personnel carriers, artillery guns, and logistical support vehicles continue to stream down from Russia and across the deserts of Iran in what can be termed as nothing other than a full military invasion. The saber-rattling and rhetoric that has continued between the Global Republic and the Chinese-Russian Alliance over the past seven years seems to have finally come to a head. His Majesty has given every opportunity for the two hold-out nations to enter the fold and join the rest of the globe in the Aquarian age of prosperity and peace. He has sent delegation after delegation, all of whom have been rejected by a headstrong people who seem to have chosen all-out war over dialogue and reason."

"Did I miss something? Who has had peace and prosperity in the last seven years?" Courtney crossed her arms tightly.

"I'm sure Angelo Luz and Pope Peter have fared rather well over the past few months." Rabbi Hertzog chuckled.

The reporter proceeded with his communication, "It is important to note that the open call for military enlistment is primarily for support roles rather than active combat positions. Analysts expect most of the active fighting by the Holy Luzian Empire to be done by advanced robotics such as drones and remote attack vehicles or hybrid soldiers which have been developed in anticipation that this conflict with the Alliance would ultimately culminate in a hot war.

The hybrid soldiers or supersoldiers have been bred from test tubes using human genetic components along with enhanced features from other species both from this planet and from the

Watchers. Of course, cross-species compatibility was achieved through the CRISPR Cas9 gene-editing process.

Since part of the soldiers' biological make-up comes from the Watchers, it is only fitting that His Majesty should invite three of the Watchers to act as generals in the Holy Luzian Empire's Army. The three who were chosen to come assist our race in defending against this horrendous attack are all personal friends of His Majesty Angelo Luz's father. Their names are Semyaza, Azazel, and Amezarak."

"Hmm." The rabbi's brows knitted tightly together.

"You know these guys?" Courtney asked.

"From the Book of Enoch. Azazel was the Watcher who taught men to make swords. Amezarak taught the art of witchcraft and spells. Semyaza is their leader." A deep tone of concern filled the rabbi's voice.

The British reporter's monologue persisted. "Pope Peter will make a televised introduction of the three Watchers tomorrow night, but it is important that viewers not allow themselves to be troubled by their appearance. Remember that they are not of this world and consider that our kind may look just as peculiar to them as they do to us. Like us, they have two eyes, two arms, two legs, though they are significantly larger in stature. Perhaps the most obvious difference will be in their eyes, greenish skin tone, hairlessness, and forked tongues.

A very rudimentary description of their species has been reptilian, but that terminology ignores their far-superior intellect."

"Three unclean spirits like frogs." Ali set his food aside to flip to the back of his Bible. "For they are spirits of demons, performing signs, which go out to the kings of the earth and of the whole world, to gather them to the battle of that great day of God Almighty." He looked up from the book. "Really, it is so amazing! What an honor it is to be living in these final hours."

Everett twisted his mouth to one side. "I'm glad you're enjoying the ride. If I had to do it over, I'd have definitely caught the first bus out. I would be content to watch the whole thing from the balcony."

"Ditto," Courtney said in a snarky tone. "Front-row seats are highly over-rated."

"But we must get a television. We have to see these creatures, these demons that Luz intends to pass off as saviors." The rabbi held up his hands excitedly as he spoke.

"We did not bring television," Ali replied. "We had only room for essential."

"All the buildings in town looked abandoned. I'm sure we'd have no problem salvaging a television. The people probably left in search of food or water. I doubt TVs were high enough on the priority list for most folks to take with them." Everett reclined against the wall behind him.

"There's a café across the street from the entrance to the underground city. I'm sure they had a TV for soccer games," Courtney added.

"Yes, all café in Turkey have TV for football."
Ali raised one finger in the air. "And have satellite dish."

"Think you'll be able to hack the signal?"
Everett asked.

"I can do it." Ali nodded.

The four friends finished their meal, then passed along the information from the report to the other people living on the first level with them. Rabbi Hertzog would disseminate an abbreviated summary of the broadcast at the beginning of service on the following day. The Saturday assembly would certainly have the highest turnout of the week.

Everett, Courtney, and Ali spent the following days coordinating with the security teams from the other underground cities. Everett specified which teams would send assistance in the instance that any given city was attacked. All of the cities utilized by the Jews sat in a fifty-mile radius, so none were onerously remote, yet Everett wanted to keep the plan as efficient as possible. The fifty-mile distance from the two farthest cities meant that the hand-held walkies used by the security teams would never reach from end to end, so Everett also established a communications relay protocol that would allow messages to be passed along, in grapevine fashion, from city to city.

Ali set up Tobias' Ham radio in the shot-up Typhoon with the solar array installed on the roof of the vehicle for power. Additionally, he ran a series of extension cords down into their subterranean dwelling from the solar array which served to power the television. The satellite dish was also attached to the war-torn MRAP, giving it the appearance of a post-apocalyptic recreational vehicle.

Once the pressing chores were finished, the team kept themselves busy with menial tasks. Everett, in particular, wanted to keep his mind occupied. Otherwise, the intensity of waiting for the final grain of sand in the hourglass of time to drop would drive him mad.

CHAPTER 19

When they finish their testimony, the beast
that ascends out of the bottomless pit will
make war against them, overcome them, and
kill them. And their dead bodies will lie in
the street of the great city which spiritually
is called Sodom and Egypt, where also our
Lord was crucified. Then those from the
peoples, tribes, tongues, and nations will see
their dead bodies three-and-a-half days, and
not allow their dead bodies to be put into
graves. And those who dwell on the earth
will rejoice over them, make merry, and
send gifts to one another, because these two
prophets tormented those who dwell on the
earth.

Revelation 11:7-10

Everett's heart broke when he turned on the television. "Oh no."

They'd just returned from surface patrol, making sure no one snooped around the entrance to their below-ground dwelling. Courtney leaned her rifle against the wall of their living quarters. "What is it?"

"Luz. He's killed Moses and Elijah. GRBN is showing the footage. He shot them himself."

Courtney turned her attention to the television. She gasped and covered her mouth as tears welled up in her eyes.

Ali slipped off his boots and joined the two of them. He shook his head as the image of Angelo Luz personally firing a fully-automatic M-4 at the two prophets of God played over and over. "You know that this is not permanent. Like our Lord, they will rise again in three days."

Everett sighed. "I know Ali. We'll all rise again, but I'm so tired of watching the people I love die. Over and over, one by one, they keep getting killed. And I'm left here to suffer through."

"With your beautiful wife." Ali had a gentle way of rebuking Everett without it sounding like a reprimand.

Everett turned to her and put his arm around Courtney. He knew Ali was right, and he was being entirely ungrateful.

Everett pulled her close and kissed her on the

head. "With my beautiful wife . . ." He looked back to Ali. ". . . and my wise companion."

Ali smiled with his lips pressed tightly together. "I know Elijah was like father for you. Perhaps I was little insensitive. I am sure it is difficult thing for you to watch. I am sorry if I mis-speaked."

Everett put his other arm around Ali and pulled him close for a group hug. He chuckled. "You didn't mis-speaked."

Having mastered the art of ascending and descending stairs on crutches, the rabbi hobbled into the room. His expression became sorrowful as he watched the small television perched on the nook which was carved into the soft stone wall. "This is a terrible thing." He shook his head.

The camera cut from the video loop of Elijah and Moses being gunned down to GRBN reporter Harrison Yates. "A spontaneous celebration has broken out on the Temple Mount. People are showing up with bottles of champagne, bags of pot, and a variety of other substances to rejoice over the deaths of the Two Troublers. I hate to take joy in the death of another human being, but I can't help but think that the world is a far better place without the Two Troublers menacing the planet, wouldn't you agree, Heather?"

The camera panned out to show Heather Smith sitting at the news desk beside Yates. "I concur completely, Harrison. In fact, if we can get some footage of the revelers congregating on the Temple Mount, you'll see clouds forming over Jerusalem as we speak. GRBN Chief Meteorologist Matt

Anderson is saying the chance of rain in Jerusalem this evening is near 100 percent."

"And in this particular instance, Heather, I can't imagine that this party will be canceled for inclement weather."

Smith laughed. "Well, I guess a festival in the rain might be fun, but I do hope if any of our listeners are planning to join in the merrymaking on the Temple Mount, please be aware of the conditions. If you see lightning or hear thunder, move the festivities indoors."

"Great advice, Heather. While we're on the topic of safety, I want to remind everyone that sharing drugs is cool, but sharing needles isn't."

Courtney shook her head in disgust. "I guess the sores are gone. I can't see a trace of scaring on his forehead or her lips. In fact, she looks better than ever."

Everett walked close to the screen and pointed at Smith's hairline. "Look closely at the individual hairs on her head. These are CGI. They've got Smith and Yates sitting in a studio up against a green screen with CGI sensors attached to their faces. The data is being patched through to a computer which is generating the image we're seeing."

"Oddly enough, the CGI Heather Smith doesn't look that much more fake than the real one." Courtney stood with her arms crossed.

Heather Smith's expression changed suddenly. "Harrison, we've got more breaking news. The

Holy Luzian Empire has just struck Moscow, Saint Petersburg, Shanghai, and Beijing with nuclear missiles. This was a retaliatory strike against the Alliance, which has been given every opportunity to withdraw their forces from Global Republic territory.

"As you know, the new Minister of Defense, General Semyaza, who has graced our planet with his presence, directed the Global Republican Army in a full-scale defensive assault against the Alliance forces in Syria, Iraq, and Turkey. For three days now, the fighting has been ongoing and the Alliance forces have actually pushed past the Global Republican Army's lines.

"I know our dear Majesty's heart, and I'm sure he is absolutely devastated at having to destroy the millions of people living in those cities, but what else can he do? His responsibility is to his own subjects."

Yates nodded pensively. "You're absolutely right, Heather. The Chinese-Russian Alliance has proven time and time again that they are unwilling to be reasoned with. I put all of my faith in His High and Most Prepotent Majesty Angelo Luz, and the Watcher, General Semyaza. I trust them without reservation. If they feel a nuclear strike was the correct response, then I believe we had no better option."

"I agree, Harrison. And I want to remind the citizens of Jerusalem that this city has the most advanced anti-missile systems on Earth. The Iron Dome 3.0 is the third-generation defense system, which is leaps and bounds ahead of the original Iron

Dome installed by the IDF decades ago."

Yates nodded. "We also have to remember one of the quantum computers that make up Dragon is on the Global Republic Space Station. That station is armed with anti-missile batteries as well. We're talking about the most advanced artificial intelligence systems equipped with the latest in military technology. It's literally like we have a god watching over us, protecting us from all harm."

Smith puckered her brow, but the CGI reduced the depth of the lines so much that the intonation of the expression was nearly lost. "It's not *like* we have a god watching over us, Harrison. We do have a god looking out from above. Dragon is the essence of His Majesty. His spirit, his very soul abides in Dragon every bit as much as it lives in his body."

Yates shook his head. "You are so spiritual. It absolutely amazes me. I tend to get so caught up in the nuts and bolts, but you seem to catch the ethereal essence of things."

Heather acted as if she'd just been insulted rather than complimented. "Why? Because I'm a woman?"

Harrison shook his head. "No, no, Heather. I don't look at people based on their biological equipment. I'm not some hayseed who believes gender is defined by anatomy. You've known me long enough to know better. I'm saying you're more spiritual because you're Heather Smith. It would be the same if you were Heath Smith or if you assumed a non-binary identity."

Courtney rolled her eyes. "Nuclear war just broke out and I have to listen to Harrison Yates apologize for making a remark that implied this computer-animated version of Heather Smith is female. I'm glad this planet doesn't have much longer. I can't imagine how much worse it would get." She picked up the remote to turn off the television.

"Wait!" Everett held up his hand to stop her. "Just try to ignore your gag reflexes for a few more minutes. I want to see if they'll tell us anything else."

Yates looked somber as he addressed the audience. "We are getting news that Russia and China have launched a significant percentage of their ICBM arsenal. While we have full confidence in Dragon's ability to neutralize those nuclear weapons, unfortunately, the Alliance has also deployed an additional attack. Chinese-Russian Alliance nuclear submarines have launched submarine-launched ballistic missiles or SLBMs. The problem with these weapons is that they can be fired from the oceans in much closer proximity to their targets. This reduces the available response time for defense systems to destroy enemy missiles."

Heather Smith shook her computer-generated head. "Word is coming in now. One of the missiles fired from a submarine in the Atlantic has just detonated in Paris. I'm afraid the City of Lights is no more."

"Another missile, possibly from the same

submarine, has just hit London," Yates added.

Everett tapped Ali on the shoulder. "Come on! We have to get the Ham radio out of the Typhoon, seal off the entrance and the ventilation shafts. Ankara is less than 200 miles from here, and it will definitely be a target for the Alliance. If a high-yield nuke goes off in Ankara, we could get the fallout.

"Courtney, go around and let everyone else on the security team know what's going on. Send them to the surface to help us get the city sealed off."

She looked less concerned than Everett. "What difference will a little fallout make? We won't be around long enough to contract cancer or have mutations."

Everett hurried toward the stairs. "Maybe not, but we will be around long enough to get radiation poisoning. And of all the ways there is to go, it's one of the worst."

Everett raced to the surface with Ali on his heels. Before shutting down the Ham radio, Everett used it to put out a call to the other underground cities in the area. He informed them of what was happening and the precautions Kaymakli would be taking, urging them to take similar precautions. The other operators on the relay network thanked Everett for the heads-up and assured him that they would pass along the information to the cities which were out of range for Everett's radio.

Afterward, Ali and Everett disconnected the Ham radio and carried the components down into the city. Once they were stowed, Everett said, "Next we need to set up the solar panel near the entrance and get the rest of the pieces underground."

"It is possible that nuclear blast could create EMP and destroy solar array if we leave panels outside?" Ali followed Everett back to the surface.

"The nearest target is Ankara. The altitude at which a nuke is detonated to destroy a city is too low to generate an EMP this far away. The Alliance would have to be specifically targeting for an EMP to affect us here. The nuke would have to be a hundred miles overhead. A standard nuke detonation is less than a mile high usually." Everett crawled on top of the Typhoon and began removing the solar panels.

"But it is possible?" Ali removed the charging cables from the panels and reeled them up.

"Possible but not likely. Jerusalem is the only city in the entire Holy Luzian Empire that has a functioning electrical grid. An EMP on any other city would be shooting a dead horse at this stage of the game." Everett relocated the panels to the enclosure just above the entrance.

The two of them positioned the charge controller, the batteries, and the inverter several feet inside the entrance to the city since they did not have enough cable to run the entire setup down to the first level.

"What will we use to block off the entrance and the ventilation shafts?" Ali asked.

Everett tested the inverter to make sure the connections were good. "Sandbags would be best, but we'll use whatever we can find. At this distance, radiated particles getting into our air supply is the biggest threat. We've got enough food and water.

We can literally stay in our bunker until Jesus comes back."

"What about air? How will we breathe?" Ali walked behind Everett.

"There's a lot of air down in the city."

"Enough for 3,000 people for two months?"

Everett sighed. "Maybe we can figure out some type of filtration device."

"Perhaps we can build frame and put on it blanket to cover openings."

Everett thought about Ali's suggestion. "Yeah, that might help just enough to keep us from getting radiation poisoning. Like Courtney said, we don't have to worry about long-term effects."

"And we can put water on blanket. Perhaps that will stop more of the water-soluble ash particles from passing through the blanket."

"Great idea, Ali." Everett turned to see the dozen or so troops Courtney had sent up to help. He explained the plan and asked them to scavenge wood, metal, comforters, blankets, and sheets to assist in constructing some primitive air filters. Everyone went to work in teams of two, searching for materials to be used in the project.

The sun had set long before Everett and the others completed their mission of building the rudimentary filtration devices. Once the job was finished, Everett thanked the other members of the security team and retired to his quarters.

He sat down on his sleeping bag and kicked off his boots.

Ali took a seat near the doorway. "Where is

Rabbi Hertzog?"

Courtney had continued to monitor the television broadcast since the inverter had been reconnected to the battery bank. "He couldn't stand to watch anymore. He went to bed."

Everett reclined on his sleeping bag and watched the TV. "What did we miss?"

"The Chinese-Russian Alliance nuked Brussels, Zurich, Milan, Munich, Vienna, and Cairo."

"What about Luz?"

"He took out every major city in China and Russia. Chongqing, Tianjin, Shenzhen, Novosibirsk, everything."

"High yield bombs?" Everett was tired, but he still felt compassion for all the lives lost on this fateful day.

"Yeah. 100 to 200 kilotons each. Everything has been reduced to ashes."

"That is big?" Ali looked to Everett for more clarification.

Everett nodded somberly. "The bomb dropped on Hiroshima was fifteen kilotons. We're talking ten times the destructive power."

"Oh." Ali lowered his gaze.

"You haven't heard anything about a strike against Ankara?" Everett asked.

"No." Courtney held her head in her hands as if the news was sucking the life from her veins. "General Semyaza hit Aleppo and Damascus with tactical nukes, but they were low-yield devices detonated only a few hundred feet from the surface. They won't give off enough radiation to give us a problem."

"Aleppo and Damascus?" Ali inquired.

Courtney nodded, then turned to Everett. "You were right about MOC joining forces with the Alliance. Marwan Bakr had suicide bombers positioned inside Jerusalem that attacked GR Peacekeeper bases all around the cities. They were coordinated with the nuclear attacks."

"So Luz hit their known strongholds." Everett could have never imagined that the final world war would be so complete in its destruction of the human race. Speaking on behalf of his father, the Father of Lies, Luz had promised peace and security while delivering destruction and death.

Courtney stood to get her canteen from the corner of the room. "Semyaza hit Bagdad and Mosul also."

"No nuclear bomb reach to Jerusalem?" Ali repositioned himself against the wall.

"Not yet. So far, the Iron Dome is working," she replied.

"Any news on the invasion?" Everett asked.

"They're not talking about it on GRBN which tells me the Alliance is advancing toward Jerusalem. If the empire was winning, Yates and Smith would be singing praises to Luz."

"You mean the republic," Ali corrected her.

"I mean empire. Most republics eventually devolve into empires—Rome, America; this one just happened to do it a little faster."

Everett added, "And as the republic devolves into an empire, its citizens devolve into subjects. Of course, with the new world order, the people were citizens in name only from the beginning."

"Yes. GRBN has been using all those terms for some time. Republic, empire, citizen, subject. They say like all words mean same thing," Ali observed.

"If you want to take down a civilization, you have to attack the language and the meaning of words. Once you've done that, no one can argue with you. Nothing they can say has any meaning because the words themselves have been deemed to be worthless." Everett considered the long, tiresome spiral the world had been on since he'd become aware of what was going on. He felt a sort of comfort that it would all be over soon.

Suddenly, the feed cut and the television lost its signal.

Everett sat up, anxious about what may have caused the outage.

"What happened?" Courtney asked.

"Could be anything." Ali looked less concerned than Everett and Courtney. "Could be raining. Could be satellite was hit. Could be station sending signal to satellite was bombed. Anything can interrupt signal at any point in system. Nuclear war is going on all over the world." Ali stood up. "I am surprise that we have signal as long as we did. I see you in the morning. Good night."

Everett waved at Ali as he left and tried to put it out of his mind.

Courtney looked perplexed as she picked up the AM/FM radio and scrolled through static finding no stations. "Do you think it could have been a nuke on Ankara? Maybe the shock wave knocked out the satellite signal."

Everett watched her futile attempt to get a signal.

"I suppose that's possible. But we don't have any way of finding out."

"Can you try the Ham radio?"

"No one would know anything this soon. Besides, the only people who speak English on the Ham radio around here are the people in the underground cities. Anyone else would be speaking Turkish. I'd need Ali to communicate with them. We'll see what we can find out in the morning."

"So what do we do now?"

"Now?" Everett thought for a moment. "Now, we trust in God." He pulled out his Bible, turned to the book of Psalms, and read aloud to his wife. Soon, the soothing words of God's Word had quieted their fretful spirits, and they both fell fast asleep.

CHAPTER 20

And after three days and an half the spirit of life from God entered into them, and they stood upon their feet; and great fear fell upon them which saw them. And they heard a great voice from heaven saying unto them, Come up hither. And they ascended up to heaven in a cloud; and their enemies beheld them. And the same hour was there a great earthquake, and the tenth part of the city fell, and in the earthquake were slain of men seven thousand: and the remnant were affrighted, and gave glory to the God of heaven. The second woe is past; and, behold, the third woe cometh quickly.

Revelation 11:11-14

Friday afternoon, Everett stood behind Ali as he listened to men speaking Turkish over the Ham radio. "Are they saying anything about Ankara? Do we know if it was nuked?"

Ali held up his hand signaling for Everett to be quiet so he could hear the rest of the transmission. Once the chatter ceased, Ali replied, "They don't say nothing about Ankara. Three days I listen—four or five hours a day. If something happen over there, I am sure the people will talk about it."

"Can you ask? Maybe one of the Hams have heard something. It would be good to know one way or the other." Everett was vexed by not knowing. No one in any of the underground cities had anything that could act as a Geiger counter so they were all in the dark about potentially harmful radiation levels.

"No, Everett!" Ali looked at him like he was crazy. "These are not Ham radio operator like you are accustomed to in America, or even like people who use radio back in Batumi. Probably all people we are hearing on radio are Martyrs of the Caliphate. Last thing you want to do is tell them we are nearby."

Everett felt stupid for not having considered such an issue. "Yeah, we don't want to do that. Is anyone talking about what is going on in Jerusalem?"

"Caliph Marwan is connecting with Alliance in Megiddo. Chinese-Russian Alliance forces are being held back from Israel by GR army on the eastern front, but Alliance have broken through on northern front. China and Russia push down through Lebanon and have taken control of Haifa and Nazareth. MOC is coming in from east, across Syrian border. Plan is to meet in Megiddo for final push toward Jerusalem. All around Megiddo is much open, flat farmland. Is good staging area for launch assault."

Everett replied, "It makes for a nice open battlefield also. I'm guessing General Semyaza will bring the battle up to Megiddo and save them the trip."

Ali smiled. "You are not guessing, Everett. You know. You have already read the ending."

Everett tussled Ali's hair. "You got me. I read the end of the book."

"I also read end of book. This is why I want to get television fixed today. It has been three days since Luz kill Elijah and Moses. I want to see what Smith and Yates will say when God raises them to life and calls them up in the clouds. I think perhaps little adjustment with satellite dish can bring back signal."

"I'd like to see it also, Ali, but we don't know what the radiation levels are. Even if Ankara wasn't hit, the polar and the subtropical jet streams could be pulling radiation from the explosions across Europe straight for us."

"Even if this is true, it will be too diluted to make radiation poison." Ali grinned showing his big white teeth. "I make deal for you. I will wear garbage bag on legs, head, arms, and body."

"You're going to make an NBC suit out of trash can liners?"

"And little bit of duct tape."

"No way." Everett shook his head.

"Come on, Everett. I will be outside like five minutes at most." Ali looked at him as if he were waiting for Everett to change his mind. "According to your calculation, we have less than two months before New Millennium begin."

Everett pressed his lips together but said nothing.

"Shabbat begin at sunset. Seventh Vial will be poured out upon earth. This is big one, Everett. If we can get even one piece of information from television, it could be difference between life and death for many people in the underground cities."

Everett looked at Ali out of the corner of his eye. "That's a good point, but it has nothing to do with you trying to convince me to let you go outside. You just want to see the reaction of Luz and all his followers when Elijah and Moses stand up in the streets of Jerusalem."

Ali nodded to cede the debate. "Can be both things."

Everett neither granted nor denied Ali's request. But he also said nothing as Ali gathered the trash bags and duct tape, then began fashioning his suit. First, he made a poncho out of one bag. Next, he punched leg holes out of another, which he pulled up around his waist and secured it to his body with a belt of duct tape.

Courtney walked into the area where they were. "What's this one doing? Dressing up like a raisin?"

Everett sighed. "He's going outside to adjust the satellite dish."

"And you're letting him?"

"I can't exactly stop him."

She stood with her hands on her hips. "You're the defacto administrator of Kaymakli. You *exactly* can stop him."

"He made a really good case for getting the television back on."

"Tell me it's not the entertainment value of watching Elijah and Moses come back to life. We'd all get a kick out seeing the GR's reaction to that one, but surely you both know it's not worth risking Ali's life." She lifted her hands momentarily and snapped them back on her hips as if to doubly emphasize her displeasure with Ali's scheme.

"It's not just that." Everett held up his hand.

"Not *just* that?"

Everett knew he should have taken more time to formulate his reply. "It's not that. Not that at all. The Seventh Vial will begin sometime after sunset. This is the quake that will level every mountain and destroy every island. Seventy-pound hailstones will be falling from the sky. This is heaven's grand finale in the fireworks show we've been watching over the past seven years. I guarantee it's going to be big. The smallest piece of information from the television could save the lives of thousands if we hear something and are able to take action on it."

"Please, Courtney," Ali said. "Everett already try many times to stop me. Do not be mad at your husband. I want to do this."

"Leave your irradiated raisin suit outside when you come back in." She huffed and walked away.

An hour later, Everett found Courtney on the

second level of the underground city in Rabbi Hertzog's living quarters. "We've got the television signal back if you two want to come watch the news."

"Yes, yes!" The rabbi had mastered his skill of scrambling up from his cot and onto his crutches.

Courtney likewise leaped up from her seated position but quickly tempered her enthusiasm. "If that's what everyone else is doing, I suppose I'll tag along."

Everett rolled his eyes without her seeing and led the way back upstairs. Ali was sitting against the wall watching TV when they arrived.

"Have they risen yet?" Hertzog let himself down to sit on a bucket and leaned his crutches against the wall.

"No mention of it yet." Ali did not turn from the screen.

Everett took a seat next to Courtney on her sleeping bag. He took her hand in an effort to quell the squabbling.

Heather Smith's computer-generated image issued an urgent update on the ongoing war between the Global Republic and the Chinese-Russian Alliance. "General Amezarak has successfully pushed Alliance forces back across the Jordanian and Saudi Arabian borders and is pursuing them into Iraq. At the same time, General Azazel is bringing GR supersoldiers, artillery weapons, armored vehicles, and supplies to northern Israel from Tel Aviv and Ashdod. A buildup of Alliance troops and supplies crossed over the Lebanese

225

border into northern Israel. They appear to have been using Megiddo as a staging area from which they planned to attack Jerusalem.

"The Alliance and MOC fighters tried to split their forces in order to attack on multiple fronts. Minister of Defense, General Semyaza, told GRBN earlier today that this was the fatal mistake he has been waiting for. He hopes to defeat the Alliance armies on both fronts by the first part of next week. He said in a radio interview this morning that both the Martyrs of the Caliphate and the Chinese-Russian Alliance have no remaining population centers able to provide provisions to the dwindling armies, and it is only a matter of time until they come crashing down under the pressure of their own lack of logistical support and much-needed supplies. Even so, he pledged not to let up his counter-attacks against the two entities who have spawned what has turned out to be the most destructive war in the history of the earth. In the course of one week, ninety percent of the world's cities, by population, has been reduced to soot and ash.

She looked up with a fabricated look of remorse. "Our hearts and wishes go out to those who lost loved ones in last week's attacks."

Suddenly, her fake frown turned upside down to form an imitation smile. "In other news, the celebration over the deaths of the Two Troublers has reemerged into the streets of Jerusalem. With Christmas, Saturnalia, and the Winter Solstice still months away, merrymakers have dubbed this momentous occasion the Festival of Hedonism and are celebrating by presenting each other with gifts and warm wishes. Pope Peter has not yet issued an official statement about the Festival of Hedonism, but sources inside the Ministry of Religion say it is likely to become an official week-long annual religious holiday."

"That's right, Heather." The screen pulled back to include Harrison Yates with a picture in picture live shot of the party going on at the Temple Mount. "One of the ways people are celebrating is by making straw or paper effigies of the Two Troublers, then burning them in the streets. Only time will tell which of these activities will become a tradition and which will be replaced by even more creative forms of expression."

"That's so true, Harrison. His Majesty recently reminded us that it was for Tammuz, the divinely incarnated god-child born to Semiramis, for whom the Christmas tree was first put up and decorated. It was only after decades of persecution upon pagan cultures at the hands of radical Christians that they stole the idea of the Christmas tree and the winter holiday altogether, that this sacred symbol was perverted into the celebration of the birth of Jesus. Whom, I might add, many historians say never existed."

"You'll find out soon enough." The rabbi sat with his arms crossed, glaring at the lying woman on the television.

Harrison looked closely at his monitor. "Heather, did you see that?"

"I'm afraid I don't know what you're talking about," she replied.

Yates giggled. "Take a close look at your monitor. There is a group of party goers dancing around the rotting corpse of one of the Troublers. And I could have sworn his hand just moved!"

She squealed. "Oh, no! Don't tell me. I bet they've tied fishing line to the hands and feet of the Troubler. There's probably someone in a crane above them that is going to make them dance around like marionettes. It's all so macabre—I just love it. This festival is going to turn out to be like a second Halloween. If there's one thing we need, it's another All Hallows Eve. It's absolutely my favorite holiday."

"I don't see any strings, but his leg just moved." Yates didn't seem to be paying attention to Heather Smith.

"Oh yuck. I hope it's not a rat under there gnawing away at his corpse. Everyone thinks it's a good idea to leave dead people in the street until the vermin show up." She rolled her eyes.

"Or the zombies." Harrison looked perplexed. "Would you look at that. He's standing up!"

Heather Smith abruptly ran out of clever things to say. Her jaw hung open like a frog trying to catch flies as she stared at her monitor.

The picture-in-picture shot of the Temple Mount showed Elijah standing up from the pavement where his body had been left three days prior. One by one, the drunken revelers realized what was happening and backed away from him. Moses walked into view and brushed the dust off the front of Elijah's robe.

The television provided no sound from the scene at the Temple Mount, but the entire crowd looked up toward the sky at something which had gotten their attention. Moments later, cascading light flowed down from above onto the two prophets, and they both ascended into the sky. The warm light quickly faded, and darkness fell upon the Temple Mount.

The partiers scurried about gathering their half-empty liquor bottles and hurrying to leave like teenagers fleeing a house party where the police had just arrived.

The Temple Mount had mostly cleared out when the camera began to shake. The television showed one wall of the new temple collapsing. Likewise, the qubba over the Dome of the Rock fell in from the violent shaking. Then, the feed cut.

Heather Smith began speaking, but there was no picture to accompany the audio. "Folks, I'm not sure what we just saw there, but evidently an earthquake just hit the Temple Mount. We're even feeling it here in our studio, and it seems to be causing some technical difficulties. Just bear with us for a moment until this thing passes."

"Is that it? Is that the Seventh Vial?" Courtney looked worried.

Everett looked at his watch and shook his head. "We've still got another hour before sunset in Jerusalem. That was probably a foreshock. We'll feel it here when the big one hits. Everyone should have something to cover their head and face with."

"I thought you said we'd be safe down here," the rabbi said.

"We'll be safer here than anywhere, but we could still have some dust and debris falling." Everett patted the old man on his back. "It's just a precaution."

The sound on the television went out, and a static image on the screen read, "Please stand by."

Everett tapped Ali on the shoulder. "Let's pull the satellite dish and the solar panels from the surface. We should have just enough time to get that done before sunset in Jerusalem."

CHAPTER 21

And the seventh angel poured out his vial
into the air; and there came a great voice out
of the temple of heaven, from the throne,
saying, It is done. And there were voices,
and thunders, and lightnings; and there was
a great earthquake, such as was not since
men were upon the earth, so mighty an
earthquake, and so great. And the great city
was divided into three parts, and the cities of
the nations fell: and great Babylon came in
remembrance before God, to give unto her
the cup of the wine of the fierceness of his
wrath. And every island fled away, and the
mountains were not found. And there fell
upon men a great hail out of heaven, every
stone about the weight of a talent: and men

blasphemed God because of the plague of the hail; for the plague thereof was exceeding great.

Revelation 16:17-21

Everett placed the hammer and chisel in his backpack. "You should go ahead and put your helmets on."

Ali and the rabbi complied without question.

Courtney continued packing her own pack. "I've got six MREs, a gallon of water, plus my canteen. Do you think that will be good enough?"

"I hope so. The important thing is that the four of us not get separated when the shaking starts."

Rabbi Hertzog put his arms through the straps of his pack. "We have food and water inside the city, Everett. Even if we get trapped inside, we'll still have our supplies."

Everett slipped his gloves on his hands and positioned the tactical goggles on his helmet. "Theoretically, you're right. But the city is made of soft, porous rock. Sections of the walls and ceilings could collapse. We could get trapped in some corridor or stairwell without access to supplies. I want to make sure we have enough for at least forty-eight hours while we dig ourselves out."

"Is it not better to stay outside until the quake passes?" Ali quizzed with a nervous voice.

"If we knew the quake and the seventy-pound hailstones weren't going to happen at the same time, that would be a fantastic plan. But, given the threat from above, I think this is our best option."

"You said the destructive waves of the quake should stay on the surface." Courtney also sounded worried.

"In theory." Everett stuck a second flashlight in the side pocket of his cargo pants. "But like I said before, this quake is unlike anything the world has ever seen."

"Would we be better off on the second level?" Courtney fastened the chin strap of her military helmet.

"Not if we have to dig our way back to the surface." Everett clipped the waist belt of his assault pack.

"What about all of the food and water buckets here in this room? If walls begin to give way, this would be the best room to be stuck in." Hertzog motioned toward the eight buckets of supplies lined up on the back wall of Everett's living space.

"That's why I have them here." Everett positioned the dust mask on his helmet behind his goggles. "But if this ceiling starts crumbling, we'll leave. We've pre-positioned food and water buckets on each level."

"And where will we go if ceiling cracks?" Ali loosely adjusted the shemagh around his neck.

"Either up or down. It will depend on what's happening and what possibilities are available to us." Everett looked at the rabbi's single crutch. "How's the leg?"

"Much better. I've been getting around with just the one crutch."

"If it comes down to it, could you move faster if you had both crutches?"

"In an open field, yes. In these tight passways, no. It's why I've been using only one."

"I'll be in front, Courtney will be behind me. Ali, you follow the rabbi and give him a hand if he needs it."

Everett looked at his watch. "Jerusalem is one hour ahead of us. It's 6:40 there. The sun will be setting on the Holy City in the next five minutes."

"But the quake could come anytime in the next twenty-four hours." Courtney fidgeted with the straps of her backpack.

Everett nodded. "It doesn't even have to come then. It's just that the last six vials have begun at sunset on the past six Fridays."

Rabbi Hertzog pulled his goggles down over his eyes. "I fully expect that it will occur in the next twenty-four hours."

Ali put on his gloves and checked the headlamp on his helmet. "If it does not happen by ten o'clock tonight, we can take shifts sleeping and keeping watch."

"Good idea, Ali." Everett took hold of Courtney's hand.

She squeezed his fingers tightly. "Can we at least listen to the radio while we wait? I'll lose my mind if I simply wait here to be buried alive."

Everett reached over to the bucket where the small AM/FM radio was and passed it to her. "Keep the volume low. I want to be able to hear the rumblings when the quake begins."

"Is it okay if we sit down?" She took the radio.

"Sure." Everett watched as the others found seats on the buckets containing the dry-storage food, but he remained standing.

The radio came to life. The female GRBN reporter with a French accent spoke softly. "I am coming to you this evening from the GRBN studios in Marseilles. If you are just tuning in, I am sorry to inform you, but the GRBN headquarters in Jerusalem has been rattled by another terrible earthquake.

"There has been some speculation by the Global Republic Ministry of Geology that we may continue to experience a few mild tremors, which could be triggered by the unprecedented nuclear explosions all around the planet. The amount of force imposed upon the Earth by such awesome weapons has the potential to vibrate tectonic plates in such a way as to release energy stored at the convergence of these plates. While we can see seismic events set off by the bombs anywhere on the planet, the most vulnerable areas continue to be in the ring of fire, which runs along the west coasts of North and South America, China, and north-eastern Russia.

"The positive news is that The Holy Luzian Empire has annihilated Chinese-Russian Alliance forces in northern Israel and dispersed troops into Iraq. Today's decisive battle in Megiddo will prove to be the single incident future historians will look to when marking today as being the end of this final world war.

"His High and Most Prepotent Majesty Angelo Luz was expected to make a public statement this evening declaring the empire victorious over our adversaries, but due to the quake, the Ministry of Media Relations is rescheduling the press conference for the first thing tomorrow morning.

"Pope Peter spoke from the Vatican only minutes ago issuing this statement. I quote, 'With our opponents subdued and a host of global cataclysms behind us, we can now begin to rebuild. So many inherent vulnerabilities were built into our old social structure, infrastructure, and shared worldview that such a devastating series of calamities was necessary that we might clear away the fallacies, mistakes, and malignant ideas of the past in order to recreate a world made in our own image.

"'We can now look forward into a future bright with potential and possibility. A clean slate; a fresh start; a true genesis has been afforded us by the goddess Shiva who destroys so she might create again anew. As the prophet Isaiah spoke, the bricks are fallen down, but we will build with hewn stones: the sycamores are cut down, but we will change them into cedars.

"'My children and fellow worshipers of His Majesty Angelo Luz, your faith has brought you this far, and now we are on the cusp of a new beginning. Do not lose hope in the one who sustains you through his mercy and love. We must persevere, showing ourselves to be worthy of his compassions and his eternal care.'

"These healing words spoken by the pope remind us to stay true to ourselves and in so doing, stay true to His Majesty and the seven heads of

Dragon which constitute the Image of Angelo Luz.

"I leave you with these final words of encouragement from GRBN, the worst is behind us and it always seems darkest just before the dawn."

"Turn it off." Everett raised his hand.

Courtney quickly complied. "Tell me about it. I thought I was really going to vomit this time."

"No." Everett stood with his arms stretched out and his hands lifted. "Did you feel that?"

The walls, floor, and ceiling vibrated. Microscopic bits of dust fell from tiny holes in the porous stone.

Ali pulled his goggles over his eyes and lifted his shemagh pulling it tightly over his mouth to act as a dust mask.

Courtney stood up and put her goggles on also. "It's happening!"

The rabbi lifted himself up and placed his weight on the single crutch.

The low rumbling grew in intensity, shaking more dust from the ceiling and walls.

Holding Courtney's hand, Everett stepped into the hallway and walked over to the stairwell. He looked up to see a small crack in the wall grow. As the fracture increased in size, silt poured from the fissure onto the floor, forming a dust cloud. He looked down at the second level and saw no movement. "Come on, let's go down into the chapel."

Courtney pulled away. "I'm just going to grab the radio."

"There's no time! Ali, help the rabbi down the

stairs," Everett directed.

Courtney emerged from their living quarters with the radio as the dust cloud began to fill the air and drastically reduce visibility.

Everett pushed her toward the stairwell behind the rabbi. He saw the form of three other security team members in the hallway and yelled out. "Quick! Get down to the second level."

The four of them rushed down the stairs to the landing of the second level. Everett looked down the shaft to level three, then back up at the first level. The other soldiers were filing down the stairs.

Everett addressed his team, "Stand up against the wall so the others can get by."

When the IDF troops reached the second level, he instructed them, "Go to the chapel. I'll let you know if this level looks like it's not going to be safe."

The shaking became more intense. "Stand back, get away from the stairwell," Everett said to his team. He continued to observe the structural integrity of the floors above and below. Another crack shot like a bolt of lightning from the stairwell on the first floor above him to the corridor which led to the entrance. Rock, and sand, and dust, and silt crashed down from above, billowing into a cloud of haze and grime, filling the air.

Everett led his team past the chapel and called out to the security personnel, "The first level is collapsing. We need to move lower!"

Everyone followed him to the rear stairwell where they descended to the fourth level. Once there, Everett could no longer feel the earth shaking, but he could still hear the activity echoing through the ceiling.

"Where to now?" Courtney stayed close to her husband.

"The tunnel to Derinkuyu on the fourth level. If the first and second level both collapse, it will be easier to travel through the tunnel and use an exit in Derinkuyu than it will be to dig out of Kaymakli."

"You're pretty calm considering we were just buried alive." The rabbi hobbled briskly behind Everett.

Courtney took the liberty of responding to Rabbi Hertzog's comment. "As sad as it sounds, this isn't our first time being trapped underground by an earthquake."

Everett pressed his back up against the wall allowing all those who'd followed him four stories below ground to pass by. He remained near the rear stairwell, listening to the ground rumble far above him and waiting for it to stop.

"How long can it last?" Ali assisted the rabbi in finding a spot out of the way of the other people streaming orderly down the staircase.

Everett glanced at his watch, then back up toward the surface. "It's been going for five minutes."

Courtney pressed her backpack against the wall and her shoulder against Everett's. "And it's still going strong?"

"Yep." Everett ducked out of the stairwell as several pieces of rock dropped down from the first level.

"I wish I knew whether the hailstones were

dropping. I'd like to know what's happening in Jerusalem." She gently tugged on his arm to get him further from the falling rock above.

Everett stepped away from the threat only slightly. He was mesmerized by the duration of the mega-quake going on overhead. The last of the occupants of the second and third levels cleared from above. The remaining security personnel found safety near Everett and his team on the fourth tier. Most of the others continued lower.

After a significant length of time had passed, he checked his watch again. "Ten minutes and it's still shaking."

According to his timepiece, eight more minutes passed before the steady reverberations finally ceased.

"Is it over?" Courtney still held his arm tightly with her hands.

Everett craned his neck to look up the stairwell and listened intently. "It seems to be. But we could have aftershocks. We'll hang out down here for at least an hour before we go back up to inspect the damage."

CHAPTER 22

And after these things I saw another angel come down from heaven, having great power; and the earth was lightened with his glory. And he cried mightily with a strong voice, saying, Babylon the great is fallen, is fallen, and is become the habitation of devils, and the hold of every foul spirit, and a cage of every unclean and hateful bird. For all nations have drunk of the wine of the wrath of her fornication, and the kings of the earth have committed fornication with her, and the merchants of the earth are waxed rich through the abundance of her delicacies.

Revelation 18:1-3

Everett cautiously ascended the staircase with Ali and Courtney behind him. He'd had to insist to keep the rabbi from coming along. "Keep some distance from each other. If a section of the stairs give way and takes us all down at once, there will be no one left to go for help."

"Yes, Everett." Ali slowed his pace, putting half a flight of stair between them.

Everett reached the second level where the chapel was. A few pillars had cracked and some had fallen into the hallway, but the ceiling appeared to be sound. He stepped over several large stones, pieces of the wall that had cracked and fallen, but none were larger than two feet in diameter. As he passed the chapel, Everett paused to look inside.

Courtney caught up to him and took a gander as well. "Hardly any damage at all."

"Yes. It looking pretty good." Ali surveyed the ceiling and the walls of the large open room.

"Since this is one of the areas with the most rock excavated from within, it should have been the weakest room on this level." Everett toured through the chapel area, inspecting the cracks in the walls up close. "If it didn't cave in, the rest of level two should be in fairly decent shape."

"Do you think our area is still livable?" Courtney stuck the blade of her knife in one of the larger cracks to test the depth.

"We can check it out, but I wouldn't get my hopes up if I were you." Everett led the way out of the large open room, down the hallway, and to the front staircase. It was more difficult to maneuver. A three-foot tall stone blocked the passageway, forcing Everett to crawl over it. Once on the other side, he assisted Courtney and Ali in getting over it. Then, the three of them made their way up to the first level.

"Could be worse." Ali slid his foot along the floor, piling up a quarter inch of sand and gravel with the sole of his boot.

Everett saw no major cave-ins as he glanced down the hallway toward their living quarters. However, when he looked up toward the entrance, it was filled with rock and rubble.

"Let's just take a quick peek at our room." Courtney stepped around a large boulder from a collapsed wall and headed up the hall.

Everett kept close behind her. When they arrived, the room looked to be in acceptable condition. The back wall had a huge crack running floor to ceiling but seemed to be structurally sound. Like everything else, all their belongings were covered in dust, but that would be easily remedied by a good cleaning.

"I know it will be a lot of work to dig out, but couldn't we give it a shot?" Courtney dusted off her rolled-up sleeping bag. "We've got less than two months until the New Millennium, and I'm really tired of moving."

Everett took a deep breath and looked at his wife with care. Being a man, he was more of a hunter-gatherer, and she was more of a nester. Still, even he was sick of the constant relocation; he could only imagine what it must be like for her. "I'll put an exploratory team together tomorrow morning to assess how hard it will be to get out. But we have to make sure we at least have some ventilation shafts open. Otherwise, we only have a few days' worth of air for so many people. If we can't verify our air source, I'll have to move everyone to Derinkuyu."

She hugged him. "Thank you. You're a good husband."

He gave her a kiss.

Ali cleared his throat to remind them that they were not alone in the room.

Everett slowly pulled his lips away from hers and looked around the room. "We'll have to get the solar panels set back up as soon as possible also."

"I wonder if radio stations are still broadcasting?" Courtney retrieved the AM/FM radio from her pack and began scrolling through.

Everett looked on as she did so, but he was certain none would be on, at least not this soon after the mega quake.

The three of them organized cleaning tasks and promptly had their living space cleaned up enough to sleep in that evening. Afterwards, the three friends swept and dusted the silt and grime from the rabbi's room on the second floor. Once that mission was completed, Ali assisted Rabbi Hertzog back up to his room where the four of them enjoyed a meal together before bed.

Saturday, Everett determined that it was worth a shot at trying to dig out of Kaymakli. Like Courtney, he'd grown accustomed to his space and really hated the thought of relocating to Derinkuyu, which had many more people than Kaymakli. However, he was only able to recruit a small number of people from the security team to assist him in the chore. Most assured him that they would join in after sundown, but for the time being, they would keep the Sabbath.

Ali tried to reason with some using Galatians chapter three but was met with resistance by several Jews who claimed the sabbath pre-dated the law since it was first mentioned in Genesis chapter two, verse two.

So, with only seven other able-bodied people to help, Everett began the task of breaking up the rocks into manageable stones which could be moved out of the way and set aside until they had an opening through which they could remove the rubble.

"You take it easy on that shoulder," Courtney warned.

"It's been three weeks. I'll be fine." Everett replied.

"And according to the doctor, you weren't supposed to be doing any heavy lifting for at least another three."

"The hammer isn't heavy," he disputed.

"You know what I mean."

Courtney worked right behind Everett, passing stones back to Ali, who passed them to a former IDF troop behind him. "The rock is really easy to break up, huh?"

Everett kept his goggles on and his mouth covered with a face mask. He struck the chisel with the hammer. "It's a lot easier to bust than that slab we had in the cave."

"If that was the case, we'd just move to Derinkuyu." Courtney kicked the smaller stones to either side of the stairs.

After an hour, Everett switched with Ali, who chiseled for the next sixty minutes, then handed the tools off to Samuel, the soldier working behind him. Everett returned to the chisel once four other men had taken an hour-long shift.

Just before seven o'clock, fifteen new men showed up, with Ruben as their leader. He'd been the man debating whether or not to keep the Sabbath with Ali earlier.

Ruben called out to Everett from the bottom of the steps. "The corridor is too narrow for all of us to work at one time. Why don't you people call it a day and let us work through the night? You can resume your shift at seven in the morning."

Everett accepted the generous offer. "Thank you, Ruben. I appreciate it."

Everett, Ali, and Courtney brought their sleeping bags down to the chapel on the second level. With all the banging and beating of rocks and chisels through the night, the first level would not be the best place to get a much-needed night's sleep.

The project continued Sunday, with Everett's group working diligently through the day. Reuben's relief team took over at seven o'clock Sunday evening.

Exhausted by the day's toil, Everett was out like a light shortly after eating supper.

He was awoken on the chapel floor right around

midnight.

"Mr. Carroll . . ."

He rolled over to see a headlamp affixed to a helmet shining in his eyes and preventing him from identifying his harasser. He held a hand up to block the bright light. "Who's there?"

The man instantly understood his mistake and removed the elastic band holding the light on his helmet. "I'm so sorry, sir. It's Ruben. We broke through to the other side." Ruben switched the headlamp on to the green-light mode making its illumination much less intense. "I thought you might like to know."

Everett immediately forgave the man for having interrupted his slumber. "That's great!" he exclaimed, paying no attention to the volume of his voice.

"What's great?" Courtney flicked on her flashlight and directed it at Reuben.

"They broke through." Everett exited his sleeping bag and slipped on his boots.

Courtney wore a velour tracksuit for pajamas. She stuck her feet in her black combat boots without lacing them up and followed Everett.

Ali had obviously been roused by the excitement as he trailed behind as well.

They followed Ruben up the stairwell to a three-foot-wide-by-three-foot-tall tunnel which led to the surface. Everett emerged from the hole like a meerkat. He sniffed the fresh air as if he were one of the small, fur-bearing, desert creatures checking for danger. The moon was three-quarters full and provided more light than he'd seen since being buried below ground two days ago.

The destruction of the buildings surrounding the entrance to the Kaymakli underground city was absolute. The Typhoon wasn't in the best shape when they'd arrived, yet now it was absolutely destroyed by the impact of the hailstones. The large blocks of ice were gone, but the destruction left in their wake served as evidence enough.

No fragment of a wall stood more than three feet in height. Every single structure had been reduced to piles of rubble less than waist high. Not a single tree remained with branches. At most, a few stripped tree trunks jetted up from the barren earth six or seven feet tall, like monoliths left by some ancient culture who'd once inhabited this un-recognizable planet with a moon that closely resembled the one on Earth.

"This world is not our home." Everett turned around, examining the ruins on every side.

Courtney took a deep breath. "Thank God for that."

"Heaven doesn't have much competition now." Ruben glanced from one section of the eradicated landscape to the other.

"It never did." Ali's head turned upward, looking beyond the wreckage of earth, past the moon and stars, as if he could see straight into the throne room of God.

Ruben turned around. "My crew will continue to excavate throughout the night. We'll clear as much of the rubble as we can."

"Why don't you guys call it a night? We'll all take a break tomorrow and pick up where we left off on Tuesday." Everett patted Ruben on the back.

Ruben knelt down to crawl back in the hole. "We'll work the rest of the shift, but you guys take the day off. After all, we took Saturday as our Sabbath." Ruben turned to Ali. "And one man esteems one day above another, yet another man esteems every day alike. Let every man be fully persuaded in his own mind. Isn't that right?"

Ali smiled big, showing his large white teeth. "Romans fourteen."

Ruben offered a friendly nod and descended into the opening.

Everett, Courtney, and Ali followed after Ruben and swiftly returned to their beds. Despite the excitement, one-by-one, they all resumed their interrupted slumber.

Everett knew they needed to rest on Monday, so he fought the urge to set up the solar panels and began scanning information channels for news about the rest of the world. Instead, his team slept in, ate some extra MREs, and attended Rabbi Hertzog's devotional service.

Tuesday, however, Everett got an early start on his task list. After a short time of personal prayer and reading a couple chapters of his Bible, he got to work setting up the solar panels and the Ham radio antenna. Courtney assisted Everett while Ali focused on reinstalling the satellite dish.

All three of them agreed that most terrestrial antennas were probably destroyed by the quake and the hailstones, but if there was any signal to be found, it would likely come from a Global Republic satellite. After all, a liar isn't happy if he doesn't have anyone to lie to.

Once the various pieces of equipment were erected, Courtney scanned the AM/FM radio, Ali worked on the satellite dish, and Everett tested the Ham frequencies. He was unlikely to understand anything being said if he were to intercept a communication, but he'd quickly call Ali to interpret.

The three of them spent several hours looking for signals but found none. The remainder of the day was spent helping the security team clear the rock and gravel from the city entrance.

In the days that followed, Everett's team would spend an hour each morning, an hour at mid-day, and an hour each evening scanning for signals with no success. The security team eventually cleared the tunnel down to the original steps to the entrance.

Finally, on the Friday morning one week after the Seventh Vial, Everett heard the faint crackling of voices on the Ham radio. "Ali! Come quickly! I've got something."

Ali hurried to the radio located in a nook a few yards inside the city entrance. "What is it?"

"Turkish, I think. Listen." Everett adjusted the volume slightly higher.

Ali sat still and quiet. The transmission was of poor quality, but he seemed to be making out the gist of the conversation.

Everett waited patiently while Ali jotted down a few notes on a scrap piece of paper stored beside the radio for just such a purpose. The conversation ended, and Everett looked up with anticipation. "What did they say? Did you hear anything about Jerusalem or Angelo Luz?"

Ali looked at his notes with his eyebrows pressed closely together. "No. This guy was MOC fighter at Megiddo. He escaped from GR forces. He was talking with his uncle in nearby town."

"And?"

Ali shook his head. "Very strange what he talk about. He say GR have vehicle at Megiddo he never see before. And he talk about the GR supersoldier he see in the fighting. He say MOC and Chinese-Russian Alliance never have a chance against these guys. He say they are like three-meter tall."

Everett chuckled. "Seriously? That's what, ten feet tall? Giants?"

Ali shook his head pensively. "I don't know. Whatever this guy see make him very afraid."

"He could have been injured in the fight and hopped-up on some local medication. Or, he could just be plain ol' hopped-up on drugs."

"Maybe." Ali's voice showed that he was deeply considering what he'd heard over the radio.

Later that evening, Everett, Courtney, and Ali met the rabbi on the second level for dinner in his quarters.

Everett relayed the unusual conversation they'd overheard that morning.

"Hmm." Rabbi Hertzog nodded his head as he listened.

"You look like you're buying this story." Everett was surprised by the rabbi's reaction.

"Messiah said that as it was in the days of Noah, so would it be at the time of his coming. The passage in Genesis that speaks of the days before the flood specifically mentions giants. It also mentions crossbreeding between the sons of God and the daughters of men. These beings are called the Nephilim."

Everett waved his hand dismissively. "Yeah, but Jesus was talking about the general state of wickedness being similar to the days of Noah."

"The Global Republic Broadcasting Network had been touting their genetically engineered supersoldiers which they admit are hybrids of humans and the Watchers. Genesis chapter six specifically says the Nephilim were warriors of renown. That sounds oddly like a supersoldier to me." The rabbi put another cracker in his mouth.

Courtney sat up straight. "So, you think these supersoldiers are the same as the Nephilim spoken of in Genesis chapter six?"

Hertzog took a long drink from his canteen. "I do. But, HaShem wiped them from the face of the Earth before, and he will do it again. At this point in the game, they are of little concern to me."

Everett pressed his lips together tightly. He hoped that the voice over the radio was not speaking the truth of the matter, but his thoughts were plagued by how quickly the Global Republic had won the war against such a vast collection of armies. They'd not only defeated China and Russia in a week, but they'd managed to put a decisive end to radical jihadis, something all of their predecessors had failed to do.

But what worried Everett the most was that he'd managed to step in just about every dung heap prophesied concerning the Great Tribulation. If there were indeed Nephilim on the planet, he had a bad feeling that he wouldn't get through the next two months without a confrontation with them.

CHAPTER 23

And Cush begat Nimrod: he began to be a mighty one in the earth. He was a mighty hunter before the Lord: wherefore it is said, Even as Nimrod the mighty hunter before the Lord. And the beginning of his kingdom was Babel, and Erech, and Accad, and Calneh, in the land of Shinar.

Genesis 10:8-10

Everett found living underground in Kaymakli to be several rungs lower on the ladder compared to the cottage in the mountains outside of Batumi. He had no picturesque view of the river, no fresh fish, no garden, and no scenic cliffs in the background.

But it was a significant step up from life in the cave, back in Virginia. The cavern near Woodstock had only the low ceiling area near the entrance, a short passageway to the main living space, the great room which they'd labeled the cathedral, and the narrow tunnel they'd used for storage.

The underground city had several different rooms on each of the eight levels. The ability to go from room to room aided in fending off claustrophobic notions. The opportunity to visit with folks for a time and then retire to a secluded space for privacy kept tensions in check while still warding off loneliness. Everett had found being trapped in the same space with the same people for months on end to be the most psychologically oppressive element of cave life.

The fact that the underground city had been designed with the purpose of human habitation in mind made it feel more civilized as well. The cave had felt a little too primitive; too cavemanesque. That small difference in Kaymakli subconsciously encouraged residents to act according to their highest nature in regard to their neighbors. Folks treated each other civilly, spoke with kind words, and were generally polite. Everett felt sure that lesser conditions would have added to the stress of confinement and left the people behaving toward one another in a much more base manner.

Everett's twenty-second day in Kaymakli was a Monday. On this particular evening, he held the walkie-talkie up to his mouth as he looked at the blank television screen. "Still nothing."

Ali's voice came over the radio. "What about

now?"

Everett had performed this fruitless ritual every evening for the past week; Ali adjusting the satellite dish ever so slightly, and Everett calling over the radio to let him know that they did not have a signal. "There's nothing, Ali. I don't think you're going to be able to . . . wait! What was that? Go back!"

"What did you see?"

Everett pressed the talk key. "It was a brief flash of a news desk. It was heavily tiled, but it was definitely something. Whatever you were doing ten seconds ago, do that."

Everett stared at the television waiting for the image to reappear. "Right there! We've got a signal!"

Courtney came in the room. "It's working?"

"Yeah, go get the rabbi!"

She scurried out of the room.

Ali rushed in to see the product of his handiwork. "GRBN! I was sure they would find way to put broadcast on satellite."

Courtney and the rabbi soon joined them. "Good work!" The rabbi came in the room with only the assistance of a cane. Since wood for canes was in short supply, Moses' staff doubled as his walking stick.

Everett looked at the CGI images of Heather Smith and Harrison Yates. They no longer seemed to be controlled by real people. They were more artificial than before; lifeless, hollow, dead.

"Those two look extra creepy today." Courtney stood behind Everett like a frightened child at a haunted house.

His lip curled as he listened to the broadcast.

"I couldn't agree more. It really is eternal life." Yates said, "Like Heather, I uploaded my consciousness into the Nirvananet, inside of Dragon, prior to the quake and the bombardment of the giant hailstones. So, even though our physical bodies were destroyed in the disaster, we will live on for eternity in the mind of Dragon."

"That's right, Harrison. And His Majesty Angelo Luz has made this gift available to all who will believe. Most of the Global Republic administration buildings around the world were destroyed ten days ago, so those who procrastinated are going to have to prove that they are worthy of the gift. The Global Republic Emergency Operation Center is located at the Shinar Military Research Base. The fifty-square-mile military facility is completely underground and totally self-sufficient."

Yates took over the report. "General Semyaza has opened a large section of the installation to support a civilian refugee center on the surface above the base. The research base has endless stockpiles of food, water, medical equipment, tents for shelter, blankets, and clothing. If you can get here, we will welcome you with open arms."

The real Heather Smith would have put some personality into her presentation, but not this one. The CGI reporter continued her part in the broadcast. "The base is located roughly 500 kilometers southeast of Bagdad, Iraq. If you are coming from the south, it is about 50 kilometers

---

northeast from the Persian Gulf coast of Iraq.

"No one will be turned away. And the best part is that you can still take the pledge to His Majesty and have your consciousness uploaded to the Nirvananet, granting you eternal life within Dragon."

Courtney shivered. "They have eternal life alright. They'll be burning in the lake of fire forever and ever, not in some computer program. Getting rid of Luz is like killing a cockroach infestation. He just won't go away."

Everett looked at the rabbi. "You nodded like you were expecting them to announce that they had an underground research center."

"I was nodding when I heard the name," Hertzog said.

"Shinar?" Ali listened closely.

"Yes." The rabbi wrapped his hands around the staff as he spoke. "It means *country of two rivers*. The location indicated by the news broadcast is near the convergence of the Euphrates and the Tigris.

"Babel, as in the Tower of Babel, was in the land of Shinar. And Babel, which means gate of the gods, was Nimrod's throne. It was here that the Babylonian system first began. Additionally, when the prophet Zechariah had his vision of wickedness personified, it was to the land of Shinar that she was taken to build a house for herself.

"It was in Shinar that Nimrod and his wife, Semiramis, developed Mystery Babylon, the false religion which has infected the Earth ever since.

"After Nimrod's death, Semiramis was

258

impregnated by one of her priests, but she claimed that she had been divinely seeded by Nimrod himself. The child who was born, Tammuz, was worshiped as Nimrod reincarnated. Nimrod was the original false god who came to be known as the sun god Baal. His wife came to be known as the goddess of fertility and sexuality, Ashtoreth. Tammuz came to be associated with the cycle of death and rebirth. The three of them are represented by various names in every pagan culture on earth.

"Going backward, Nimrod was the grandson of Noah's disobedient son, Ham, who may have secretly brought forbidden esoteric wisdom onto the arc, preserving it through the flood. Ham may have passed down this secret knowledge of the Watchers to Nimrod. It could have been this hidden mystery of the fallen angels which Nimrod intended to use to open up a portal to the underworld.

"I believe that is the reason God confused the languages of the Earth at Babel. There was little threat of a physical tower reaching the heavens. After all, God has allowed skyscrapers, air travel, and space exploration without consequence."

Courtney sat with her finger pressed against her lips as she listened. "And you think the Shinar Research Facility has opened some kind of portal?"

"I believe it is the place where the CRISPR Cas9 gene-editing process was perfected to make it possible for the sons of god to breed with the daughters of men once again. I think this achieves the same goal as the Tower of Babel portal. It allows the Watchers to have a more-direct physical grasp of this realm."

Everett was growing tired of the Great Tribulation and hoped he could get through it without another battle. "So, Shinar—you think this is where Luz has his army of supersoldiers; the Nephilim?"

"I do." The rabbi drummed his fingers on the staff.

Everett sighed as if resigning to a thing that was far from his circle of control.

CHAPTER 24

And Enoch also, the seventh from Adam, prophesied of these, saying, Behold, the Lord cometh with ten thousands of his saints, To execute judgment upon all, and to convince all that are ungodly among them of all their ungodly deeds which they have ungodly committed, and of all their hard speeches which ungodly sinners have spoken against him.

Jude 14-15

Friday afternoon, Everett pulled the batteries out of the charger, which was plugged directly into the inverter from the solar array. He walked outside and positioned the solar panels to the best angle in order to get the last remaining sunlight of the day.

Afterwards, he returned to the first level, stuck the fully-charged batteries into his and Courtney's flashlights and replaced the tail caps.

"Aren't you getting ready?" Courtney put on her best jeans and favorite sweater, which she'd hand-laundered the day before.

"I don't know if I'm going." He inspected their walkie-talkies, both of which had freshly charged batteries.

"It's Rosh Hashanah! Rabbi Hertzog has been preparing his message for tonight's service all week. And the women have been preparing the meal since this morning."

Even though it wasn't turned on, Everett stared at the television as if he expected it to get up and walk away at any moment. "You better not let the rabbi hear you call it Rosh Hashanah."

She rolled her eyes. "Yom Teruah, whatever. Everyone else down here calls it Rosh Hashanah."

Everett took a seat on the inverted bucket next to his sleeping bag. "I guess old habits die hard."

"Whatever you call it, you have to go. The service will be short, then the meal will be served, and you can be back in the room by nine o'clock to listen to the news.

"Fifteen people spent the whole day yesterday scratching around in the ruins of the city on the surface just to scrape up enough firewood to make a hot meal for tonight. It's been a month since we ate hot food, and it might be our last chance to have a warm meal on this planet."

"You go. Enjoy yourself." He took her hand and kissed it.

She interlaced her fingers with his. "It won't be the same without you. Please come."

He sighed. "I really believe Messiah will return tonight. I've been waiting for this moment for seven long years. Seven very, very long years."

"Then what better place to be when he returns than worshiping Him in a congregation of fellow believers or awaiting his return at a huge celebration? Rabbi Hertzog has been teaching on the glorious appearance ever since we arrived in Kaymakli. Everyone there is hoping for the same thing you are. And we'll be together."

She lowered her head giving an expression that begged for his consideration. "We don't know how all of this is going to play out, Everett. But whatever happens, and whenever it happens, I want to be by your side for the entire thing. Please go with me tonight."

His heart melted and his resolve faded. Everett stood up and embraced his wife. "You're right. I won't miss anything by not listening to the GRBN broadcast. Besides, whatever they report will be a lie wrapped in deception and covered in falsehood."

Everett found his most presentable pair of pants and put on the shirt Courtney had washed for him the day before.

Ali walked in the room. "I will see you at the service. I am helping some people with the food preparation."

"See you there." Courtney waved.

"Helping people with the food preparation?" Everett pursed his lips as he repeated the phrase.

"What?" Courtney continued brushing her hair.

"You were an NSA profiler. He's going to help the ladies, not some people. That didn't sound subversive to you?"

"I was a sub-contracted profiler. His English isn't perfect."

"He knows the word for lady, girl, and woman."

"Maybe he wants to be useful but because of his middle-eastern culture, he doesn't want to point out that he is working with the women."

"You're being naive. It's a girl."

"So, what if it is a girl?"

"We've got forty-five days until the clock runs out on time itself. Why bother trying to strike up a relationship?"

"So, if you had just met me today, you wouldn't try to talk to me because we only have six weeks left?"

Everett had painted himself into a corner and there was only one way out. He kissed her tenderly and said, "You win. If we only had six hours left on the clock, I'd spend every second trying to win your heart."

She smiled like a cat with a mouse firmly under her paw, then finished getting ready.

Everett checked his watch. "It's five o'clock. The sun sets in Jerusalem an hour ahead of us. It should be setting in twenty minutes. The service doesn't begin until 6:30. Maybe we can hear something from Jerusalem before we go."

He monitored his watch, not wanting to turn on the television until the seconds before the sun was to set in Jerusalem. The television was a significant drain on the battery bank, and Everett was unsure what the skies would look like after their Creator had split them wide open.

At precisely 5:20, he turned on the television. All he saw was the CGI versions of Yates and Smith droning on with the same Global Republic propaganda, inviting survivors to come to the Shinar refugee center in southern Iraq, or as Everett liked to call it, Luz's concentration camp.

No additional news had been reported an hour later when Courtney tugged his hand. "Come on, I want to get a good seat up front. Your TV will still be there when we get back."

Everett wasn't so sure about that, but he'd committed to go, so he went.

When they arrived in the chapel on the second level, Courtney whisked Everett to the front, claiming three spots on the floor where they would sit. "We'll save a spot for Ali." She stood, facing the entrance to the chapel.

Everett spotted the young Arab's dark hair before Courtney did. He also noticed a girl about Ali's age a few steps behind him. "You better save two." Everett took three paces away from Courtney to make room for whoever the young woman was since the chapel was beginning to fill up.

Ali saw Courtney waving and instructed the girl to follow him down front. When they arrived, Ali held out his hand toward Everett. "This is my brother and sister, my family, Everett and Courtney." He motioned to the girl with long black hair and olive skin. She had a strong nose, but she was very pretty. "This is Ilia."

"Pleasure to meet you." Everett shook the girl's hand.

"Likewise," she said.

"Just to clarify, we're Ali's brother and sister in Christ, not by blood." Courtney shook Ilia's hand. "Otherwise, it'd be kinda weird because I'm married to this one." She motioned to Everett with her thumb.

The choir came in and led the congregation in four acapella worship songs. Afterward, Rabbi Hertzog delivered his Yom Teruah message from Matthew chapter twenty-five, speaking on the parable of the wise and foolish virgins, and encouraging the congregation to persevere in their faith until the very last second.

After the message, the rabbi prayed, then a man stepped forward to blow the shofar. A chill ran through Everett's bones as he considered that the same sound would soon emanate from heaven, and Yeshua would return to claim His Kingdom.

The man finished blowing the shofar and returned the way he'd come in. Before the congregation gathered in the chapel and had a chance to begin conversing amongst themselves, another sound was heard. Once again, it was the sound of the shofar, but off in the distance.

Everett listened closely as a smile of anticipation grew across his face. "That's it!" he whispered to Courtney. "Come on! Let's go to the surface!"

Everett quickly got ahead of the crowd and made it to the stairwell with Courtney in tow. Ali an Ilia followed close behind. The four of them charged up the stairs with everyone else behind them. Everett dashed out of the entryway and stared up at the sky. A brilliant, bright-white cross glowed in the heavens. It shined so bright, it drowned out the light of the stars so intensely, they were washed in pure white light as if the sun was shining.

Everett recalled Matthew chapter twenty-four, verse thirty and recited it aloud. "And then shall appear the sign of the Son of man in heaven."

"Now what?" Courtney asked.

Everett waited, looking excitedly at the cross in the sky. "I don't know, but whatever it is, it won't be long now."

The sound of the shofar faded, and twenty minutes later everyone living in the underground city was outside looking up at the sky. Spontaneous worship broke out, with the entire group singing song after song and dancing for joy.

Everett sang along with his eyes on the sign of the cross above, but no other momentous events occurred.

An hour later, the food was brought up to the surface and the communal meal was enjoyed al fresco. Everett, Courtney, the rabbi, Ali, and Ilia shared a bed sheet spread out on the ground like a picnic cloth as they ate.

Once they'd finished eating, Everett tapped the rabbi on the shoulder. "I'm anxious to know what's going on. Would you like to come down and see if GRBN is reporting anything?"

"Oh, yes." The rabbi accepted Everett's help in standing, then used the staff to assist in his walking.

Everett then helped Courtney to her feet. "Ali, are you and Ilia coming?"

"I have to help with the dishes. But thank you for the invitation," Ilia declined politely.

"And I will help Ilia." Ali looked at her with the gaze of a man falling in love.

Everett fought his grin. "You know where we'll be. Come on by when you're finished."

Once Everett, Courtney, and the rabbi arrived in their living quarters, Everett quickly powered on the television.

The computer-generated image of Heather Smith had exaggeratedly large eyes and it was speaking entirely too loud. This was obviously the effect Dragon was trying to achieve with the broadcast, but Everett adjusted the volume lower.

Smith's bugged-eyed likeness said, "While the alien invasion is a cause for concern, by no means is this a time to panic. General Semyaza personally assured GRBN that the alien race which began their encroachment upon our planet shortly after 7:00 PM Jerusalem time is a sect of interplanetary menaces that he has dealt with and defeated before. While the extraterrestrial beings assaulting Earth may look human, General Semyaza's top aide, Major Kokabiel, says they are actually closer genetically to the race of the Watchers. Major Kokabiel is a full-bloodied Watcher himself, and he said the inferior size of the Invaders is evidence of their lesser abilities.

"Major Kokabiel said we can place full confidence in the Global Republic's supersoldiers to defeat the Invaders. He promises that our weapons and troops are far more advanced than the Invaders, and that the war will be little more than a prolonged skirmish. Generals Semyaza, Azazael, and Amezarak have pledged to eradicate the universe of this plague known to our planet only as the Invaders. General Semyaza granted them generous and amicable terms when the Watchers won the last conflict, but the King of the Invaders has broken the treaty and proven that he is not to be trusted."

As the AI machine controlling the image of Harrison Yates caused him to show an expression of unbelief, Dragon tipped its hand that it did not fully grasp what it means to be human. Yates' mouth hung open, and his head bobbed around in a manner that the real Yates would never have acted in. Yates said, "Alien invasion? Heather, this sounds like something straight out of a science fiction novel. But I suppose that while we've expected it for centuries, it was only with the arrival of the Watchers that we learned definitively we are not alone in the cosmos. Still, it's a lot to take in."

"That's true, Harrison. We're still adapting to that revelation, and it can be a lot to take in for some people. We have to be thankful to the father of His Majesty Angelo Luz for being the first extraterrestrial to make contact with our species, and to His Majesty himself for being the mediator. I don't even want to think what would be happening right now if General Semyaza and the other Watchers hadn't come and we were on our own to fight the Invaders."

"Heather, did Major Kokabiel give any indication as to why he thinks the Invaders came?"

"Yes, Harrison. He said they abused their planet's atmosphere and resources to the point where it was no longer able to support their race. Much like climate-change deniers of decades past, the Invaders had the scientific evidence that they needed to alter their behaviors, but were unwilling to make those changes."

Yates shook his head. "I hoped that was a problem that only we had to deal with, but I guess it's the same story wherever you go."

Courtney sat with her arms crossed. "Like you said, lies wrapped in deception and covered in falsehood."

Everett expected no less. Satan had begun the grand drama in the garden with a set of lies. It would be quite uncharacteristic of him to not see his strategy through to the end.

CHAPTER 25

And I saw heaven opened, and behold a white horse; and he that sat upon him was called Faithful and True, and in righteousness he doth judge and make war. His eyes were as a flame of fire, and on his head were many crowns; and he had a name written, that no man knew, but he himself. And he was clothed with a vesture dipped in blood: and his name is called The Word of God. And the armies which were in heaven followed him upon white horses, clothed in fine linen, white and clean. And out of his mouth goeth a sharp sword, that with it he should smite the nations: and he shall rule them with a rod of iron: and he treadeth the winepress of the fierceness and wrath of

Almighty God. And he hath on his vesture and on his thigh a name written, King Of Kings, And Lord Of Lords. And I saw an angel standing in the sun; and he cried with a loud voice, saying to all the fowls that fly in the midst of heaven, Come and gather yourselves together unto the supper of the great God; That ye may eat the flesh of kings, and the flesh of captains, and the flesh of mighty men, and the flesh of horses, and of them that sit on them, and the flesh of all men, both free and bond, both small and great. And I saw the beast, and the kings of the earth, and their armies, gathered together to make war against him that sat on the horse, and against his army. And the beast was taken, and with him the false prophet that wrought miracles before him, with which he deceived them that had received the mark of the beast, and them that worshipped his image. These both were cast alive into a lake of fire burning with brimstone. And the remnant were slain with the sword of him that sat upon the horse, which sword proceeded out of his mouth: and all the fowls were filled with their flesh.

Revelation 19:11-21

October passed, November came, and Everett continued to monitor the television. He heard only lies about how the Watchers would soon secure a victory over the Invaders. GRBN aired no footage of the ongoing final battle, and the fighting did not come near the Cappadocia region of Turkey where Everett and the rest of God's people were staying.

On occasion, Ali would intercept a transmission over the Ham radio of someone who'd left the conflict zone near southern Iraq and the Persian Gulf. They told stories of otherworldly soldiers riding on horseback, wearing armor made of a nearly-impenetrable, brilliant-white material. According to the Ham transmissions, the weapons of the Invaders were far superior to those of the Watchers and the Global Republic's supersoldiers.

Everett marked off his calendar on Monday morning. "Today is the day. It's been 1335 days since Luz broke his treaty with the nations. According to the book of Daniel, we've reached the end of time."

Ali held Ilia's hand tightly as they sat together on Everett's sleeping bag. "I am ready to meet the King!"

Courtney stood and embraced Everett, holding him tightly. "Me, too."

Everett ran his fingers through her hair and sighed, thankful that he'd made it to the end with no more conflict.

Rabbi Hertzog stood up from the bucket he'd

been sitting on. "I'll arrange a special time of worship this evening. I want to be singing His praises when He arrives."

Ruben rushed into Everett's living quarters carrying a walkie-talkie. He was on watch with one of his men. "Mr. Carroll, the underground city in Kayseri was just attacked!"

Everett's heart stopped. He wasn't sure what to expect on the final day of history, but it certainly wasn't a strike against the neighboring city. "Do they need reinforcements? Who's assaulting them?"

"The Global Republic. I think it's too late for reinforcements. Their security team put out a call about a minute ago, but by the time I called the other cities on the grapevine, Kayseri was already being overrun."

Everett grabbed his load-bearing vest and began stuffing magazines in the pockets. "What's the situation? Are they being slaughtered?"

"Just the fighters who resist. The others are being taken hostage."

Everett put his single-point sling over his shoulder and attached his HK G36C rifle. "Hostages? What's the point in that?"

Hertzog spoke as he stepped out of the way allowing Courtney to get her vest and rifle. "Perhaps this is Luz's final play. It could be that he and his father are on their last leg in Shinar and about to be taken by the armies of heaven."

Ali slipped his chest rig over his head and began loading magazines as well. "I do not understand why he takes hostage."

The rabbi continued. "It's Luz's last-ditch effort,

perhaps to negotiate with the King for the lives of His children."

Ilia reluctantly let go of Ali. "But why? He has already lost the final conflict."

Rabbi Hertzog took Ilia's hand and pulled her close to him to comfort her so Ali could finish preparing for battle. "Child, he lost the war two thousand years ago, but he won't stop until Messiah has bound him with chains and cast him into the Lake of Fire."

Everett pushed his Sig into his drop-leg pistol holster. "Kayseri is forty miles from here. They'll probably hit Ozkonak next, then they'll be on their way here. Reuben, call Derinkuyu's security team and tell them to put some charges in the tunnel and collapse it so the GR can't get through to their side once we're overrun."

"Couldn't you just blow up the entrance to Kaymakli and seal us off? Then they couldn't get to us as long as the tunnel from Derinkuyu is not accessible." Ilia hugged Ali.

Everett knew it was a plausible plan, but he couldn't use it. "If we do that, it will only send the GR supersoldiers straight to Derinkuyu. It's just not in my nature to save my own skin at the expense of someone else's. Sorry."

"What can I do to help?" The rabbi's face showed his deep concern.

"You can rally any available shooter with a gun and military experience, then send them topside. And you can pray." Everett led his team to the surface.

Once there, Everett conferred with Ruben and

his team. "We'll have auxiliary volunteers coming up soon. I'll need each of you to lead a fire team."

They all nodded letting Everett know they would do whatever needed to be done. As the volunteers arrived, Everett assigned them to the individual fire teams.

Security personnel from Ozkonak called over the radio. "The soldiers! They're huge! They've breached the entrances into the underground city. Our fighters are being massacred!"

Everett knew there was nothing he could do to help the poor souls in Ozkanak. "Courtney, Ali, take six volunteers with you and bring up the remaining shoulder-fired weapons. Bring everything we've got. Start with the PG-29V rockets first, then retrieve the RPGs."

Courtney nodded and began tapping volunteers to help with the task. Ali trailed right behind her.

Everett picked out defendable shooting positions amongst the rubble from the above-ground city of Kaymakli, which had been razed by the earthquake and hailstones. He stood beside Reuben and the other team leaders. "Some of the collapsed building have small pockets that you can get inside. They're precarious and could cave in on you, so give it a good kick to make sure it's stable before you get inside. It's not the best solution, but we don't have many other options for cover. At least the rubble will stop small-arms fire."

Reuben nodded and began allocating teams to the surrounding building with pieces of walls that still stood or man-sized air pockets within the debris.

Then, Everett waited for the inevitable.

Ali arrived with the first load of weaponry. "Where do you want I should stage the rockets?"

Everett looked at the launch tubes. There were four. "How many rockets do we have?"

"Thirty, maybe forty." Ali held two rockets under each arm.

Everett surveyed the smashed remains of the Typhoon, which still sat twenty feet away from the entrance to Kaymakli. "Our team will use the truck for cover. Put one of the tubes there, then distribute three to the other foxholes. Allocate the rockets evenly."

Courtney returned minutes later with four volunteers behind her. All held RPG launchers or several grenades. "Where to, boss?"

"Stick two launchers inside the Typhoon. Hand out the rest to the other fire teams. Try to distribute the grenades proportionately to each launcher." Everett felt the ground beneath his feet rumbling as if the Earth itself was thundering.

Reuben's voice called over the radio. "I've got a visual on eight colossal MRAPs. I'd say they're roughly twice the size of any other military transport vehicle I've ever seen. And the armor looks heavy."

Everett called back over the radio. "All teams, hold your fire until they get close enough to make a direct hit. If you can get a bull's eye on the windshield with one of the PG-29V rockets, it should incapacitate the vehicle. Otherwise, aim for the grill. The smaller RPGs probably won't do much to these vehicles unless you can knock off a wheel or blow out a tire. From what I hear, we're going to be dealing with some big boys. You may have to use RPGs to take out the supersoldiers. Utilize weapons firing 5.56 ammo for cover fire. That round may not be very effective against these guys unless you can get a headshot. Anyone shooting AK-47s should try to make the kill shots. The 7.62 round is going to have a lot more punch."

Everett released the talk key and turned to Courtney. "Can you run back downstairs and get those full auto AK-47s the sheik sold us?"

"Sure." She turned to the entrance and hurried away.

Everett pointed at four of the IDF volunteers beside the wreckage of the Typhoon. "You guys go with her. Bring up all the ammo and all the magazines."

Ali stood beside Everett. "I have already AK."

"Good." Everett patted him on the back. "But we're going to be operating the shoulder-fired weapons, at least until we run out of ordnance."

Everett pressed the talk key. "Reuben, how far out are those MRAPs?"

"Quarter mile, and moving fast."

"Okay, if you get a shot, you're clear to fire." Everett released the talk key and crawled inside the Typhoon through the missing front windshield. He checked the various latches to the top openings. All had been irreparably jammed by the hailstones except one.

"Ali!" he called out once the hatch was open. "Pass me the Vampir launch tube."

Ali climbed up on the hood of the Typhoon with

the rocket launcher in tow. "Here! It is already armed."

"Great. Bring the rockets inside the truck and feed them to me from below." Everett took the six-foot-long launch tube and found his first target. He wasn't sure how far away the vehicles were because of their enormous size. They seemed to be about an eighth of a mile out. Everett directed the crosshairs to the fourth vehicle in the convoy, figuring the other fire teams would deploy their rockets toward the first, second, or possibly third MRAP in the line. Unsure about the flight time of the rocket in relation to the speed the MRAPs were traveling, Everett didn't have the confidence to try to put the rocket through the windshield, so he centered the sights on the grill.

SWOOSH! The rocket took flight, impacting with the front end of the intended target. BOOOOM! Fire and smoke engulfed the front of the vehicle, but it kept coming!

Two other rockets from Everett's troops made their way to the first and second vehicles. The first smashed through the windshield and exploded, bringing the MRAP to a halt. The other hit the front tire, slowing the second vehicle down significantly.

"Rocket!" Everett reached below where Ali slapped another projectile into his palm.

Everett rapidly loaded the next rocket. The GR convoy began to fall out of line and take up firing positions. Everett took aim at the same truck he'd shot moments earlier. But now it was closer and had come to a stop. This time he placed the crosshairs over the windshield. SHROOOFP! The rocket blazed to the MRAP, crashing through the front glass and exploding inside.

Courtney and the four IDF volunteers returned, hoisting the guns and ammo into the Typhoon's shell.

More rockets jetted out from the surrounding foxholes occupied by Everett's troops. Automatic machine gunfire poured at them from the direction of the assailants. Everett ducked for cover and took another rocket.

PING! TING! TANG! The bullets striking the side of the Typhoon were coming from large caliber weapons. They jarred the heavy vehicle with each strike.

Ali pointed at the dents appearing on the side of the truck. "Those look like fifty-caliber."

Everett plucked a piece of broken mirror from the shattered side view mirror and stuck it out the front of the truck to get a view of what was happening. "Wow! Those guys are monsters! Nine feet! And that's their primary weapons they're shooting. It looks like they have bullpup machine guns, and judging from the magazine size, I'd say they're fifty-cals."

Courtney looked over Everett's shoulder at the giants emerging from the gargantuan MRAPs "They're wearing heavy body armor too. It looks like a black stretch Kevlar suit with black steel plates affixed to the exterior, like an exoskeleton."

"Like the scales of a dragon." Everett dropped the mirror and prepared to continue his assault. Immediately upon sticking his head out from the top hatch, he began taking fire. Everett had to swiftly set his sights on one of the GR supersoldiers and pull the trigger. Swooosh! BOOM!

The explosion of the rocket sent pieces of the nine-foot-tall behemoth, swirling through the air in all directions.

"I got one!"

"Awesome! How many to go?" Courtney passed him another rocket.

"I don't know. Eight trucks and probably ten soldiers per truck." Everett considered the time he'd need to be exposed in order to reload the launch tube. "I better go with a regular RPG. That will allow me to pop up and fire."

Ali exchanged the rocket in Everett's hand for an armed RPG launcher. "Tell me when you are ready to shoot, and I will also shoot other RPG from opening in windshield."

"Good plan. Remember, just target the individual supersoldiers." Everett waited for Ali to get into position.

"Go!" Everett popped up through the hatch and instantly had rounds flying past his head. He focused on his breathing, took aim, and fired. He watched the fiery wake of the RPG as it made a direct impact with another of the giant supersoldiers. Everett wasted no time getting out of the line of fire and dropping back into the battered hull of the Typhoon.

Ali's eyes were as wide as pancakes when he ducked back into the truck. He breathed frantically.

"Did you get one?" Everett asked.

Ali forced a smile as he gave a fast nod.

"Can I give you guys some cover fire?"

Courtney offered.

"No. You keep the grenades coming." Everett motioned to the IDF soldiers. "But you four can. Slip out the front windshield and crawl down underneath the Typhoon. All the tires are flat and the front axle is broken, so it sits only inches from the ground. It would take a sniper sitting still to hit you beneath the truck."

The four volunteers dutifully complied.

Everett and Ali reloaded. Everett looked at his accomplice. "Ready?"

"I am ready." Ali stood prepared to spring into action on Everett's command.

"Go!" Everett repeated the maneuver, striking another of the humongous Nephilim warriors dead.

Reuben's voice came over the radio. "The foxholes on our right and left flanks have both been neutralized by the enemy supersoldiers. They're closing in on my position. If anyone has a shot, I could use a little help."

Cover fire rang out from below, and Everett took another grenade from Courtney. He placed it in the launcher and turned to Ali, who also held an armed RPG launcher. "Go!"

Once again, Everett lunged through the top hatch while Ali stuck his weapon out the front windshield. Everett now fired at a team of Nephilim warriors shooting at the collapsed building, which Reuben's team was using for cover.

WHoooosh! Shwooofp! Booom! BOOM! Everett and Ali each eliminated one soldier, but in so doing, had finally brought the attention of the giants on themselves.

Everett dropped down and took the grenade Courtney had waiting for him.

"Only two grenades left after this round." She handed another warhead to Ali, also.

Everett breathed anxiously. "That's not good. We've got another forty supersoldiers."

BOOOM! An explosion from under the Typhoon flipped it on its side. Everett, Courtney, and Ali were tossed against the side wall of the truck like Tic-Tacs being shaken in their container. He saw black for a brief moment but quickly regained his composure. Everett knew the IDF troops providing cover fire from under the truck were probably dead. He looked to Ali, who had his RPG and was crawling toward the opening. Everett glanced at Courtney. "Are you okay?"

A thin trickle of blood was dripping from her forehead. "Yeah, I'm good." She reached around and picked up her AK.

Ali fired his rocket. Boom. "Quick! They are coming!"

Everett took a grenade from Courtney and crawled to the windshield opening since the top hatch was now facing the entrance to the underground city, the opposite direction of the Nephilim.

Everett passed the grenade to Ali and crawled past him. Seven supersoldiers were charging toward him. He fired. BOOM! Two giants dropped from the fragmentation effect of the grenade, but the other five now had six more Nephilim behind them, joining in the assault. All of their rifles barked out large-caliber automatic fire, pelting the bottom of the Typhoon, which lay on its side.

Everett rolled out of the way for Ali to launch his grenade. Ali fired, but his head and shoulders were riddled and torn with fifty-caliber bullets.

"Ali!" Courtney screamed in horror.

BOOOM! Another enemy rocket struck the Typhoon, ripping a hole in the bottom of the MRAP and sending the Typhoon rolling side over side.

Everything went black.

When Everett opened his eyes, he tasted blood in his mouth, his legs were numb, and his left arm was throbbing with pain. He looked around to get his orientation. The bottom of the Typhoon now faced the entrance to the underground city, which Everett could see through the gaping seven-foot long hole made by the rocket. "Courtney!"

"I'm here." Face down near the opening of the windshield, she was struggling to get up.

"You have to get into the underground city." The numbness left his legs and was quickly replaced by pulsating agony.

"I don't think I can walk." She laboriously turned herself over.

"Then you have to crawl. It's right out the bottom of the truck. I'm coming to help you." Everett stood up, but instantly collapsed under the searing pain in both legs." He called out, "Jesus! Help us!"

Just then a giant arm reached in and grabbed Courtney. Everett hoped it was Messiah answering his prayer—but it wasn't.

The hand which grabbed Courtney had six

fingers, and it held her tightly by the throat as it dragged her from the vehicle.

Adrenaline shot through Everett's veins enabling him to stand on his shattered legs and propel himself toward the windshield of the Typhoon. He stepped out with his AK-47 drawn to see the massive heap covered in coal-black armor holding his precious wife, dangling in the air by her throat, like a rabbit in the hands of a hunter. She looked so tiny in contrast to the goliath.

The monster had human eyes, human lips, a human face and human form. Other than its size and having six fingers on each hand, it was eerily human in appearance. But not its voice. When it spoke, the sound was low, hollow, demonic. And when it spoke, it addressed Everett with a teasing smile. It held the massive bullpup rifle with one hand and pointed it toward Courtney's head. "If you will renounce Jesus, I will let her live." Two other Nephilim clothed in black iron dragon scales stood laughing behind the one taunting Everett.

Everett shook his bloody head slowly and summoned his last bit of strength to raise his AK.

"What are you holding onto? We have won the war. Your Messiah has abandoned you, just like He has abandoned all of your friends that we have killed here today. Look around you. You've been sold a bill of goods. Everything you believe is a lie!"

"I will never deny Yeshua." Everett remembered the story of David and Goliath. He remembered the spot right between the eyes where the tiny stone had struck the filthy Philistine.

"Suit yourself." The monster pulled the trigger, releasing a stream of bullets, which pierced Courtney's body, spilling her blood and her life.

Everett pulled his trigger, knowing that he would be with the love of his life soon enough. POW! The single round from Everett's AK-47 found the very same spot David's stone had struck. The twelve-fingered beast dropped Courtney's listless body, then fell backward.

A fresh wave of gunfire and explosions rang out from all around. White metallic arrows struck the other two Nephilim in the head, dropping them near their dead companion.

Everett used his right hand and left elbow to crawl to Courtney's body. He gently closed her eyes with his fingers, then cushioned her limp neck with his arm as he lay beside her. All the gunfire, explosions, and yelling faded into the background as he remembered the first time he'd seen her. She was so soft and cute sitting at the table in the restaurant next to his friend Ken who'd arranged the blind date. He recalled how he'd nearly blown it with her by showing up late and acting a little over-confident. Then he remembered how his heart had raced when she'd kissed him unexpectedly at that initial meeting, letting him know that she was giving him one more shot. His heart ached as the memory of their small wedding at Elijah's cabin played like a movie in his mind.

Now, despite everything he'd done to try to protect her, she was dead. His worst nightmare had come true, and he'd had to watch her die.

A squad of supersoldiers ran behind the Typhoon

where Everett lay in the growing pool of blood. He looked at his rifle briefly but knew retrieving it would require him to move his arm out from beneath Courtney's head, and he simply wasn't willing to let her beautiful hair lay in the puddle of blood. Besides, he'd lost the will to fight—and the will to live. Nothing would please him more than for one of the Nephilim to send him to be with her. He missed her already.

But the supersoldiers paid him no mind. They seemed more concerned for their own lives. Someone was attacking them, and it was a much larger force than the troops Everett had been commanding from Kaymakli.

Everett heard the hooves of horses beating the ground and rushing in his direction. He turned to the six Nephilim who were using the overturned Typhoon for cover. They fired their weapons at the charging force, emptying their magazines. A rider on a white horse stormed their position, swinging a sword back and forth, until he'd severed the heads of all six Nephilim. The rider wore a white armor, which was barely recognizable as ever having been white. His armor was covered in the blood of the slaughtered Nephilim. The horse neighed with fury, raising up on its hind legs.

The rider brought the horse back down and turned toward Everett. His eyes blazed like fire. His hand with which he gripped the reins had a long scar as if it had been pierced. Instantly, Everett recognized him as being the same man he'd seen on the mountain back in Virginia speaking with Moses and Elijah. Everett's strength left him as it had before, leaving him just enough energy to mouth a single word. "Messiah."

This time, however, Everett did not lose consciousness. His eyes streamed with tears as he locked his gaze with the rider's.

The rider nodded at Everett and smiled compassionately before kicking the horse with his heels and charging off to finish the battle.

Everett fought to breathe as if he'd fallen flat on his back, but soon, his strength returned. His arm wasn't throbbing. And his legs didn't hurt. He ran his tongue along the cut in his mouth that had been bleeding, but he couldn't locate it. What was more, the pool of blood he'd been lying in was gone. Everett gently lowered Courtney's head and came up to a sitting position. He looked all around him, but there was no blood anywhere. "Did I imagine that? No, I saw him shoot her."

Everett looked out toward the dead Nephilim to make sure he'd not just awoken from a dream. Sure enough, they were all there. The six killed by the rider, the one he'd killed and the other two with the white metallic arrows in their heads and necks. Where they lay, there was blood—blood in abundance.

He looked back to Courtney who'd previously lost the color in her face. Her cheeks were pink, not white. Her lips were rosy, not the pale hue they'd been only moments ago. Everett inhaled deeply, but he dared not hope. "Could it be?"

Her eyelashes fluttered, and he ran his hand along her soft, warm face.

"Courtney? Can you hear me?"

Her lashes batted again. This time, her eyes opened. She focused on him.

He exhaled and began to sob as he embraced her, picking her up into his arms.

"What happened?" she asked.

"Jesus, that's what happened. He was here." He held her close. Out of the corner of his eye, he saw Ali stirring around.

The young man stood up on his feet and brushed himself off. He looked at Everett. "Are we winning?"

"Yeah." Everett heard more horses charging in their direction.

One of the riders called out, "Check behind that truck. I see GR uniforms sticking out from behind it."

A woman's voice added, "And watch out! It could be an ambush."

The voices sounded vaguely familiar to Everett, but he couldn't be sure. The events of the past five minutes had been utterly surreal.

The horses galloped to the edge of the Typhoon.

Everett called out to the riders. "Hold your fire! We've got three friendlies back here. All the hostiles are dead."

"Everett?" a voice called out.

Everett turned, still holding Courtney in his arms to see one of the troops from the army of heaven walking around the corner. His suit of armor was brilliant-white. Form-fitting, but thick. It was made of a material that Everett had never seen before. The man wore boots and gloves of the same material. He held a bow and wore a quiver filled with the white metallic arrows like the ones which had killed the two Nephilim. Then he looked at the man's face. "Kevin?"

The woman walked around the side of the truck after the man.

Courtney squealed and jumped to her feet. "Sarah!"

Two more men dismounted their horses and came around to the side of the flipped MRAP where the reunion was taking place.

"Ali!" one of the men called out.

"Tobias!" Ali called out with joy. "And Gideon! Dinah, she is here, in the underground city. You must come in. She will be so happy to see you!"

"She's here—in Kaymakli?" Gideon sheathed his white metallic sword and looked at Tobias.

Tobias put his hand on Gideon's shoulder. "Go see her."

"You don't think Michael will mind?"

Tobias shook his head. "The General won't care. The battle is over—the war is over. We're just mopping up at this point. Go ahead. I'll watch your horse."

Gideon waved at Everett and the others, then rushed into the entrance of the underground city.

Everett took Courtney in another embrace. "All those verses about God's protection—every time I watched someone else I cared about die, they seemed to be less and less true. They just didn't make sense. Then when you died, my faith was pushed to the edge. But now I understand."

He turned to Ali. "I'm sure there is someone who would like to know you're still alive."

Ali smiled, his white teeth glowing in the sun. He shook his finger at Everett. "Not still alive, Everett. Alive again!"

"I stand corrected. While you're down there, will you let Rabbi Hertzog know the war is over and that everyone can come out?"

"Sure." Ali hurried down the stairs behind Gideon.

Everett held his wife a few minutes longer, wondering what the New Millennium would be like. He looked down at the ground to see a small patch of wildflowers blossoming beside his left foot.

Courtney looked down to see what he was staring at. "I don't remember seeing flowers anywhere around here before."

"Me either." Everett recalled a verse from Isaiah and recited it to her. "The wilderness and the solitary place shall be glad for them; and the desert shall rejoice, and blossom as the rose."

And I saw an angel come down from heaven, having the key of the bottomless pit and a great chain in his hand. And he laid hold on the dragon, that old serpent, which is the Devil, and Satan, and bound him a thousand years, And cast him into the bottomless pit, and shut him up, and set a seal upon him, that he should deceive the nations no more, till the thousand years should be fulfilled: and after that he must be loosed a little season. And I saw thrones, and they sat upon them, and judgment was given unto them: and I saw the souls of them that were beheaded for the witness of Jesus, and for the word of God, and which had not worshipped the beast, neither his image, neither had received his mark upon their foreheads, or in their hands; and they lived and reigned with Christ a thousand years. But the rest of the dead lived not again until the thousand years were finished. This is the first resurrection. Blessed and holy is he that hath part in the first resurrection: on such the second death hath no power, but they shall be priests of God and of Christ, and shall reign with him a thousand years. And when the thousand years are expired, Satan shall be loosed out of his prison, And shall go out to deceive the nations which are in the four quarters of the earth, Gog, and Magog, to gather them together to battle: the number of whom is as the sand of the sea.

Revelation 20:1-8

DON'T PANIC!

Inevitably, books like this will wake folks up to the need to be prepared, or cause those of us who are already prepared to take inventory of our preparations. New preppers can find the task of getting prepared for an economic collapse, EMP, or societal breakdown to be a source of great anxiety. It shouldn't be. By following an organized plan and setting a goal of getting a little more prepared each day, you can do it.

I always try to include a few prepper tips in my novels, but they're fiction and not a comprehensive plan to get prepared. Now that you're motivated to start prepping, the last thing I want to do is leave you frustrated, not knowing what to do next. So I'd like to offer you a free PDF copy of *The Seven Step Survival Plan.*

For the new prepper, *The Seven Step Survival Plan* provides a blueprint that prioritizes the different aspects of preparedness and breaks them down into achievable goals. For seasoned preppers who often get overweight in one particular area of preparedness, *The Seven Step Survival Plan* provides basic guidelines to help keep their plan in balance, and ensures they're not missing any critical segments of a well-adjusted survival strategy.

To get your **FREE** copy of ***The Seven Step Survival Plan***, go to **PrepperRecon.com** and click the FREE PDF banner, just below the menu bar, at the top of the home page.

Thank you for reading
The Days of Elijah: Book Four
The Seventh Vial

Reviews are the best way to help get the book noticed. If you liked the book, please take a moment to leave a five-star review on Amazon and Goodreads.

I love hearing from readers! So whether it's to say you enjoyed the book, to point out a typo that we missed, or asked to be notified when new books are released, drop me a line.

prepperrecon@gmail.com

Stay tuned to **PrepperRecon.com** for the latest news about my upcoming books, and great interviews on the **Prepper Recon Podcast**.

Available Summer 2018!

Ava's Crucible

The deck is stacked against twenty-nine-year-old Ava. She's a fighter, but she's got trust issues, struggles with depression, and despite her natural beauty, doesn't score well in the self-esteem department. Her personal complications aren't without merit, but America is on the verge of a second civil war, and Ava must pull it together if she wants to survive.

Ava has just lost her adoptive mother to cancer. Her adoptive father walked out on his family for the sweet young thing at the office fifteen years ago. Ava's fiancé broke off the engagement shortly after her mom got sick. Her natural mother died during child birth, and she has no idea who her biological father is. With such a long history of abandonment, it's understandable why she's hesitant to put her faith in humans, but now it's affecting her relationship with God.

The tentacles of the deep state have infiltrated every facet of American culture. The public education system, entertainment industry, and mainstream media have all been hijacked by a shadow government intent on fomenting a communist revolution in the United States. The antagonistic message of this agenda has poisoned the minds of America's youth who are now convinced that capitalism and conservativism are responsible for all the ills of the country. Violent protest, widespread destruction, and politicians who insist on letting the disassociated vent their rage will bring America to her knees, threatening to decapitate the laws, principles, and values on which she was founded.

Ava refuses to give into fear, but she simply cannot survive on her own. She must deal with her crisis of faith and trust other people, or she'll never make it through the deadliest period in the history of America.

If you liked *The Days of Elijah*, you'll love the prequel series,

The Days of Noah

In *The Days of Noah,* you'll see the challenges and events that Everett and Courtney endured prior to this series. You'll read what it was like for the Christians in their final days before the rapture, and how the once-great United States of America lost its sovereignty. You'll have a better understanding of how the old political and monetary system were cleared away, like pieces on a chess board, to make way for the one-world kingdom of the Antichrist.

If you have an affinity for the prophetic don't miss my EMP survival series, *Seven Cows, Ugly and Gaunt*

In *Book One: Behold Darkness and Sorrow*, Daniel Walker begins having prophetic dreams about the judgment coming upon America for rejecting God. Through one of his dreams, Daniel learns of an imminent threat of an EMP attack which will wipe out America's electric grid and most all computerized devices, sending the country into a technological dark age.

Living in a nation where all life-sustaining systems of support are completely dependent on electricity and computers, the odds for survival are dismal. Municipal water services, retail food distribution, police, fire, EMS and all emergency services will come to a screeching halt.

If they want to live, Daniel and his friends must focus on faith, wits and preparation to be ready . . . before the lights go out.

You'll also enjoy my first series,

The Economic Collapse Chronicles

The series begins with *Book One: American Exit Strategy*. Matt and Karen Bair thought they were prepared for anything, but can they survive a total collapse of the economic system? If they want to live through the crisis, they'll have to think fast and move quickly. In a world where all the rules have changed, and savagery is law, those who hesitate pay with their very lives.

When funds are no longer available for government programs, widespread civil unrest erupts across the country. Matt and Karen are forced to move to a more remote location and their level of preparedness is revealed as being much less adequate than they believed prior to the crisis. Civil instability erupts into civil war and Americans are forced to choose a side. Don't miss this action-packed, post-apocalyptic tale about survival after the total collapse of America.

CPSIA information can be obtained
at www.ICGtesting.com
Printed in the USA
BVOW08s2253191217
503281BV00016B/680/P